Acclaim

"A very sweet romance amidst a story of dynamic family relationships that will leave you feeling all the emotions. With its large cast of characters, there is always someone to root for and someone to root against. This is my kind of book! "
—KASIE WEST, author of *Better Than Revenge*

"A sweet beach love story for all of us longing for somewhere to belong. I read this in the dark, cold of winter and was reminded all over again of how love, like hot chocolate, can warm us from the inside."
—LISA-JO BAKER, bestselling author of *Never Unfriended* and *It Wasn't Roaring, It Was Weeping*

"This is one of the best beach reads I've ever read. I loved every single thing about this book, from the large, extended family, to the family that was found by the end of the book. A must read!"
—APRIL J. SKELLY, author of A LETHAL ENGAGEMENT

"Poetic and romantic, *Seashells & Other Souvenirs* shimmers with heart and hope. Filled with nostalgia, every poem and page and chapter feels as comforting as wise words from a grandmother. Soothing and insightful, it's like the silence of a best friend or the steady, soft swell of waves upon shore. The story unfolds beautifully, reminding us that as surely as those waves come and go, or the summer sun takes its time to set, time flows ever forward and it's up to us to treasure the beauty set before us. And like a touch of grace, Rachel shows us that while bright memories pass below the horizon, joy in this moment isn't beyond our reach. A true delight, this story will steal your heart and then help you find it again. An absolute treasure."

—BRITTANY EDEN, author of the Heartbooks series

"*Seashells and Other Souvenirs* is a charming love letter to childhood, family, and friendship. It's filled with the sweet discovery of the true meaning of love, but most of all, it is a nostalgic tale of growing into adulthood with all its aches and joys."

—AMBER KIRKPATRICK, award-winning author of *Unleashed*

"I laughed, cried, and gasped my way through this brilliant debut. Lawrence has an amazing way of crafting characters who are complex and completely endearing. I felt like I knew Alex's heart, and by the end of the book, I was a sobbing, happy mess. *Seashells and Other Souvenirs* beautifully addresses the fears anyone thrust into a new chapter of life will appreciate: What if change makes us forget the people, places, and memories that formed us?"

—ANDREA RENAE, author of *Where Darkness Dwells*

"*Seashells and Other Souvenirs* is a heartwarming story about the innocence of childhood love and the ways we examine and redefine those memories in adulthood. This story felt like a warm hug or the perfect day at the beach with rich characters, settings, and storytelling. I didn't want it to end."

—ERICA WYNTERS, author of The Camelot Flowers Mystery Series

"Lawrence's debut is a breath of fresh sea air! *Seashells and other Souvenirs* is a cozy story about first crushes, deep relationships, and the devotion of family. With past events meshing seamlessly into the present, we are reminded of the nostalgic beauty of childhood and how it forms us as adults, and how remembering and moving forward can sometimes go hand in hand. A delightfully funny and sweet beach read full of heart, sand, and endearing characters everyone will fall in love with!"

—EMILY BARNETT, author of *Thread of Dreams*

"Rachel Lawrence has a way of crafting words—both in poetry and prose—to make you feel like you're sinking into a hug on a familiar beach. Nowhere else is that more obvious than in *Seashells & Other Souvenirs*! The way she weaves the plot through past, present, and poetry is magnificent, and the story it tells is exactly the kind of romance I adore: slow-burn friends-to-lovers with beautiful moments wrapped in a sweet plot. These are characters you'll want to carry with you like your own little literary souvenirs.

This book is for all the folklore girls, those who relate to Jo March, and who see the world in nostalgia-tinged glasses. I will be reading everything Rachel Lawrence writes!"

—HANNAH CARTER, author of *Saltwater Souls* and *The Depths of Atlantis*

"*Seashells & Other Souvenirs* is such a gem of a read! Perfect to tuck into your bag for a weekend at the beach. I loved how the story mixes a yearning for how things used to be with journaling! It follows a relatable and poignant main character who's trying to make sense of how her family used to be and who they're all becoming, while she's seemingly left behind. It's super relatable and really hits home about how tough it can be to hold onto the past while also trying to step forward into what life has next. This book beautifully shows how we can treasure our memories while still making room for new adventures. It's a sweet and heartfelt read that will stick with you long after you finish it!"

—ALLISON BYXBE, founder of The Inky Collective journaling community

"Lawrence captures the elusive and intangible magic of childhood memories and weaves an unforgettable story of family, the aches and joys of growing up, and the unforgettable adventure of finding a life you can love again. As sweet and fun as it is poignant, *Seashells and Other Souvenirs* is a story you will want to come back to again and again."

—KATEE STEIN, Author of *Glass Helix* and the Of Earth and Sky duology

SEASHELLS AND OTHER SOUVENIRS

Seashells

and Other

Souvenirs

Seashells and Other Souvenirs

a novel

Quill & Flame
PUBLISHING HOUSE
IGNITE

Rachel Lawrence

For Samantha, Becca, & Ally
who are part of all my favorite beach memories
The *best* part

Chapter 1

They say if you put your ear
To a seashell
You can hear the ocean
But I hear
The beating of my own heart
The voices of four little girls
Laughing and sharing secrets
Making memories
As countless as grains of sand
And wishing that joy
Could be bottled up
Forever

Wendy's Wild Water Park was an awfully flashy name for two rickety blue slides that fed into half a swimming pool. Even so, we spent an entire day every summer hauling squeaky foam mats up an astroturf ramp for the thrill of taking the plunge again and again.

I was ten the summer my cousin Sutton decided it was time the four of us girls graduated to the Tall Slide.

"Seriously." She gave her soggy strawberry blonde curls a shake. "If the boys can do it, we can too." The oldest of us at eleven and a half, Sutton likely could have convinced us to follow her off the edge of a cliff if she'd had a mind to.

Rebekah sidled up to me in the line. "You okay, Alex?" She knew I was terrified of being up so high. And of the tunnel that enclosed the top half of the slide. She knew most everything about me. We were more like sisters than cousins, and people often mistook us for twins. Born only four months apart, we shared the same straight golden hair and freckled faces. But she was always at least an inch taller and a whole lot braver.

"I'm fine," I lied as I tucked my mat under my arm and fidgeted with the paper bracelet stamped with the words ALL DAY PASS.

The female teenage lifeguard held out a hand to stop the spunky cousin with dark pigtails in front of us. "Hold on; I need to measure you. How old are you, sweetie?"

Elle squared her shoulders and stood on her tiptoes. "Almost nine."

The lifeguard squinted at the yardstick in her hand. "And almost tall enough. Next summer." She smiled sympathetically. Elle's face fell.

"Oh, come on, Kels," the boy behind us yelled. "She's close enough. Let her slide."

Elle took the lifeguard's sigh and momentary pause as permission and plopped down on her mat, pushing off the sides. Sutton laughed at her triumphant whoop echoing down the tunnel, and the boy smiled and pumped his fist. My stomach churned.

"You go next, Alex." Sutton tugged me forward by the corner of my mat. I closed my eyes and took a breath, then gingerly placed my mat in the swirling water flowing from the entrance of the slide.

"Don't overthink it," Rebekah encouraged. "Just do it this first time, and it will be easy after you see how much fun it is."

I slowly lowered myself into a sitting position and waited for the lifeguard's okay. "Whenever you're ready." She nodded.

I turned around and started to stand. "I think maybe—"

But Sutton's hands clamped over my shoulders and sat me back down. "You'll thank me later." I hardly had time to register her words before she gave me a hard shove. I flew forward, barreling toward the water below and reaching above my head to hang onto the mat that had slid right out from under me. I'd only just seen the start of my second decade of life, and this was how it was going to end?

I didn't even have the presence of mind to scream as my body was flung up and down the sides of the tunnel like a towel in the old dryer under the beach house. I struggled to hold on to my top with one hand and grasp the runaway mat with the other. If I was going to die, I wanted to do it with my bathing suit and my dignity intact. As I whipped around the last curve and shot out into the open bottom stretch, the bright sun momentarily blinded me.

And then my feet hit the water.

My body twisted around, the mat flew into the air, and my forehead collided with the edge of the slide.

The last details I registered were one of my aunts shouting my name, a copious amount of blood in the water, and a flash of annoyance at myself for ever listening to Sutton. Everything went black.

"Alex!" Sutton greets me excitedly at the front door and pulls me in for a hug. "How does it feel to officially be on summer break, Ms. Henry?"

I pull back and narrow my eyes at her. "Whose car is that in the driveway?"

"Just Chris's friend from work." She grabs my hand and drags me toward the kitchen. "He likes to read, and he's great with the baby," she whispers. "And he's *very* handsome."

"Oh my gosh, Sutton," I hiss. "You have to stop doing this."

We round the corner to find the two men playing peek-a-boo with a chubby eight-month-old in a high chair. I have to admit, it *is* very cute. Sutton flashes me a triumphant grin as the men stand and she introduces us. "This is my cousin, Alexandria. And Alex, this is Bryan."

"Nice to meet you, Alex." Bryan holds out a hand and offers me an apologetic wince. I'm relieved that he seems to feel as awkward about this whole scheme as I do.

"I hope you guys came hungry!" That's my cue from Sutton to sit and let her play matchmaker in exchange for another dinner that

Chris cooked but is letting her take credit for. My honorary niece's tiny toothy smile makes it worth it. Usually.

"So Sutton tells me you're a teacher?" Bryan ventures.

"Yep. High school literature." I spoon some mashed potatoes onto my plate. "I hear you like to read?"

"I do." He takes the bowl from me and serves himself. "But I can't say that I was very interested in literature back in high school. Then again, I didn't have a pretty teacher either."

I inwardly cringe.

"Alex is going to publish a book of poetry soon," Sutton interjects.

"Is that right?" Bryan winks across the table. "I'd love to read it."

I set my fork down, irritated at my cousin's presumptuousness. "Well, I have to actually *write* it first. But if you're still working with Chris when the time comes, I'll have Sutton pass along the information." The baby starts to fuss, and I scoot my chair back to intercept Chris. "I'll take her upstairs and change her. Come on, Marcail." I hoist her onto my hip and escape to the staircase, pretending not to hear Sutton following me.

I lay Marcie on the changing table and turn to locate a clean diaper. Sutton, arms crossed, scowls at me from the doorway. "Why can't you at least make an effort, Alex? I'm trying so hard."

"Which no one asked you to do."

She sighs dramatically. "I just hate to see you selling yourself short. There's a whole world out there and you won't let yourself see it. Refusing to let anyone in. Teaching at the same high school you just left a few years ago. Stuck in this tiny town—"

"The town that's so boring that you chose to move here?"

"Because I fell in love."

"You're welcome for that by the way." I snap up Marcie's jumper and hand the baby to Sutton.

"I'm trying to return the favor! But it's like you don't even *want* to be happy!"

I bristle. "So I can't be happy without a guy? I can't be happy with this simple life I've chosen?"

"Of course you can." She kisses the top of Marcie's head. "But *are* you happy, Alex? Really?"

I push past her but linger at the top of the stairs, studying the carpet until she speaks again.

"You know I love you, Al. And if this is what you really want, how you want to spend your life, I'll support you one hundred percent. But I can't stand this feeling that you've put your future on pause. That you've written this perfect story in your head of how you think things *should* be and have shut out any other possible route to happiness."

"And you think Bryan is the route to happiness?" I scoff.

"I think Bryan is a more plausible possibility than a boy you kissed on the beach when you were sixteen and haven't spoken to since."

I'm suddenly back at the top of that water slide, Sutton's hands at my back, ready to push too far. My fingers move to the pendant around my neck, and my thumb traces the outline of the silver sand dollar hanging from the chain.

"I'm sorry," she relents. "Let's just finish dinner. Chris said Bryan was planning to ask you to go to the company picnic next week if tonight goes well. Maybe you could give him at least two dates before you write him off?"

This isn't about dating, but I don't know how to make her understand that. I meet her eyes, a rare spur-of-the-moment decision firming up by the second. "Unfortunately, I won't be here next week."

Her forehead wrinkles in confusion. "What do you mean?"

"I'm leaving this boring little town for the summer, Sutton. To finally write my poetry book."

Chapter 2

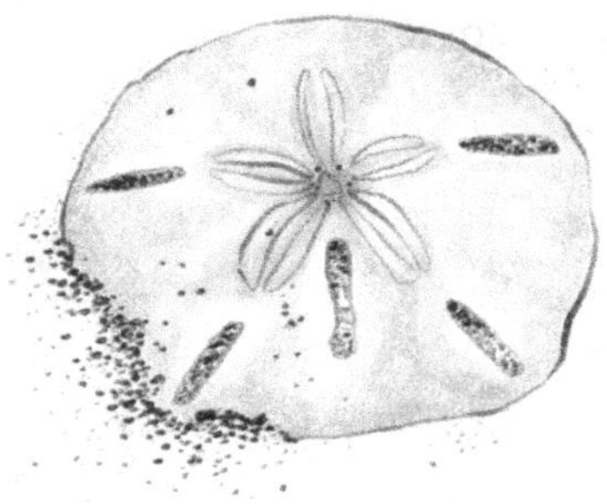

I was eight the fateful July day the pink boogie board snapped in half. The four of us had finally agreed on a color, pooled our wrinkled dollar bills, and talked my Aunt Mary into driving us off the island to the little beach store to make the purchase.

We'd only stopped by the house afterward long enough to shed the clothes we'd worn over our suits and to throw some juice boxes and crackers into a canvas bag before making a beeline for the beach.

"Don't forget to put on sunscreen!" my mom called from her post at the kitchen counter as she tore off another long sheet of aluminum foil and covered a dish. It was her night to help make dinner for the masses. She didn't even ask about which adult would be supervising us because it was a given that someone's mom was sitting in a foldout chair in the sand at all times.

Our flip-flops popped on the asphalt as we crossed the little street that separated us from the ocean. "Who's going first?" Elle adjusted the Little Mermaid towel slung over her shoulder.

"Oldest to youngest," Sutton stated matter-of-factly. Of course.

Rebekah rolled her eyes at me, but none of us argued.

The sun was high in the sky and the moat around our sand-castle was almost finished by the time I unfastened the sandy Velcro strip from my wrist and offered it to Elle.

"Oh, can I have a turn?" Rebekah's brother Elias jumped up from the pile of shells in front of him.

"After me!" Elle smiled, one front tooth missing. "Come on!" The two of them ran into the waves, Elle wobbling under the weight of a board almost as big as she was.

I'd just sat down on my striped towel and torn open a pack of peanut butter crackers when Elle came running back up the beach sobbing. Elias jogged behind her, a piece of the broken board in each hand. "I'm sorry, Elle. I said I was sorry!"

All three of us found our way to her side, as usual. "It's okay, Elle." Rebekah rubbed her back while Sutton wiped the stream under her nose with the corner of a towel. I pulled out a cracker; food was a love language we shared.

"I didn't mean to," Elias defended himself. "I just wanted to see what would happen if I tried to stand on it like a surfboard."

Rebekah took our broken treasure from his hands and set it reverently by our feet. Elle burst into fresh tears.

"Don't cry. You can borrow ours." The unfamiliar voice was a surprise; we weren't used to encountering many people not related to us on this strip of shore.

Two boys stood to our left. The taller one with shaggy blond hair smiled sympathetically at Elle, and the younger one with short brown hair and glasses held out a green boogie board with the silhouette of a palm tree printed on top.

"We live next door to the house you guys stay in every summer," he blurted out. "Well, one of them. How many people are in your family anyway?"

"Don't be rude." His brother cut eyes at him. "I'm Gavin," he said. "And this is Jude."

Jude, who looked like he couldn't be much older than our Elle, was undeterred. "But seriously, we tried to count once when you were eating dinner in the backyards. There's, like, a *lot* of you."

"Forty-nine," Sutton said proudly. "And counting."

"Whoa."

Sutton smiled at the awed look on Gavin's face.

"Are you guys all brothers and sisters?" Jude asked.

"We wish," Rebekah said. "Elias and I are siblings. But us girls are cousins. Our dads are brothers. There are eight of them all together. And then, with all their kids plus our grandparents and our two great aunts' families and *their* kids . . . my dad says we'll need a fifth house next year."

"That's really cool." Gavin squinted and shaded his eyes from the sun. "But eight brothers? I'm not sure I could handle more than the one I've got." He shoved Jude's shoulder playfully, and I decided I liked him.

"So you guys rent the house next to ours? The blue one?" I asked.

"No, we don't rent it. It's our house."

"Wait. You *live* there, live there?" Sutton gasped. "Like all the time?"

Both boys nodded eagerly, clearly sensing our excitement.

"That's so cool!" Elle had forgotten all about the broken board. "Wouldn't it be awesome to live on vacation?"

"Well, it wouldn't be vacation then," Sutton explained. "So it's just the two of you?"

"And our big sister Kelsey. And our dad." Gavin looked at Jude, but the younger boy just stared at his sand-coated toes.

"So." Gavin turned to Elle. "Are we boogie boarding or not? I can show you how to catch the good waves."

And that's how our friendship with the Alford brothers began.

"You're sure you can't come stay with me? It'd be fun."

"I wish!" Rebekah's voice echoes over the speakerphone as I turn on my signal and exit the interstate. "Do you know how hard I had to fight my boss just to get off the week of the reunion?"

"Does your boss know how many people would have come after her if she'd have said no?"

Rebekah laughs. "So where are you staying anyway? It's not like you to do something spontaneous like this."

It's true, but it still bothers me that she said it out loud. My little car bumps over a pothole in the country road I've just turned onto, and the grocery bags in my backseat rustle. "Did you just call me boring?"

"Not boring." She pauses, and I can picture her tugging on the ends of her hair like she does when she's thinking. "Just . . . cautious. Your parents were cool with this?"

"Well, considering I'm almost twenty-two, I didn't exactly ask their permission, Bek." I glance in the rearview mirror and add, "They did send me with laundry detergent, pepper spray, a wad of cash, and multiple bottles of sunscreen."

She giggles again. "That sounds more like the aunt and uncle I know. Did you pack your boogie board or are you hoping to borrow one from some handsome strangers on the beach?"

"Oh, I brought my own. It's in the trunk right next to my box of Barbie dolls."

"You joke," she retorts, "but our Barbie days were the best. Hey, I'm gonna let you go; I'm getting another call."

"A handsome med student, perhaps?"

"Maaaybe." I love that I know exactly which smile I'm hearing in her voice. "Or it could be Granddaddy calling to update me on his latest fishing trip."

"Okay, tell him I said hi. I'll call you back when my book is finished."

"You'd better call me back as soon as you set foot on the beach. And send me a picture when you go over the bridge!"

I adjust the air conditioning and reach for the phone button. "I'm telling my mom you're encouraging me to text and drive. Bye."

Twenty more minutes and I'll be on the main road of the biggest town next to our island. It's my best bet for finding an economical long-term hotel situation. If I can be careful with my savings and the money my dad gave me, I may be able to make it stretch until the beginning of August. If not, I'm sure I can apply for a seasonal part-time job and work around my writing time. It's the closest thing to a plan I have, and I can't afford to overthink it now. I close my hand around the necklace at my throat and remind myself why I need this summer, why we all need this book. Everyone else may enjoy flying down the slippery slide of time, but all I can see is the possibility of pain ahead. I'm not ready to let go yet. I have to find the words that will keep my cousins from forgetting the best days of our lives. And I don't know if I'll ever be able to move forward until I sort through everything that lies behind us.

Chapter 3

"Did you know that all the pandas in United States zoos are owned by the government of China?"

"Cool story, Jude." Gavin spun around from the front seat of the golf cart we were all crammed into. "Did you know most people don't bring a book of trivia facts to get ice cream with friends?"

Sutton stopped the cart at the crosswalk to let some late beachgoers cross the street in front of us. "Leave him alone. I think that's a very interesting fact, Jude."

"I'll bet you do," Gavin teased, his perfect teeth sparkling in the headlights of a passing car. "Hey, can we go to the slushie place instead?"

"What do you think, Alex?" Sutton deferred to me for once. "Your choice; you only turn thirteen once."

"Wow, Sutton," Elle piped up. "Did you just say two nice things in a *row*?"

Rebekah elbowed me. "She's only being so nice so we don't rat her out for doing something illegal."

"Please." Sutton waved her purple fingernails in the air dismissively. "I don't need a license to know how to drive one of these things. Besides, we're on the island; there isn't even real traffic here."

"So what do you say, Alex?" Gavin winked, and my insides melted. I'd have agreed to just about anything to see him smile at me like that again. But ice cream was *tradition*. And I wasn't ready to throw that away just because Gavin Alford made me forget my own name sometimes. Letting them come on our annual ice cream outing was a big enough concession.

"How about both?" I shrugged. "I mean, Sutton's right; you only turn thirteen once."

"Yeahhhh!" While Elle cheered from her perch on the rear-facing backseat and Sutton nodded her approval, Gavin high-fived me behind his back.

By the time we were finishing our second desserts, the conversation had turned silly. "So what happens when your family gets so big you fill all the beach houses for rent on the whole island?" Gavin asked.

"Then we stage a takeover of any other houses we can find." Sutton swiped a bite of his peanut butter cup ice cream, and I was tempted to hate her for how easily she flirted with him.

"Except for ours, right?" Jude looked up from his book and flashed his silver braces at us.

"We'll work out an alliance," Sutton reassured him. "And once Gavin and I get married, we'll have the blue house anyway."

Gavin raised his eyebrows, but Rebekah jumped in before he could share his thoughts. "How come you get to marry Gavin? Alex and I aren't that much younger than you guys. Why couldn't it be one of us?"

"Because Sutton Alford sounds the best, and you know it. Plus, imagine how gorgeous our children would be."

If I didn't know my cousins so well, I would have been shocked they were having this conversation in front of him, even in jest.

"What about me?" Elle grabbed a napkin from the middle of the picnic table and wiped her mouth. "I'm not even in the running?"

"One of you could marry Jude." Sutton's eyes lit up. "Then we can be sisters for real." Jude choked on his bite of cookies & cream.

"You guys are ridiculous." I passed Jude a napkin.

Gavin didn't miss a beat. "Elle, it wouldn't be fair if we got married. Can you imagine how much better our kids would be at boogie boarding than everyone else's? We wouldn't want to burden them with that kind of limitless talent and fame."

Everyone laughed, and I closed my eyes and breathed in the sticky, salt-scented air, memorizing the moment, adding it to my collection.

I crack the cover of my comfort read and let myself get lost in the world of Darcy and Elizabeth for a while. Considering the afternoon I've had, I need to escape. I drove over the bridge a few hours ago, desperate to see the row of familiar houses that share a backyard, the ones that frequent my dreams even more than the house I grew up in.

But seeing their driveways crowded with unfamiliar vehicles made me feel sick.

The rational part of me has always known that other renters stay there all but one week of the year, but I've never wanted to believe that this place could belong to anyone else the way it does to us. I passed the houses twice before I parked my car on the gravel in front of the only empty one on the street, then climbed the wooden stairs up to the porch. It's funny how, even never having been inside, I feel like I have permission to be here. The fact that it's still not a rental makes me think the Alfords still own it, but it's been years since we've seen any of them. The house has stood hauntingly quiet the last few summers, and the only sign of life has been a white car parked there once or twice. Rebekah decided it must have been a house cleaner.

Ironically, Elizabeth is just touring Pemberley when I hear footsteps on the staircase of the blue house's porch. I close my book and jump up from my borrowed rocking chair. Peering over the edge of the railing, I find the white mystery car parked next to my still unpacked black one. Before I have time to form an excuse for being here, a boy with dark hair and glasses stands in front of me, his familiar brown eyes filled with questions.

All of a sudden, I'm eight years old again, and everything is going to be just fine.

"Jude!" I lurch forward and throw my arms around his neck. "I can't believe you're here!"

He tentatively pats my back before taking a step away, laughing quietly. "I live here, Alex."

"Right." I shake my head, embarrassment fighting to take over my initial shock of joy at seeing his face. Sure, he's taller now, and his braces are gone, but he's still the fifteen-year-old kid who ate chocolate cupcakes with us. The twelve-year-old who taught us most of the random facts we know. The nine-year-old who knocked over my sandcastle and felt so bad about it he helped me rebuild a better one. The seven-year-old who shared his board with us when ours snapped in half. "It's just been so long since I've seen you. How are you? How's . . . your family?"

He leans against the railing and blinks a few times, a tiny sad smile twitching at the corner of his mouth. "Good. Gavin lives in Virginia now, selling real estate. He's coming to visit in a few weeks, but he seems to be doing pretty well." He looks at me as if asking whether he should continue or if this was all I needed to know. I nod, encouraging him to go on.

"Kelsey and her husband are up in Wilmington. Her little boy is five." He sighs. "And my dad is living in Georgia now. Last I heard from him." The way his voice turns scratchy makes me want to hug him again, but I'm certain that would make him feel even more uncomfortable. I settle for a tiny step in his direction.

"And you?"

He lifts his arms and scans the porch. "And I'm . . . here. Helping my friend Tyler with his business and doing a few other odd jobs. What about you?"

"I just finished my first year of teaching. High school literature."

"I thought you'd have just finished college?" His brows pinch together, and I'm unreasonably happy that he would know this, that he remembers things about our lives the way we do about him and his brother.

"I graduated early."

"That's awesome. Do you like teaching?" He scoots over and looks at the railing beside him. I move to the empty space and prop my elbows up at my sides.

"I think so. I mean, the first year of anything has its challenges, but I love the students and I'm always up for talking about books."

"You always have been." He smiles and finally asks the question anyone less patient would have started with. "So what are you doing here? You guys aren't usually around until the first week of July." He glances next door to confirm he's not missing something.

"It's just me for now. I came early to work on a project."

"Oh?"

I haven't explained it out loud to anyone except my family, but I guess he's close enough. "I'm hoping to write and publish a book of poetry. About the beach and our traditions. I thought I'd come and spend some time with our memories, kind of recreate some of them, and try my best to capture them on paper. For my grandma. Well, for us. To help work through losing her."

And to keep us from losing everything she gave us.

He ducks his head to meet my gaze. "I'm so sorry to hear that, Alex. I know you guys were close."

I bite my lip to keep from crying. I've put this poor guy through enough already today.

"For what it's worth," he speaks again, "I think that's a really beautiful way to honor her legacy."

"Thanks." I sniff. "I'm sorry I just showed up on your porch. I didn't know anyone was staying here."

He pushes off the railing. "No need to apologize. It's really good to see you. I hope we bump into each other again. Where are you staying?"

I make a face. "I'm not exactly sure. I'm struggling to find a hotel that's affordable and where I feel at least moderately safe. I underestimated the cost of staying at the beach during tourist season." I pick a piece of lint from my T-shirt. "After checking out several part-time jobs in town, I think I may need to find something with more hours to make this work. But then I might not have the time I need to work on my book." A sudden idea comes to me. "Hey, any chance you have connections with someone who's hiring here on the island? I'm willing to try anything."

"You're asking the wrong guy. I've only got an assortment of low-paying, part-time gigs myself."

I try not to let my face fall the way my hopes do.

"But why don't you just stay here?" The question seems to surprise him as much as it does me, and it hangs between us for a few seconds before he unpacks it for us both. "It's a huge house, and I'm hardly ever home. You'd have a whole floor to yourself, and you wouldn't have to worry about paying for a hotel or gas."

"I'd want to pay you something. At least help with utilities." I can't believe I'm even entertaining this idea, but it makes the most sense out of any option I've been presented with all day. And, even though I haven't seen Jude in years, the idea of staying with him makes me feel safe.

"No." His head moves back and forth adamantly. "I don't even pay rent. And I'd pay for utilities either way. I don't want your money." He tucks his hands into the pockets of his shorts. "But maybe, if you didn't mind . . ." He pauses and weighs his next words.

"What?" I finally ask.

"I want in."

"What do you mean?"

"The traditions you're recreating. All the ones we watched from a distance for years. Can I tag along? For some of them at least?"

I open my mouth, close it again.

"It's okay if you want to say no. I know how you are about keeping things sacred. You can stay here either way, no strings attached. I just . . ." He shrugs. "Your family. What you guys have is really special. And I know most people don't have anything quite like it, but we never had anything even close."

Hearing him ask for what he wants so directly is new for me; the Jude we grew up with always kind of went with the flow. He keeps talking. "My friend Ty teaches surf lessons now, but we're trying to expand the business into a whole tourism company, something that can offer families who come here the chance to make the kinds of memories that I only ever dreamed about making as a kid. I've come up with dozens of lists of activities and ideas, but what I really need to know is how to add that element of magic that was part of everything you guys did. Maybe you could help me? Share some of your secrets?"

I wouldn't even contemplate the request if it was coming from anyone else. But this is Jude. Sweet, quiet, slightly nerdy Jude. Gavin's little brother. And if I'm being honest, he's throwing me a lifeline here.

I hold out a hand, and he takes it. I shake it once. "Deal."

<h1 style="text-align:center">Chapter 4</h1>

"I'm nervous." Elle pulled at the sleeve of my former dance recital costume as we waited under the stairs for our turn to grace the backyard basketball court turned stage.

"Don't be." Sutton applied another layer of sticky lip gloss and tucked the tube into the pocket of her glittery jumper. "We're going to be fabulous. Just don't forget your lines."

It was the day before I turned nine and the night of my playwriting debut. The Henry Family Talent Show was a vacation staple, and this year, we had been preparing our act for *months*.

"But that's what I'm nervous about," Elle groaned.

Rebekah squeezed between Sutton and Elle. "You won't forget, Elle. And if you do, just make something up. Or Alex can whisper the lines to you."

I folded the script I was nervously studying even though I knew it backwards and forwards, the one I'd worked on since Christmas, painstakingly made three handwritten copies of, and mailed off to my cousins in February. It included five short scenes based on characters from our favorite movies and a dance number to cap it off.

My cousin Sean's saxophone solo ended and my Uncle Zack's loud voice boomed, "And now, we present 'Beauty and The Sea Beast!'"

"Here we go." Rebekah adjusted her mermaid tail and led us in front of the sold-out crowd.

For the next handful of minutes, we told the dramatic story of Gail Scale, the merman's only daughter who was destined to break the curse of the handsome octopus prince. We performed our little hearts out.

Aside from Sutton dropping the magical seashell once, Elle accidentally calling her Queen Sutton instead of Queen Starfish, and one slight wardrobe issue with a twisted tail, we were flawless.

We finished our dance with a flourish, breathless and beaming in our perfect ending poses. A standing ovation followed. Even the three siblings on the back deck of the house next door clapped furiously and whooped from their rocking chairs.

"Looks like we have a future writer in the family," Uncle Zack commented as we exited the stage.

My heart swelled.

"So, anything you need as far as linens or toiletries will be in this closet. Laundry room is under the house. And obviously, help yourself to anything in the kitchen."

We're standing on the beige carpet outside the upstairs bedroom filled with the bags Jude helped me carry in from my car. The room clearly used to be Kelsey's. Though the one next to it had a little more space, I couldn't handle the idea of staying in Gavin's old room.

"Anything else?" Jude's hands find his pockets again. "I mean, I'll just be downstairs if you think of anything."

It's starting to sink in how absurd and awkward this whole arrangement is, and the thought of spending the next several hours alone in this house with a practical stranger is making me sweat.

I pick at the chipped polish on my thumbnail. "You know, I was thinking I might make a quick run to the store. Stock up on some supplies."

"Supplies?"

"Yeah. If you're going to get the full experience, at the very least we're going to need some vacation food."

His body language relaxes and amusement dances across his features. "And that's different from regular food, how?"

"Regular food is practical, balanced, reasonably . . . reasonable. Vacation food is all the junk you're never allowed to buy or eat any other time of year. Trust me; it's a thing."

"Well, you're the expert here. I'll grab my shoes and keys." He starts walking but turns back around, the slightly nervous kid I once knew emerging again. "Unless you wanted to go alone. I didn't mean to invite myself."

I laugh out loud. "Jude, I showed up on your front porch and somehow ended up staying here for the summer. You can ride with me to get groceries."

"I'll drive." He smiles and disappears down the steps.

As he backs out of the driveway a few minutes later, I wonder aloud, "Isn't it crazy that the last time I saw you, neither of us could drive yet?"

"Yeah, but you probably got your license the next week."

I adjust my seatbelt and turn to face him. "I actually failed my test the first time."

"Well, I'm glad I offered to drive then."

"And I'm glad you feel like you still know me well enough to be mean to me." I turn the radio on, but he immediately reaches to turn the volume down.

"I didn't have a chance to ask about your family yet. What's everyone up to now?"

"Hmm." I tuck a stray piece of hair behind my ear. "Sutton is married now and has a little girl. She's running a nonprofit from home."

Jude chuckles. "I'd have guessed she'd be running a country by now."

Not many people could get away with a comment like this, but when he says it, fondness laces his voice.

"You're not far off." I snicker. "But once she saw there were no openings for dictators, she found that motherhood suits her just as well. She still gets to boss someone around." I cringe at the bitterness I can hear behind my words and hope Jude doesn't notice.

"She always reminded me a little bit of Kelsey. What about Rebekah and Elle?"

"Rebekah just started a job as an ICU nurse. She's a little overwhelmed, but I know she's amazing at it. She's dating a new guy, but we haven't decided yet if he's good enough for her. And Elle." I pause to swallow down the sudden lump in my throat. "Elle's been studying abroad in Spain. She flies home the week before the reunion. It's been really weird having her so far away."

"I always wondered how you guys survived in different towns when you left the beach every year." He's pulling onto the bridge.

"Oh, hold your breath!" I instruct before gulping in a lungful of air.

"What?" He looks over at me.

I puff out my cheeks and widen my eyes at him until he complies.

The second he drives over the other side, I exhale loudly and he follows suit. "We always hold our breath when we cross the bridge. Congratulations," I say. "You've just completed your first classic beach trip tradition."

"Perfect," he laughs. "I'll add Bridge Breath Holding to the tourism brochure as soon as we get back to the house." Turning left into the grocery store lot, he eases into a parking spot.

When we get inside, he frees a shopping cart and gestures to me. "Lead the way, Al." If I didn't know better, I'd have thought it was just yesterday that we were riding in a crowded golf cart, listening to the radio, and ranking our favorite Christmas movies. Any trace of unease melts away, and I'm convinced that this summer is going to be amazing after all.

I head straight for the cereal aisle.

"Starting right in the middle of the store, huh?" The cart's wheels squeak as he strolls up beside me. "Are we going in order of meals here, starting with breakfast?"

"We're not here for meals, Jude. We're here for snacks." I scan the shelves. "Except for breakfast food, which can serve as either a meal *or* a snack."

"Should I be writing this down?"

"Here they are." I proudly hold up the quintessential beach breakfast item, and Jude looks it over.

"But since you'll be here all summer, wouldn't it make more sense to buy a big box of cereal instead of eight little ones? It's cheaper."

I gasp. "You can't put a price on tradition."

He holds up his hands in mock surrender. "Of course, of course. I didn't mean that. But for my notes, what makes the little boxes special?"

"Tradition! Keep up, buddy."

"Right." He reaches for two more packs and tosses them into the cart. "Better?"

"You're a natural." I spin the cart around and take the helm. "Now, on to the snack cakes."

After a thorough search of every aisle, we pull into the check-out line with a kitchen's worth of junk food as well as a few actual meal essentials. "This should last us at least a week or two."

Jude tries not to smile but fails. "Think we got enough cheese?" he remarks as he helps unload everything onto the conveyor belt.

"Impossible. But it will have to do."

"You really like cheese, huh?"

"No, I LOVE cheese. It's basically medicinal. Ask any one of my cousins and they'll tell you that a cheese-based snack is scientifically proven to improve my mood by one hundred percent."

"Noted." He reaches for his wallet, but I step in front of him.

"This is my contribution, okay?"

He hesitates but eventually nods in agreement.

As we pack the trunk I ask, "Are you starting to wonder what kind of psychopath you just invited into your home?"

"Only a little bit."

I have so many questions for him, so much to catch up on, but I know we have time. We spend the ride back compiling a list of everything each of us can cook and which recipes include cheese. The conversation flows freely, minus the forty-six seconds we hold our breath as we drive back onto the island.

"Okay, but what is your absolute favorite pizza topping?" he asks as he cuts the engine in front of the blue house.

I don't even have to consider. "Pineapple."

Silence.

"Jude Alford. Don't tell me you don't like pineapple on pizza."

"It's not that I don't like it," he hedges. "I've just never tried it."

I cover my mouth and hang my head.

"Are you wondering what kind of psychopath you've just agreed to live with this summer?" he teases.

"Only a little bit."

Chapter 5

"What did you wish for?" Rebekah asked as I licked the chocolate frosting from the birthday candle I'd just extracted.

"I don't think she's allowed to say." Jude adjusted his glasses and peeled the paper liner from his cupcake.

"Right," Sutton agreed. "Or it won't come true."

"I'm jealous that you get to spend your sweet sixteen at the beach," Rebekah commented.

"Yeah, because *you* only got a slumber party at a fancy hotel with all your friends from school," Elle shot back.

"I told you I wanted to invite you guys! It was a last-minute thing!"

"Okay, ladies." Gavin leaned forward across the picnic table we were all sharing. "Let's not lose sight of who we're celebrating. What are our plans for the rest of the evening, birthday girl?" The way he looked at me temporarily incapacitated me. He'd always been dreamy, but somehow the fact that he'd just finished his first year of college made him even more attractive. He had an air of sophistication about him that was both mysterious and reassuring. I felt safe around him. Protected. And also terrified.

"I don't know what *your* plans are." Elle finished off her final bite. "But our last night here is always family movie night." She gestured to where two of my uncles were hanging a giant sheet from the balcony two houses over.

"That sounded a little bit harsh, Elle," I chided.

"I'm sorry, are you the same girl who always insists we never ever break tradition?" Sutton wagged a finger in my direction. "The one who had to be convinced it was okay to let Rebekah make you cupcakes in lieu of an ice cream run this year?"

"I'm not suggesting we break tradition," I defended. "I'm just saying that we don't have to be ugly to our friends about it." I turned to Rebekah. "The cupcakes are delicious, by the way."

Gavin nudged my fingers with his across the table and offered me one of his signature winks. "It's cool, Alex. We aren't offended. We'll pop some popcorn and watch from our deck like we always do. We care about our Henry girls far too much to get in the way of their traditions. You ready, Jude?"

Jude crumpled up his trash and followed Gavin back next door, throwing me one last "Happy birthday, Al" over his shoulder.

I followed my cousins upstairs to grab blankets before we settled into our camping chairs in the yard for the feature presentation.

An hour in, Elle had fallen asleep like she did every year. I studied the faces of my best friends in the flashing glow of the big screen, feeling extra nostalgic. This was all going by too fast.

A piece of popcorn hit the side of my head. Then another.

When I raised my eyes to the deck next door, Gavin jerked his head toward the street behind us.

Rebekah giggled, but Sutton just rolled her eyes as I tiptoed past them and crept around the house.

My heart was racing by the time I met him in the middle of the road. "What's up?"

"I just got a text from a friend, and rumor has it, there are going to be fireworks tonight. Want to check it out?"

I nodded, and he wrapped his hand around mine as if it was the most natural thing in the world, as if he'd done it a million times.

I let him lead me down to the beach, and we climbed the steps hand in hand. We stood there, shoulders touching, watching the waves crash into one another.

I was almost afraid to speak, scared that it would somehow spoil the magic and the moment would evaporate. But when he slid his arm around my waist, I felt invincible.

"Tell me a secret, Gavin Alford."

"Hmm." His breath tickled my ear. "What kind of secret?"

I pulled my sweatshirt sleeves over my hands and leaned into him. "I want to know the story of how you guys ended up living in the beach house." The girls and I had invented about a thousand theories over the years, but somehow, we'd never gotten the facts.

He was quiet for a beat too long, and I panicked. Maybe it was the wrong question.

"It's not exactly a secret," he finally said. "We just don't talk about it much, because Jude gets weird about things sometimes."

"Oh," I breathed, ready to drop the topic completely. But he kept talking.

"My mom's parents gave the house to my parents as a wedding gift. They said everyone needed a place to escape to every now and then. But my mom thought it was crazy to own a beach house and not live in it all the time, so they got jobs nearby and moved in. Living on an island made commuting longer, and I think they got a little lonely out here during the offseason, but my dad said she never wanted to leave. After she died, he couldn't let the house go. So, yeah, we've been here ever since." He cleared his throat. "Sorry; that was probably a much more boring story than you were hoping for."

"I'm sorry, Gavin." I looked up at him. "I can't imagine—"

"I was pretty little." He brushed off my concern. "I don't remember much from before she was gone." He sighed and turned me so I was facing him. "How about a happier secret?" he suggested.

"Okay." I smiled.

He lowered his face dangerously close to mine. "I very much want to kiss you right now."

My cheeks flushed, but I forced myself not to look away.

He kept one hand on my waist and moved the other to cradle the side of my face, gently sliding his thumb across my cheek. "Tell *me* a secret, Alexandria Henry."

I swallowed. "This," I whispered. "This is what I wished for."

"Looks like your cousin was wrong then."

"Hmm?"

"About it not coming true." He closed the miniscule gap between us and, as if on cue, fireworks lit up the sky.

We missed every single one.

The next morning, when I woke to my cousins packing their suitcases, bleary-eyed from staying up far too late talking, I was tempted to believe it had all been a dream.

But Sutton came back inside from loading her car and handed me a small gift bag. "I was asked to deliver this to you." Her usually confident voice was laced with an emotion I couldn't quite decipher.

I pulled out a white cardboard box and opened it to find a silver necklace with a sand dollar charm. The torn scrap of paper in the bottom of the bag bore six words I would read over and over again: "Happy birthday, Alex. Until next year."

But the next year, the Alfords were gone.

I sit bolt upright and squint as my eyes adjust to the darkness in the room, and it takes me a few seconds to remember where I am, how I got here. I check the time on my phone; 12:12. How have I only been asleep for an hour?

Swinging my feet over the side of the bed, I pull on a long-sleeved shirt over my tank top. I pad across the floor as quietly as I can, aware that Jude's room is directly underneath this one and not sure how heavy of a sleeper he is.

The door to Gavin's room is wide open, but I still feel like I'm trespassing as I step inside. His bed is neatly made and everything on his desk is in its place. I wonder if he was this organized when he lived here or if the room's been cleaned up since. There's a mirror-topped dresser in the corner with so many photos tucked around the edges that I can hardly see my own reflection. His smile is every bit as dazzling as I remember it as he looks back at me from dozens of moments in time captured with friends. I'm not surprised that none of us girls are in any of them, but it still makes me a tiny bit sad and jealous. The faded image in the bottom right corner grabs my eye and immediately makes me tear up. It's a young Gavin and Jude, long before we met them but unmistakably the same boys we knew. Know? They're on the beach. Gavin's arm is draped casually over Jude's shoulder, and Jude is looking up at him with a look of pure adoration in his eyes. I know the feeling.

My mind too full for sleep, I grab my notebook and pen from the room next door and go downstairs.

I'm so lost in thought that I'm only one step from the bottom before I notice Jude sitting on a barstool at the kitchen island, books spread out in front of him under the hanging light. He's clad in gray pajama pants and a white T-shirt and is typing something on his laptop. When he pauses to lift his glasses with one hand and rub the other across his tired eyes, a twinge of affection pinches my chest.

"Hey." He catches sight of me and leans back on the stool. "You okay?"

"Yeah, I'm good. I just woke up and couldn't fall back asleep. I didn't mean to disturb you."

"You're not disturbing me."

I cross the room and set my notebook and pen next to a textbook. "What are you working on?"

"Online business classes. But I think I'm done for the night."

"Oh, wow. This tourism business idea is for real then?"

He looks stung, and I feel like a jerk.

"Sorry, that came out wrong." I sit down beside him. "I love that you're doing this. I think it sounds really cool. I guess I always just pictured you becoming some kind of doctor, or like, a Jeopardy contestant or something. You were always so much smarter than anyone else in the room."

"That's a very kind way of saying I was a nerd."

I shake my head, but he smiles just enough to let me know he's not offended. "Believe it or not, 'game show contestant' is not an actual profession. And while the science of medicine fascinates me, I'm not a fan of blood."

"Oh my gosh, I forgot about that! Remember that time Rebekah cut her foot on a seashell?"

He winces. "I'd rather not."

"Sorry," I laugh. "Do you still play the trumpet?"

"What's with all the questions?" He closes his computer.

I almost apologize again, but he doesn't look upset. "It's just strange." I shrug. "I feel like I know you so well and, at the same time, don't know you at all."

"Well." He closes a book and stacks it on another. "I haven't practiced trumpet since high school marching band. But rest assured, I am still very much the geeky kid you remember." He stifles a yawn.

"I need to let you get some rest."

"It *has* been a pretty eventful day," he admits. "But feel free to stay up as long as you want. You can write or watch TV or eat cheese or whatever it is you usually do on vacation; I promise you won't bother me."

"Thanks. And maybe tomorrow, we can work on the Late Night Cheese Eating promotional materials for your future clients."

"Perfect." He stands and slides the stack of books from the counter into his arms before heading for the hallway. "Night, Alex. I'm glad you're here."

So am I.

Chapter 6

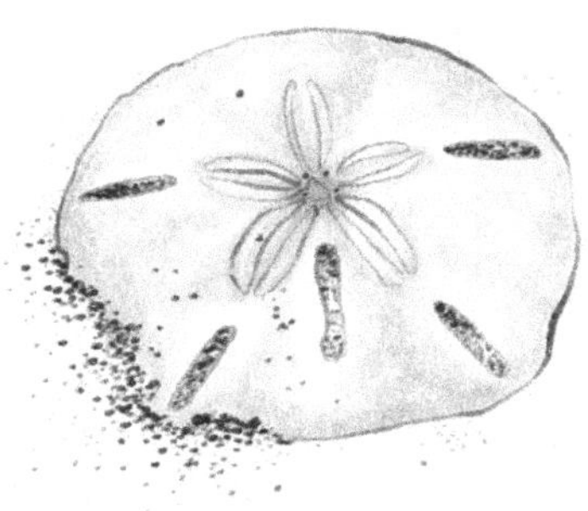

I have a box of seashells
And other souvenirs
No matter where I open it
It brings me back to here
Most of the time I keep it
Tucked high up on a shelf
For inside, there lay sacred
Fragile pieces of myself
Whispers of sweet days gone by
And people I love dearest
Lessons learned and memories
I long to hold the nearest
Sometimes I hardly can believe
I've found myself so blessed

To have these treasures buried
Here so deep within this chest

I was seven the first time I had a legitimate shot at Olympic gold.

We were in second place in the relays with one event to go. My parents and I were teamed up with Rebekah, her four brothers, and my Aunt Jane and Uncle Jeff. The only things standing between us and the podium were a handful of other relatives and the open sand.

"You guys know the rules," my Aunt Clara shouted above the roar of the waves. She pointed up the beach to where a line of sand buckets stood in the dry sand furthest from the water. "First team to fill up their bucket wins."

I looked down at the giant sponge in my hand. "We got this," Rebekah whispered.

"In your dreams," Elle answered from the huddle next to us.

My aunt gave the signal, and we were off. Our first rotation was perfect, and it was my turn again before I'd even had a chance to fully catch my breath.

I was almost to our bucket when my flip-flop broke. Had the games commenced after dinner as scheduled, this would not have been a problem. But since the weather forecast had caused us to move them to earlier in the day, the sand was *hot*.

I squeezed out the sponge and hobbled back to tag Rebekah, who more than made up for the seconds I'd lost.

"Here." She yanked her own sandal off when she returned. "Borrow mine."

We were back on track, but two turns later, in our haste to transfer the shoe we were sharing, the strap pulled away from the sole.

"Crap!"

I would have found the look Aunt Jane shot Rebekah for using that word hilarious if I wasn't so caught up in the fact that our Olympic dreams were about to die.

"What do we do?" Rebekah stood helpless with one shoe and a dripping sponge.

"Come on, kiddo." Scooping her up and throwing her over his shoulder, Uncle Jeff took off down the beach. Rebekah squealed and held on for dear life.

When the sponge was finally passed back to me, my dad was ready. I watched Rebekah's face as he carried me away and wondered if mine shone with pure joy the same way hers did.

The race ended, and we all collapsed in the sand, laughing until the tears spilled down our sunburnt cheeks.

I didn't need a medal around my neck to know we'd won.

"Just like any other hotel, I guess. I'm not sure what you want me to say. Hey, did you read that article I sent you?" I try to change the subject. Lying to Sutton had been easy, but I've always had more difficulty keeping things from Rebekah. And I'm not exactly certain why I feel so protective of the details surrounding my stay here, but I do.

"Not yet. I pulled a double shift, remember?"

"That's right. You should sleep, hero."

"You know me, saving the world one emptied bedpan at a time. K. Love you, Al. Send me pictures of your room."

"Okay." I won't. "Love you too."

I set my phone on the counter space next to the stove and study the note again. It was tucked under a house key when I stumbled into the kitchen late this morning.

Thought you might need this. Wednesdays are my long days, so I won't be home until around 8:30. Make yourself at home. At the bottom of the page, there's a drawing of a little mouse eating a piece of cheese.

The clock on the microwave reads 8:27. I fill a pot with water and turn on the burner, then open the fridge and find the pack of hotdogs we bought yesterday.

I've washed the grapes, opened a bag of chips, retrieved the ketchup and mustard, and set two places by the time he walks in the front door, looking exhausted and slightly disheveled.

"What's all this?" He motions to the table.

"I wasn't sure if you'd eaten dinner yet," I explain, suddenly feeling very self-conscious. "If you aren't hungry, that's okay."

His signature soft smile appears, and he sits. "No, I'm starving. Thank you. But you didn't have to do all this."

"It's just hotdogs, Jude." I shrug. "No big deal." But even as I say it, I wonder if it's actually a bigger deal than I realize. When's the last time anyone cooked for Jude? The last time he didn't eat alone in this kitchen?

The words tumble out of my mouth before I can stop them. "Do you ever get lonely here by yourself?"

He looks up from the perfect line of mustard he's just drawn.

"Sorry," I recover. "It's just that coming from a big extended family, I'm used to being around a lot of people, and it was so quiet around here today. I can't imagine being alone all the time." I'm making this worse.

He picks up a chip. "Well, like I said, I stay pretty busy with work. But I guess I don't really know anything different. Even when the four of us were here, everyone else was hardly ever . . . here."

I want to ask him what happened, why they suddenly dropped off the face of the earth six years ago. Despite the fact that I feel like I know him and his family as well as my own, it isn't true. And I don't want to lose them again by pushing him away. A change of subject might be best.

"I know you've had a busy day, but is there any chance you'd be up for an adventure tonight?"

He nods and swallows the grape he's chewing. "Every chance. What are we doing?"

I set my hotdog down so I can use my hands to present the words like a game show prize. "Night Castles."

"I'm not sure I'm familiar with that particular tradition," he confesses.

"Okay, so." I scoot my chair closer. "It's supposed to be a team sport, but it will work on a smaller scale for just the two of us. The basic premise is that teams randomly draw a piece of paper with the name of a famous building or landmark on it. You have a set amount of time to use sand and anything else you can find on the beach to construct it. The catch is, the only light you can use is glow sticks. No flashlights. Those are only for The Judging. You get one point for every person who can guess what your building is, one point for every correct guess of your own, and two points for everyone who chooses yours as their favorite. There's a significant amount of math involved now that I think about it. Of course, none of this will apply tonight. We'll just have to each decide what we want to build and then guess each other's."

I look up and Jude is leaning back in his seat, looking at me like he's very used to this specific brand of Henry family crazy. "Where are we going to get glow sticks?" is his only question.

I gesture to the counter with a flourish. "I'm very prepared. I'm no Night Castle rookie."

We make quick work of cleaning up the kitchen, and Jude snaps the glow sticks and makes them into bracelets and necklaces while I run upstairs for the new shovels and buckets I picked up this afternoon.

"I was thinking," he says as we make our way up the street. "Since this is my first Night Castle experience and there are only two of us, why don't we build something together? You can kind of mentor me, and then next time, I can go Anakin Skywalker and try to defeat you with the skills you've taught me."

"Did you just infer that I'm Obi-Wan? Because I take that as a compliment."

He holds up a glow stick and swings it like a lightsaber.

"You're even funnier than you used to be," I observe.

"Um . . . thanks?"

I laugh, something I've been doing much more of since I got here yesterday. A familiar place with a familiar friend is doing my heart a lot of good, I decide.

"Do you still like mint chocolate chip ice cream?" I suddenly need to know he hasn't changed *too* much.

"I'm not a monster, Alex. Of course I do."

"And do you still like being summoned with an off-key rendition of your favorite Beatles song?"

"I never liked that, and you know it."

"Really?" I feign innocence, recalling one of the very few times I've ever seen him get angry. He was ten at the time, so I'm pretty sure it's a safe subject now. "So from now on, I'll just say, 'Yo, Jude.' Would that be . . . better?"

"Don't do it."

I sing the last word of my question over and over to the tune, and he rolls his eyes.

We reach the steps that lead to the beach, and he turns around. "You finished?"

"I want to say yes, but . . . "

"Alex."

"Nah." I pause for effect before launching into a chorus of enthusiastic "nahs" that would make the British band proud.

A real laugh escapes Jude, and it makes me unreasonably happy. This feels right. Like maybe my childhood isn't so long gone after all.

Chapter 7

"Where have *you* been?" Elle leaned forward and around me to glare at Sutton.

Sutton ignored her and set up her folding chair in the grass next to Rebekah's. I looked over and lifted a brow, hoping that my silent question had a better chance of eliciting an answer than a thinly veiled accusation.

"I was on the phone." She smiled sardonically at Elle. "I wasn't aware I had to get permission to move around independently. I'll be sure to check in with the rest of the unit next time." For some reason, the comment stung me more than it seemed to bother Elle. The past year of high school had caused some kind of unwelcome shift in my oldest cousin, and I couldn't help but feel she was keeping things from us.

Rebekah pulled an elastic band from her wrist and twisted her hair up into a ponytail. "I hope it wasn't that dumb basketball player. I thought you were over him. I keep hoping you'll finally figure out that guys don't magically become decent in the span of a few months."

"And I keep hoping you'll learn to mind your own business," she snapped.

Sudden tears sprang to my eyes. "I hate this."

The yard, filling with family, buzzed around us, but the four of us sat in silence.

"It's not like we've never fought before," Sutton finally said.

Rebekah slid her chair close and linked her arm in mine. "We'll get over it, Al. It'd take a lot more than Sutton's witchy attitude to break up the four of us."

Sutton stuck out her tongue and made an over-the-top hateful face.

A giggle snuck out of Elle. And then another. Soon, she couldn't stop.

Rebekah joined in, and my chair shook so hard I didn't stand a chance. Sutton hung on the longest. She tried her best to stay angry, but by the time my Great Aunt Debbie sat down in the middle of the circle with her ukulele, we were all in hysterics.

The Uku-Lady, as we grew up calling her, looked our way and waited for us to control ourselves before she began.

"Any requests?" She scanned the crowd. But everyone knew we'd sing them all.

It took the skunk and watermelon songs and the first two verses of the one about the ticklish turtle before I finally let myself believe it: we were all right. And, as long as we kept showing up for each other, we always would be.

"Good morning."

I was proud of myself for setting an alarm and getting an early start today, but Jude was already fully dressed and cooking eggs. I should have guessed that he'd be a morning person.

"Morning." I open the cabinet and survey the tiny cereal box collection. "How long have you been up?"

"Not long. I just went down to the beach to check on Ty's surf lessons and take a few pictures for the website. You want an omelet? I'm using the good cheese."

He turns around just as I pull out the fruit loops. "Don't judge me; I'm on vacation."

"Never." He holds up the spatula. "I was honestly thinking about a bowl of that chocolatey kind myself."

"Excellent choice." I reopen the cabinet and grab the box, then open a couple of drawers, trying to remember where to find spoons.

I locate bowls and set them on the island, and by the time I've retrieved the milk from the fridge, he's cutting the omelet in half and transferring it onto two plates.

"Was the Taj Mahal still standing?" I ask as I pour my cereal.

"Sadly, no. I wanted to get a picture before the tide came in." He frowns. "But we'll always remember how perfect it looked by the light of a dozen glow sticks."

"We'll build a better one next time," I promise.

"Here." He slides a piece of paper across the counter. "I thought this might be helpful." I study the calendar page with a surfboard logo at the top. "It's the template I use to keep Ty organized, but since my work schedule is kind of unusual, I put all my shifts for the next couple weeks on here so you'll know when I'll be around. My phone number is at the top in case of emergency. And down here is the schedule for trash pick-up and all that kind of stuff." He pauses and runs a hand through his hair. "And now I'm realizing that this seems kind of weird, like I'm trying to be your landlord or something. That wasn't my intention."

"No." I set my spoon down and offer him a reassuring smile. "This is very considerate, Jude. And it will help with planning all the fun stuff. Can I borrow a pen?"

He opens the most organized junk drawer I've ever seen in my entire life and passes me a pen. I go through the calendar and add things like "crab hunting," "shell painting," and "postcards to celebrities" in between bites of the cheesiest, most delicious omelet I've ever eaten.

"So you don't go in until this afternoon to . . . wait tables?" I consult the chart. "What restaurant?"

He averts his eyes, and I don't miss the color that creeps into his cheeks. "I'm not ready for that conversation yet."

"You know that only makes me want to know even more, right?" I lean forward. "Is it something scandalous? Illegal? Do you have a secret double life?"

He starts clearing the dishes. "Anyway," he changes the subject, "do you think we have time to squeeze in a traditional beach activity this morning? Or do you have plans already?"

"Well, the weather is gorgeous today. It would be perfect for a beach swap, but seeing as I only brought two books, we might need to hit up the used bookstore first."

"Hmm." He turns off the sink. "Want to explain that one for me? What's a beach swap, and why do you need books for it?"

"It's something the four of us started a few years ago. Everyone brings a favorite book, and we trade. We spend a couple hours reading together on the beach, and then we give our honest reviews over a bag of tortilla chips when everyone's done."

"Why tortilla chips?" He catches himself. "Right. Tradition."

I nod approvingly.

He leans against the fridge, considers for a moment, then says, "Okay. Come with me."

I follow him down the short hallway, my curiosity piqued.

I'm not sure what I'm expecting, but when he swings open the door to his bedroom, my hand flies to my mouth in shock. "Oh my gosh! JUDE."

Floor-to-ceiling bookshelves line an entire wall and are filled with books organized by color. There must be hundreds of books in here. My feet act before my brain has a chance to process, and I think, too late, that I probably should have asked his permission before running my hands across the spines and pulling a few from the first shelf to read the backs.

I look up. He's watching me admire his collection with a look of pure pride. It isn't unwarranted.

"This is amazing," I squeal. "Is it okay—?" I look down at the book I'm holding.

"Of course. How else are you supposed to pick one for the beach reading tradition?"

"Okay, first of all, forget the beach swap. I'm trying to figure out how to convince you to swap *rooms* with me. And secondly, *you're* supposed to pick which book I read." I slide the book back into its place. "And now would probably be a good time to tell you that you'll either be reading *Pride and Prejudice* or a rom-com Sutton loaned me."

"If I admit that I've read the first a handful of times already, does that automatically mean I end up with the rom-com?"

"No, Mr. Bingley, it does not. It is impossible to read any Austen book too many times. And this one is my comfort read." I scan the titles in front of me. "What's yours?"

He crosses the room to stand next to me. "You promise you won't laugh?" He chuckles and shakes his head. "I guess you already know I'm a nerd anyway . . . "

"Jude." I point to the bookshelves. "You are the coolest person I know right now."

"Is that why you called me Bingley?"

"Well, you're too nice to be Darcy," I confess. I mean it as a compliment, but I'm not sure if it comes across as such. "Okay, so your comfort read . . . ?" I prod.

He reaches above my head, selects a yellow book, and places it in my hands.

"*Little Women*?" I trace the intricate lettering with my index finger. "Why would I laugh? This is one of the best stories ever written."

"It doesn't seem like a very manly choice, I guess." He raises his shoulders and lets them fall again. "But it's oddly comforting to escape to the March household sometimes. It actually makes me think of you Henrys."

I laugh. "That makes me very happy." I wince. "Although, I think all four of us might be some combination of Jo and Amy. There's not a mild-mannered Meg or Beth amongst us."

"You aren't wrong." His countenance softens. "And Laurie didn't have a geeky younger brother tagging along either, so it's not a perfect analogy." He reaches to the right and picks out his own copy of *Pride and Prejudice*. "We should get going," he suggests. "Those tortilla chips aren't going to eat themselves."

Two hours later, I carefully mark my spot in Miss Alcott's story with a gum wrapper and turn in my beach chair. "Just so you know, you guys were both our Lauries."

He smiles and keeps reading.

Chapter 8

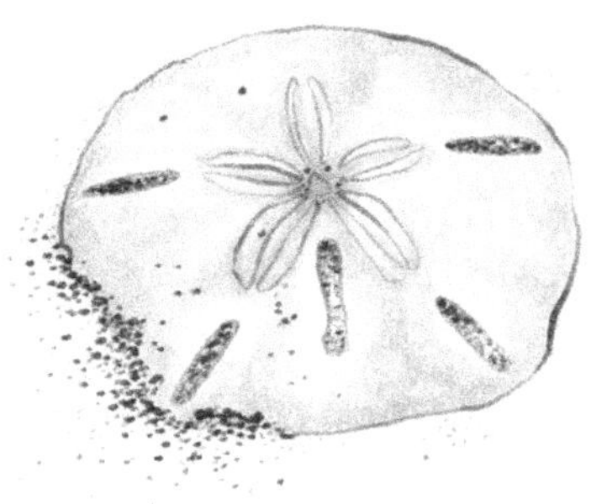

"Hold on." I examined the top card on the deck. "I played a five!"

"Right, but you can't win with the same number you won with on the last turn," Sutton explained as if I were much younger than my nine years.

"You're just making this up as we go along!" Elle accused. "So you always win!"

"Guys." Sutton pulled out her cheetah print notepad and pointed to the third line scribbled in bright green gel pen. "The rules that we *all* agreed upon clearly state that you can win with each number only once a round."

"Fine." Elle threw down two sevens. "Gubbins!"

"Wait a minute." Sutton checked the two piles in front of Elle and referred to her notes several times before finally admitting defeat.

"Okay." She scribbled a tally mark in the second column. "But Bekah and I are still up by three."

Everyone tossed their remaining cards into the middle of the table, and I gathered up the deck. "I'll shuffle this time. Then maybe you guys won't end up with all the hearts."

"See? What did I tell you?" My Aunt Jane walked into the room. "A little rain is good for the imagination."

"You're right," I told her. "Sutton and Rebekah are doing an awesome job imagining they have a chance at beating us."

Elle bumped my fist with hers before cramming another handful of gummy worms into her mouth.

"So queens are wild, right?"

"Right," I confirm. "And the six of clubs."

"This is the most complicated game I've ever played." He discards two cards and draws new ones. "And if you lay two down together, it's their total value minus one?"

"Unless they're nines."

"In which case, you automatically win."

"Yes. Unless someone on another team has two nines also, but that hardly ever happens."

Three plays later, he says it quietly. "Gubbins."

"Seriously?!" I check the cards. "Okay, either this is crazy beginner's luck, or you and I are going to swindle my whole family when they come in July."

He shuffles. "I'll just randomly show up on game night, and you'll volunteer to teach me to play. They'll never suspect a thing."

"You joke, but I'm counting on you. Don't let me down."

"Aren't you guys pretty strict about partners though? You think they're gonna just let me in?"

"They'll have to. Elle and Elias refuse to play with anyone but each other since their winning streak a few years ago. And when Sutton brought Chris in, Rebekah became *my* partner. But this year she's bringing Dr. McHandsome, so I'll need a new teammate."

He starts dealing the cards again. "So you're really not a fan of Rebekah's new boyfriend, huh?"

I fidget with my necklace. "It's not that I dislike him. He seems like a good guy, and he makes Bekah happy. I don't know."

He stops dealing and gives me time to say more, if I want to. I do.

"Sometimes I worry that things won't ever be the same, you know. We all used to be so close. And now Sutton has Chris and Marcie, and Rebekah's with this doctor guy. And Elle—Elle has the whole world. And I'm happy for them; I *want* them to be happy." I shrug. "I just don't want them to be happy . . . without me. Does that make me sound like a terrible person?"

"No, it doesn't." He abandons the cards and adjusts his glasses. "But it absolutely confirms the fact that you're the real Jo."

I study the ceiling and blink a few times to keep from crying. "Does that mean I'll end up publishing my book after all?"

"Oh, I have no doubt." He picks the deck of cards up again. "I'm saving it a spot of honor on my shelves."

He waits to make sure I'm really all right before he casually says, "Hey, speaking of family, Gavin's been talking about coming down the weekend after next to visit some friends. Will that be . . . okay with you? If he stays here?"

I beg my face not to show any of the dozen emotions that simultaneously assault me. "Of course. You don't have to ask my permission for your brother to come visit you in your own house." It takes a second for me to process what this would mean. "Oh, but I can totally leave for a few days if that'd be better."

"No, that's not why I brought it up. And maybe I shouldn't have. I just didn't want it to be weird for you." I suddenly wonder how much he knows. "Seriously, Alex, it's not a problem at all for you to stay; I'm sure Gavin would love to catch up with you." I feel my face heat. "I just wanted to give you a heads up, is all."

"Okay," I breathe, feeling lightheaded and racking my brain for a change of subject.

Jude rescues me. "Hey, how many houses do you all rent now?"

"Nine." I push Gavin as far from my mind as I can. If Jude can already tell that this mention of his brother has struck a nerve, I'm in trouble. "The four on this street and then three more a few blocks down toward the pier. And this year, both sides of that duplex on the corner."

"Wow. You guys really are taking over the island." His voice is still tinged with concern, and I want to tell him I'm fine, but I'm still not quite sure I am.

The quiet lasts long enough that I'm starting to feel awkward. "I've got an idea." Jude stands up. "If you're up for it."

I really don't feel like going anywhere today, but I nod anyway.

"After all these years, I'm still trying to figure this nation of a family out. If I grab a piece of paper, will you talk me through who's who?"

I'm *always* up for talking about my family. "Let's do it." I feel better already. "But you're going to need more than one piece of paper."

I appreciate him giving me a minute to pull myself together. He comes back with a notebook and pencil along with two bottles of water and a bag of cheesy chips. "Okay." He flips to a blank page. "I can't promise I'll get all this the first time."

"That's all right. There are people *in* our family who still don't have it all straight." I open my water and take a sip. "Okay, so my Uncle James is the oldest. He has four kids." I list them off and move on to my Uncle Kenneth's family.

I make it all the way to the seventh brother before I can tell I'm losing him. "Let's take a break," I suggest.

"No, I think I've almost got it." He scribbles down another name. "I just needed to see how the four of you girls fit into all this; you've always been my reference point."

I freeze, and hot tears fill my vision without warning.

"That." My voice catches. "That's exactly what I was trying to explain earlier." He looks up from the page, and I'm desperate to make him understand why I feel so lost. "The four of us have always been *my* reference point. For everything."

Chapter 9

The ocean soothes me with her song
When I feel alone
afraid
adrift
She never drowns out the voices
Of those I love
She plays them back for me
Over
and over
and over
Until I remember them
Until I memorize them
Until they meld into my own
And I start to find the rhythm

Of my words
Again

"Four . . . five . . . six . . . seven . . . eight . . ."

Elias's voice faded as Rebekah and I took off in the same direction, looking for a hiding place no one had used yet.

Elle was already under the picnic table where my mom and several aunts were sitting and talking, and Sutton must have found a good spot because I had no idea where she was.

Rebekah pulled me past the little row of hedges and under the blue house.

"I don't think we should be over here." I glanced behind us to see if our moms were watching. "This isn't our house."

"Gavin and Jude won't mind." She kept walking.

"We only met them two days ago, Rebekah. We can't just invite ourselves to their house."

"We're not going into their house." She checked the doorknob beside the outdoor shower and pushed it open to reveal a washer and dryer. "Just in here."

"I feel weird about this." I hesitated.

"You'll feel better when we win. And I don't even think anyone's home."

The sound of my cousin's "Ready or not, here I come" made the decision for me. I scurried into the laundry room behind Rebekah and pushed the door shut.

"Leave it cracked," she whispered. "Not enough to see, just enough to hear what's going on."

"Okay." I reached for the door handle.

It turned but wouldn't budge.

"It's stuck." I panicked.

Rebekah's eyes got big. "You think it locks automatically?"

"It's not locked." I wiggled the handle again. "It's just jammed or something."

She pushed my hands out of the way and tried it herself. Nothing.

My panic turned to full-fledged fear. I balled my hands into fists and started pounding on the door, yelling at the top of my lungs.

I turned to Rebekah for some kind of reassurance, but she had started to cry. "We're going to be in so much trouble."

"*Help!*" I was frantic. How had none of the dozens of relatives next door heard us? What if they never found us? Or perhaps more concerning, what would happen to us if they did?

"Hello?" A tentative voice called from the other side of the jammed exit.

Rebekah found her voice. "We're stuck! We can't get the door open."

"Okay, hold on. Let me see if I can open it from this side."

I watched the handle move up and down a few times. "Hmm. I might have to kick it or something. Can you stand back?"

Rebekah and I both moved away. There was a loud thud and then another. The door hardly shook.

"Let me go get some help," our would-be rescuer suggested.

"But we don't want to get in trouble!" Rebekah's tears had disappeared. "Can't you just try one more time?"

"Okay, just a second."

Everything was quiet for a moment. Rebekah reached over and held my hand.

The sound of rapid footfalls approached, followed by a crash. The door swung open, and Jude's small silhouette stood in the doorway and rubbed at his shoulder as our eyes adjusted to the sunlight pouring in.

"Are you okay?" Rebekah rushed toward him, and he stumbled backwards a little.

"Yeah. Yeah, I'm okay." He sounded like he was still trying to convince himself. "I can't believe that worked." A slow grin spread across his face and briefly lit his eyes with pride before he noticed the splintered wood of the doorframe and winced.

"We're gonna be in So. Much. Trouble." Rebekah's tears returned. And, of course, seeing her cry made me start too.

Jude looked more frantic than we did mere minutes ago. "Don't cry! You won't get in trouble. Really. I'll tell my dad it was my fault."

Rebekah wiped her nose with the back of her hand. "But it wasn't. It was our fault."

"It's not a big deal." He stepped to the side so we could move out of the laundry room. "We get in trouble for stuff like this all the time. And I don't mind being grounded, because I like to read anyway. Listen, I'll make you a deal: you guys stop crying and I promise no one will even know you were over here today." He held out a hand.

Rebekah half laughed, half sniffled as she grabbed it and shook it up and down.

"No, not like that," Jude corrected. "That's how you shake someone's hand when you meet them. For making a deal, you just need one firm shake. Like this." He extended his arm to me next and shook it decisively when our hands met.

"Alex? Bekah?" Elle's voice echoed.

"Quick." Jude shuffled aside. "Around the bushes at the front. I'll keep an eye out over here for you."

We took off. At the end of the driveway, I stopped to mouth, "Thanks, Jude."

He straightened his glasses and shrugged. Almost like he knew it wouldn't be the last time he fixed things for us.

"Why does it smell so good in here?" Jude walks in the front door, and it's all I can do not to bombard him with all the words I've had no chance to share with anyone else today. It's nearly nine p.m., and he's been gone since I woke up this morning.

"Lasagna's in the oven." I set down the salad bowl and reach for an oven mitt.

He tosses his keys in the little basket and frowns. "I thought we might just order pizza or something tonight."

"Oh." I close the drawer in front of me. "I'm sorry."

His cheeks color the way I've noticed they do when he feels misunderstood. "Please don't apologize. I love lasagna. I just don't want you to feel like you have to cook every night. I'm used to fending for myself."

"Well, I'm used to living in a house that isn't a short walk away from the ocean, but I'm not complaining."

His shoulders relax, and he leans against the counter. "How can I help?"

"You want to mix up the salad?"

He moves to the sink to wash his hands. "Talk to your cousins today?"

"Only Bekah for a few minutes. She was on her way back from Sutton's." I place the steaming lasagna on a trivet. "This will need to cool for a few minutes."

"Mmm." He closes his eyes and breathes deeply. "That seriously smells incredible." He adds dressing to the leaves and starts tossing the salad. "Hey, do your cousins know you're staying here?"

I look for something to busy my hands with, not sure how to explain this to him. "No, actually. I didn't know if—" I search for the right words.

"If they'd think it was weird?"

"More like if they'd ask me a million follow-up questions. Or maybe even if they'd invite themselves to move in too." I force a laugh and change the subject. "How was your day?"

"Long," he admits. "Saturdays are pretty full." I'm starting to realize that all his days are pretty full; even with the schedule he gave me, I'm still not straight on how many jobs he's working.

"What did you have today again?"

"I helped Ty early this morning with some end of the week stuff and then cleaned houses as people started checking out around nine. I left there around two-thirty and then worked two dinners."

"At your mystery waiting job?" I interject. He cuts his eyes at me, and while I know he isn't angry, I can also tell he's still not ready to tell me more. I switch tracks. "I've always thought it would be interesting to be a housekeeper on the island. Is it strange to think about the stories of all the people who've just spent one of the best weeks of their year in the houses you're cleaning?"

He chuckles. "Well, I'm not a writer like you, so I usually do less thinking about people's stories and more thinking about how to get stains out of the carpet or gallons of sand out of the bathtub. In fact, the state of some of these houses would make you happy you don't know the stories behind them." He shivers.

"That bad, huh?"

"Not always. But I've . . . seen some things." He yawns and stretches his back.

"Here." I take over the salad. "You sit down. I'm tired just hearing about your day."

He hesitates but doesn't argue. "How was your day?" he asks while I fix his plate. "Did you write?"

"I did." I finish serving my plate and sit down next to him.

"So you're probably exhausted too, just in a different way." I'm struck by the way this simple observation rolls off his tongue so effortlessly but makes me feel so *seen.*

"Yeah, actually. I'm kind of spent emotionally."

He cuts into his lasagna and asks, "You feel like talking about it, or do you need to think about something else?"

I do feel like talking to him about it. I've always felt like I could talk to Jude about pretty much anything. Minus his brother.

"Have you ever had the feeling," I ask as I set down my fork and pick at the edge of the napkin in my lap, "that everyone and everything around you is moving on, and you're just kind of . . . stuck? Like you've been left behind?"

He wipes his mouth and nods. "Alex, I grew up in a beach house where my neighbors, when I had them, moved in and out on a weekly basis, with a family that never really felt like what I supposed a normal family should. And then *they* moved out. I know that feeling very well."

"Of course. I'm sorry, Jude. I didn't—"

He bumps his knee against mine. "Stop apologizing to me tonight, okay? You have nothing to be sorry for. I'm just telling you that I understand how you feel, and it sucks."

He turns back to his dinner, and it makes me happy to see that he's enjoying it.

I study him for a few beats before saying, "I keep coming back to how therapeutic the ocean is for my heart. Do you ever feel that? Or is it so commonplace to you now that it's lost its effect?"

He swallows the bite in his mouth and sighs. "Impossible. I could live *in* the ocean and never get enough of it."

"Good. I really hoped that was the case."

"Speaking of which." He checks the time. "Is it too late to squeeze in a beach tradition tonight?"

"We already have." I smile.

"Yeah?"

"One of my favorite Henry family vacation traditions: ending a long day talking over a meal with some of your favorite people in the world."

I can tell he almost doesn't ask the next question, but I'm glad he does. "Does that mean I'm included in your list of favorites?"

"Of course you are, Jude. Pretty close to the top of it, in fact."

"So, like, somewhere between your cousins and cheese?"

"Let's not get crazy." I spear a cucumber with my fork. "There are days when I'd rank cheese above at least two of my cousins."

His laugh is the most comforting sound I've heard all day.

Chapter 10

We'd been helping Grandmama make her famous chocolate oat-meal cookies since before we could read, but the summer I turned twelve was the first time we were entrusted with making them by ourselves. She was not in the kitchen to supervise, she said, but merely to visit with us while we worked.

I could recite the steps in my sleep, and the recipe was one composed of fewer actual measurements and more instincts and estimates. Still, we took the task very seriously; we wanted to make her proud.

Sutton stood at the stove, watching over the pot and stirring constantly to ensure that not a single batch burned. Rebekah and I took turns rationing out and pouring in each ingredient. Elle transferred hot spoonfuls of chocolatey heaven onto the waiting sheets of tin foil and then popped each cookie free as it cooled, adding it to a paper plate. Our granddaddy and various aunts, uncles, and cousins were emptying the plate almost as quickly as she could fill it.

We all held our breath when Grandmama reached over, plucked a sample from the latest batch, and popped it into her mouth.

She closed her eyes and sighed contentedly. "Girls, these may be the best cookies I've ever tasted; far better than any I've made." She caught my eye and winked. She had dozens of grandkids, but I always got the impression I was her favorite. And I suspected that Elle, Rebekah, and Sutton all had the same theory about themselves. I was pretty sure this was intentional on my Grandmama's part.

"These things are going *fast* this year," Elle observed as she used a spoon to remove more treats from the foil.

"I told you." Grandmama beamed. "They're special."

"Or maybe it's because our family keeps growing." Rebekah filled a teaspoon with vanilla extract.

"We really are blessed." Grandmama's eyes shone.

"Or because Uncle Alvin's daughters all brought their boyfriends this year," I grumbled to Rebekah under my breath.

"I don't think we have enough cocoa for another batch." Sutton peered into the container I'd just set on the counter.

"I bought at least five containers this year." Grandmama walked around and rustled through a cabinet. "You girls really did make a ton of these today!" She lifted a towel from the edge of the sink and reached over to squeeze Sutton's shoulder. "Y'all deserve a break; I'll clean up. And if you decide you want to bake again tomorrow, we can ride over to the store." She picked up the roll of foil and tore off a sheet, nestled some cookies inside before folding it closed.

"Y'all ought to take a couple of these over to the family that lives in that blue house."

Elle wiggled her eyebrows at Sutton.

"When you have something special," my grandmother whispered as she put a gentle hand on my back and entrusted me with the shiny bundle, "it's good to share it with other people. Some things can never be divided, only multiplied."

It's Monday morning, and there's a muscular, half-naked man standing in Jude's living room.

"Um, hi." I feign normalcy as I walk past him to the kitchen. He follows me.

"Hi there. You must be Alex." He rests the hip of his lime-green swim trunks against the counter and picks up an apple from the basket next to him. "I'm Tyler."

"Ah." I flip the switch on the coffee maker. "Surf lesson Ty." I contemplate a bowl of junk cereal but feel self-conscious enough to opt for a piece of fruit instead. "Are you looking for Jude?"

He crunches into his apple. "Nah. We've been down at the beach all morning." I check the clock; it's only a quarter after eight. "He just wanted to grab a quick shower before we do some work."

As if on cue, Jude's bedroom door squeaks open, and he emerges into the hallway with wet hair and a band camp hoodie above his cargo shorts. I look from him to Ty, and the contrast almost makes me laugh out loud. They are exactly the kind of unlikely best friends I would expect to find in a book.

"Good morning, Alex. I see you've met Ty."

"Yep." Ty walks around the island and pulls Jude's laptop from its spot. "We were just sharing a bite to eat, and I was about to convince her to sign up for a few lessons."

"Absolutely not." I set down my uneaten apple and open the mug cabinet. "You want some coffee, Tyler?" I offer like this is my own kitchen or something.

"Not a coffee drinker." He makes a face and runs a hand through his messy, long hair. "But I'd love a glass of water if you don't mind."

Jude watches me fill a cup at the sink and hand it to Ty before he takes a seat.

"Thanks." Ty flashes his toothpaste commercial-worthy smile.

I fix two cups of coffee and try to add the same amount of milk to Jude's that I've watched him pour in the past couple days. I place his mug in front of him and hold mine up. "Is it okay if I take this upstairs?"

"Of course. But you don't have to leave."

"Yeah, come take a look at this." Ty angles the computer and scoots over so I can take the barstool between them.

I leave my coffee beside Jude's and sit in front of the screen. "Wow." I scroll through the open website's home page. "This is really cool."

Ty points to the toolbar at the top. "If you click here, you can see all the activities Jude wants to offer when we officially launch. And here." He moves his hand next to mine and drags the cursor over to a tiny surfboard logo. "These are my client testimonials. See? Right here it says even a beginner can learn basic skills in just *one* lesson."

"I'm not taking surf lessons." I laugh. "Jude, do you surf?"

"Not well," he confesses and sips his coffee.

I explore the site for another minute. "And you guys designed all this yourselves?"

"Nope." Ty takes over the keyboard again to show me the handful of things I've missed. "Jude designed the whole thing. And came up with all the ideas. He also does all the admin stuff and bookkeeping and has been applying for loans. Oh, and he manages all the marketing."

"Who took the photos? These are gorgeous." I bite the inside of my cheek and hope he knows I'm referencing the beach and not his chiseled physique riding the waves.

"Jude."

"Whoa." I elbow Jude. "I didn't know you were a photographer too. No offense to Tyler, but you're basically running an entire business singlehandedly. This is incredible."

"None taken." Ty smiles. "I keep telling him he doesn't need me. I think he only keeps me around for advertising purposes." He stands and flexes his muscles. "But I'd do that for free; this website is essentially a dating platform for me."

"That's not true," Jude disagrees. "I mean, the dating thing maybe. But Ty's surf business is what really started all this. And he does more than he takes credit for."

"I'm just saying." Ty slides the computer away from me. "Jude could do pretty much anything he decided he wanted to. He's a man of many talents."

I like this guy. Not for the classic surfer boy charm, but for the way I can see he cares about my friend and recognizes all the amazing qualities that even Jude himself doesn't.

"So, Jude's been telling me you've been helping him figure out how to give families the full vacation experience," Ty goes on. "Sounds like your giant fam is the authority on all things tradition?"

"Kind of," I admit proudly. "But I really think we have so many more options because of our numbers. If you guys run the same kinds of events and let each family bring their own team to the competitions, people would see how much fun it is and sign up every year for sure. And people could pick and choose what they want to do based on their schedules, ages, et cetera." When I realize I've started to talk with my hands, I tuck them into my lap. "It would give families who vacation the same week every year a chance to connect with other families and form friendships." I nudge Jude again. "*We* met some of *our* favorite vacation buddies here, anyway."

An amused smile dances across Ty's face. "I think we just found our hype person, Jude."

"Sorry." I blush. "I just get excited talking about this stuff."

"As does Jude." He pulls up a new window on the computer and logs into his email. "Which is why I keep telling him to take the plunge and do this full-time. I never see him get this jazzed about cleaning houses or his pirate gig."

I reach around a frozen Jude to retrieve my coffee mug and try to keep my expression neutral. "Pirate gig?"

Jude sighs, and Ty barks a laugh. "You haven't told her? I don't know why you're so secretive about this, man. It's just a job."

I swivel around on my seat toward Jude and wait for an ex-planation. He sets his empty mug next to my nearly full one and sighs dramatically. "Fine. Have you ever heard of Ye Olde Dragon's Treasure Cove?"

"Stop it!" I grab Jude's arm with both hands. "You mean the dinner show I've been trying to talk my cousins into going to with me for *years*? Oh my gosh, this is the coolest thing *ever*. Why didn't you tell me?"

At this point, Tyler is cackling, and Jude has turned beet red.

"I'm booking a ticket right now." I let go of his arm and stand. "When's your next shift? Tonight?"

"Please don't," he groans.

"Why not?" I sink back onto the barstool, deflated.

"Because it's embarrassing." He rubs a hand across his forehead, leaving his damp hair sticking up at odd angles. It's sort of adorable, and I feel slightly guilty for teasing him.

"I don't think it's embarrassing. I think it's awesome." I force myself to take a sip of coffee to give myself time to gauge whether or not he's genuinely upset. I'm relieved when his eyes tell me he isn't. "Are you in the show?" I ask cautiously, my curiosity winning out. "Do you get to fight the animatronic dragon? I've heard it looks very realistic."

"Right." His signature timid grin returns. "Because there are so many real dragons to compare it to. And no, I'm not in the main show. I just wait tables."

"Dressed as a pirate?"

Tyler snickers again.

"Yes."

"Do you sing or dance or anything?" I press further.

He doesn't answer. I want so badly to beg for details but decide I might have more success without Tyler here, so I switch courses. I have no shortage of questions about this venue. I pick the first that comes to mind. "Have you ever seen anyone get engaged there?"

"Um . . . no? What kind of question is that?"

"I just think it would be a romantic place for a proposal. Like, something you'd see in a book or movie."

"I assure you, it would not."

"Think about it though. The guy tells the girl, 'Your heart is the greatest treasure I could ever be lucky enough to discover.'"

Tyler nearly spits out his water. "'I'd fight a thousand dragons for you, my pirate queen,'" he suggests when he recovers.

"See? Ty appreciates the value of a grand gesture."

"I didn't say *that* exactly," the surfer boy counters. "But it would make for a great story."

I put a hand over my heart. "'Sail off into the sunset with me?' Tell me that's not a little bit sweet, Jude."

He scans my face and then Ty's, appearing resigned to the fact that he's clearly outnumbered.

"Oh, how about this one?" Ty slaps the counter. "'Surrender your booty, my lady.'"

"Okay." Jude scoots back from the counter as I giggle and takes his mug to the sink. "I think maybe we should get some work done."

I pick up my now-lukewarm coffee and stand. "I'll head upstairs, but just to be clear, I'm not done with this conversation."

"I didn't assume you were." Jude chuckles. "Let me know if you need anything."

I head across the living room to the stairs. "I need to see this pirate costume but other than that . . ."

"It's the earring that really makes it," Ty calls.

"See you later, Alex," Jude yells, hurrying me along.

I'm in the bedroom doorway when Ty's deep voice wafts upstairs. "She's cute, man."

"Don't," Jude warns. "You're a great guy, but I know you're not looking for something serious. And she's special. She's practically family."

"I meant for *you*, dude."

The quiet seconds that follow give me time to close the door so I won't hear his answer.

Chapter 11

Why is it that the things we could never live without
Are the things we could never hope to have full control over:
The sun
The sea
The ones we love
Our own hearts?

I cried on and off the whole day of my fourteenth birthday. It was the first year I really felt the weight of leaving childhood behind and realized that some things would never be as they once were. Bekah had started regularly wearing makeup, and Elle had stopped putting her hair in pigtails. And it didn't help that Sutton had been shamelessly flirting with Gavin all day.

After dinner and a trip to get ice cream, we were in the backyard throwing bean bags into holes on wooden boards. Several of our other cousins had joined in, and everyone was acting extra competitive. No one even noticed when I slipped away.

I had intended to walk the beach to clear my head, but by the time I reached the ocean, I was too tired to do anything but sit cross-legged in the sand and listen to the waves throw themselves against the shore again and again.

Jude joined me as the sky grew darker. He didn't say a word, just settled in a couple feet away and methodically moved the squares of the Rubik's Cube he'd carried in his hands all evening.

I stared at a piece of washed-up seaweed and let the salt water carve paths down my face.

The breaking of the waves and the steady clicking of the puzzle in Jude's palms held a soothing sort of rhythm.

I dabbed at my runny nose with the shoulder of my T-shirt. The clicking stopped.

In the blurry periphery of my vision, I registered his hand extending the nearly perfectly aligned colorful cube toward me. I took it, thankful for a new object to focus on. I spun the rows this way and that, watching the colors scramble, making a mess of any progress he'd managed. If he minded, he didn't let on.

Had I been on my own, I may have been tempted to break the thing. Or chuck it into the sea. Instead, I kept clicking and turning and spinning my frustration out. It was oddly therapeutic.

At some point, I realized I'd stopped crying. I let out a breath and passed the cube back to Jude, watching as he strategically rearranged each row in what first seemed like random patterns. I don't think even five minutes passed before he smiled, rolled it around to show each solid-colored side, and laid it down in the sand between us.

I was equally impressed and envious of his ability to take something so jumbled and make sense of it. I looked away.

"If you want to be alone, I can leave." His changing voice still held the same timid kindness.

I had nothing to say but knew that I didn't want to be alone, didn't want his steady presence to disappear.

"No."

He waited a minute and then asked, "Do you want to talk about it?"

"No."

He picked up the Rubik's Cube, mixed it up, and began to solve it again. I closed my eyes and listened, trying to tune out everything else.

"I peed my pants at band camp last summer."

My eyes snapped open and I turned to find his face painted with shock, like he was as baffled by this spontaneous admission as I was.

He averted his gaze and let the story tumble out. "It was blazing hot, and everyone kept drilling us with the importance of staying hydrated. I drank so much water. *So* much. But we had this one instructor who refused to let us take a break until we'd gotten this certain piece perfect. The clarinets were coming in late. We must have done it twenty times; I was in agony. I wasn't the only one, and we were so drenched in sweat at that point that it was hard to tell. But still. I was mortified." I was sure his face was maroon under the dusk that had just descended. "Thankfully, we have this pact: what happens at camp, stays there. But I had a nightmare once that

Gavin found out." He shivered and pushed his glasses up on his nose.

I studied his profile and fought down the urge to giggle, because I didn't want him to think I was laughing at his expense. "Why are you telling me this?"

"Because if you ever do want to talk about . . . anything, I want you to know that I'm safe. Now you know my secret, so you have something on me. And if I ever betray your trust in any way, you have my full permission to ruin my high school career with this information. Deal?"

His palm was sweaty as we shook, but I knew for a fact that I could tell him absolutely everything I was feeling in that moment. And I very nearly did.

"Alex?" Elle jogged toward us, Rebekah and Sutton close on her heels. "We were looking everywhere. Are you okay?"

She slid down beside me and slipped her arm around my shoulders. Jude nodded wordlessly and stood, taking the Rubik's Cube and leaving me in my cousin's capable hands. I started to cry again. Rebekah and Sutton caught up, and I was soon in the middle of a huddle of familiar hearts. They didn't demand an explanation either, just held me until I recovered. Like we always did for one another.

Elle's voice crackles through the phone, and I feel every single mile between us. "I just wanted to give you a heads up before I got there, so you'd have time to process it. I know how you hate change."

"I'm excited for you, Elle. Like you said, this is a once in a lifetime opportunity." The way my words quaver gives me away.

"It's just two years. And I'll do everything I can to make the beach trip again next summer. And you guys can fly over here too. Can you imagine the four of us running around Madrid? Though there's a chance they'll revoke my visa if Sutton doesn't behave." She laughs, but I don't trust myself to pretend to join in. "Hey Alex, I need to go; it's late, and my roommate just turned off her light. She's not very subtle," she whispers.

"Okay, I'll talk to you soon."

"You sure you're okay?"

"I'm fine." I'm proud of how steady I sound now. "I can't wait to hug you soon."

"Love you, Ally."

"Love you too, Elly."

I wait for her to end the call and stand there, numb. I know it isn't normal the way things like this shake me. This is a good thing for Elle, the right thing even. But I feel unmoored.

I sit on the couch for hours, staring at a blank page, willing my-self to channel my feelings into something productive but coming up empty.

When Jude's keys rattle in the front door, I spring to my feet and rush straight for him without thinking.

"What's wrong?" He steps inside and toward me, radiating con-cern, and I keep walking until my face is buried in the shoulder of his black T-shirt, and the words are rapidly spilling over between shaky sobs.

"Elle is moving back to Spain for two years but we all know it will be longer and I'm torn between wanting to see my cousins and being terrified of what this trip will be like and Gavin is coming and I feel gross and for some reason I can't write anymore and every single poem I've written so far feels stupid. I don't know what's wrong with me."

In the span of two steady heartbeats thudding in my ear—mine or his, I'm unsure—I almost have time to feel sorry for spewing all this on poor, unsuspecting Jude. But a second later, his arms close around my back and he whispers the two words I need to hear more than anything. "It's okay."

I stay until the tears stop and my breathing slows, then pull back and survey him. His shirt is wet and has snot smeared across the sleeve. I'm sure I look as much of a mess as I feel. "Sorry," I croak, gesturing to his shirt.

"This shirt smells like pyrotechnics and fried chicken anyway." He smiles reassuringly. "No pirate's afraid of a little snot."

He looks as relieved to hear my weak laugh as I am. It's okay. I'm okay. Everything is going to be okay.

All the emotions that threatened to overwhelm me this afternoon seem much less daunting now that I'm not alone with them. "Sorry," I stammer again.

"You don't need to apologize for being sad." He picks up the remote control and places it in my hands. "I'm going to get cleaned up. You want to find us a good movie or something? I don't think I have energy for schoolwork tonight."

I nod wordlessly as he leaves the room. A movie sounds nice. I grab the blanket from the back of the couch and spin myself a cocoon before pulling up a list of movies on the TV.

When Jude comes back, he's wearing his pajamas and carrying a heating pad and a bottle of Tylenol. He hands them to me.

"What's this for?"

"I just thought," he hedges. "I didn't know if you maybe weren't feeling a hundred percent." His cheeks flush and he looks away before slowly explaining, "I have a sister."

I gasp. "Oh my gosh, Jude. Are you implying you think it's my time of the month?!"

It is, of course.

"No." He backs away. "I thought . . ." He looks both horrified and confused. "I'm sorry. I was honestly just trying to help." I stare at him, unable to find words, until he offers, "I can go. I'll work in my room."

I shouldn't be mad at him. And I don't want him to go. His friendship is pretty much the only redeeming thing about this whole day. "No, I shouldn't have yelled at you. You were being thoughtful." I scoot over. "Let's watch the movie. Please?"

His eyes flicker to the screen. "*Little Women*? I thought Austen was your comfort story."

"*Pride and Prejudice* is my comfort *book*; *this* is my comfort *movie*."

"I'll be right back," he promises.

I listen to him rattle around in the kitchen while I plug in the heating pad and wait for it to warm, trying not to dwell on how ridiculous I feel. Minutes later, he re-enters the room and sets a plate on the coffee table in front of me. Two pieces of cheese toast. He starts the movie.

I burst into tears again.

Chapter 12

"It was there, I swear. I *saw* it." Rebekah stood on one of the colorful bedspreads, pointing to the bottom of the wicker dresser.

Elle and I had climbed onto the other bed when she squealed and ran, but Sutton still sat in the middle of our game of Barbie dolls, wearing a skeptical frown. "I'm sure you thought you saw something, Bekah. But I don't even think mice live at the beach."

I momentarily forgot my fear. "Why couldn't mice live at the beach? Mice can live anywhere."

"I didn't say they couldn't. I said they didn't. Too many crabs and bugs and stuff. It's not their ideal ecosystem." Sutton was always trying to use big words and things she'd heard in school to sound smarter than the rest of us.

"That doesn't even make sense."

"There!" Rebekah wiggled her finger up and down, and we all stared at the dark crack under the drawers.

Sutton crossed her arms, nonplussed. "There's nothing under there."

"If you're so sure," Elle challenged, "*you* go check it out."

"Fine." Sutton hopped up and used a bare foot to swipe a layer of tiny doll clothes and accessories out of the way, clearing a path to the dresser. She bent down and peered into the void. "I don't see anything," she reported. "Maybe—" The rodent shot out, and Sutton jumped at least three feet off the ground.

We screamed in unison, a shrill otherworldly sound. The mouse froze with only one back leg and its tail still hidden from view.

Seconds later, the door flew open, and my mom, Aunt Jane, and Grandmama all came running into the room.

"What happened?" My mom quickly scanned each of us for obvious injuries before her eyes fell to the rigid creature on the carpet.

My aunt let out a small noise of disgust, and my grandmother shook her head.

Mom grabbed a stray flip-flop next to the closet and crept toward the mouse. "I think it's dead."

She nudged the tiny gray form with the tip of the shoe and nodded in confirmation. My grandmother slipped from the room and came back with a plastic grocery bag. My aunt closed her eyes as my mom disposed of the vermin.

Rebekah sank onto the comforter and whispered in awe, "But what are the chances it would die right at that moment?"

"Did we kill it?" Sutton asked. "With our screams?"

My aunt put a hand on Sutton's shoulder before turning to leave the scene, likely to hunt down some disinfectant for the floor. "I think so. Looks like you literally scared him to death."

As she shuffled from the room behind my aunt, Grandmama stopped to offer some of her sage advice. "Remember this, girls. There's no foe you can't face when you all join forces."

We'd recount this story for years to come, the mouse getting bigger and our collective lethal scream getting louder every time. But, no matter how small our adversary truly was that day, I was more convinced than ever that, with these girls by my side, I could take on the world.

"So, do I have to wait like everybody else for your book to be published, or do I get to read some of your poetry early?" Jude leans over in his beach chair, and I instinctively cover my paper with my arm.

"Sorry." I adjust the towel I've draped over my legs, refusing to get a sunburn until family vacation week. "The idea of anyone reading any of this is kind of freaking me out right now."

He squints at me from under his navy baseball hat, and I notice that he has a fresh smattering of freckles across his nose. "But isn't that kind of the point of writing a book? For people to read it?"

"Well, yes." The corner of my page flaps in the wind, and I stop to secure it. "But that doesn't make it any less scary." I roll my pen between my fingers and consider for a moment. "I guess I probably will need another set of eyes on it at some point this summer. But I don't think I'm quite ready yet."

He stretches his legs and buries his toes in the sand. "Okay. Just know I'll be here when you *are* ready. And I'd be honored to be the first to tell you how good it is."

"Thanks, Jude." Both his offer and his confidence in me mean more than he could possibly know.

He turns a page of the book in his lap. "How are you feeling today? We can head back to the house if you want."

"I'm good. You'll be gone all day tomorrow; we have to make the most of our beach time." I straighten my sunhat and try to sound nonchalant. "Gavin still coming to visit this weekend?"

"Mmhmm." He doesn't look up, and I'm grateful. "Should get in sometime late Thursday night. He's golfing in a charity tournament with some friends Friday and Saturday morning, but he should be around in the evenings."

I scribble absentmindedly in the margins of my paper. "Did you tell him I'm here?"

"Of course." He turns another page. "He can't wait to see you."

There's no logical reason this simple statement should make my heart race the way it does. But I don't pen another word for the next hour. My thoughts are too full of blond hair, blue eyes, and memories of the night I turned sixteen.

Chapter 13

"And I'd be remiss if I didn't mention the matchmaker herself." Chris raised his glass and winked at me across the backyard of the giant beachfront house my aunt and uncle had rented for the reception. "Alex, I never would have guessed that the boy band obsessed girl I tutored in algebra would grow up to introduce me to the love of my life. You've become one of the truest friends I've ever had, and I could never thank you enough for deeming me acceptable for your beautiful cousin. I still don't feel worthy, but I promise to take care of her and to do my best every day to make her happy. And Sutton . . ." He shifted his gaze to the bride in the seat at his right and, with a voice full of emotion, began to address her.

The way she looked at him as he spoke, like she'd follow him any-where, told me everything I needed to know, everything I already knew. Sutton trusted Chris with her heart, and we could too.

It had been a long, hot afternoon, and I'd never forget standing in front of the ocean between Sutton and Elle, sweat trickling down our backs, as vows were exchanged. Or the way our family members shifted in their folding chairs, fanning themselves with the programs that Rebekah designed. Or the woman in the water behind us doing handstands that would no doubt need to be photoshopped out of all the pictures.

But Sutton would remember this as the happiest day of her life.

Chris finished his speech, leaned down, and kissed Sutton's forehead. Everyone cheered as the music started back up.

"Come on." Elle grabbed my arm and motioned for Rebekah to follow us to the little dance floor the deejay had brought along. I slid my shoes off under the table, happy to have Elle lead the way in Sutton's absence.

We danced ourselves dizzy. It wasn't until my feet started to hurt that I let my emotions catch up with me.

"I'm going to sit this next one out," I yelled over the music to Rebekah and Elle and started to cut a path back to our table.

"Where do you think you're going?"

I turned around. Sutton's manicured hand rested on her hip, her smile the same shade of white as her fairytale gown. "I know you aren't going to miss *our* song." I hadn't even noticed the first few notes of our favorite talent show number the deejay had just cued up.

"Never." I offered my own polished fingers, and she pulled me back out into the center of the party. Elle and Rebekah were already in their positions, ready to make absolute fools of them-selves in front of a couple hundred people.

It was a miracle we still remembered every single step. And yet, it didn't surprise me one bit.

When the chorus started for the second time, the crowd went wild. Chris had joined in on Sutton's opposite side, as confident in the choreography as we were. I laughed until my eyes were wet.

When the music ended, I followed Chris off the dance floor to get some water. "I can't believe Sutton taught you the dance," I laughed.

"She didn't have to. Do you know how many times she's made me watch those talent show videos?" His gaze wandered back to her, and no one could have missed how enamored he was. "I may have just pledged my life to Sutton, but she made it clear from the very beginning that the four of you were a package deal. So if I have to learn a new dance every summer, it's more than worth it. And Al?" He gave me his full attention and waited for mine. "Sutton always told me that growing up with only brothers, you guys were the sisters she always wanted. I feel the exact same way."

"Ugh, Chris." I shoved his tuxedoed arm away. "You're going to make me ruin my makeup again."

It's nearly one in the morning when inspiration strikes. I gather my writing supplies and tiptoe downstairs, happy to see the kitchen light is still on.

I don't have to ask if it's okay to join him; he's already scooting his stack of paperwork over on the counter to make space for me. I don't want to keep him from his work, and I'm lost in my own world of words anyway. But after spending the whole day alone, I just want his company.

I'm not sure how long we work side by side in silence, but at some point, he brews a pot of coffee and sets a full mug in front of me. Sometime later, he gently shakes my shoulder until I lift my head from the countertop. "We should get some sleep," he says. I drag myself, notebook in hand, back up the stairs to bed and sleep harder than I have in a long time.

I don't know what time of day it is when I wake up with the sun in my face. I rummage under my pillow for my phone; only eight o'clock. When the front door hinges squeal, I jump out of bed and run to the top of the stairs.

"Are you leaving already?" I call down.

Jude smiles up at me from the doorway, and my brain registers for the first time that I must look like a mess. I reach for my unruly bun and tug the elastic band out, then start smoothing it with my hands to pull it back up.

"I was just going to run a few errands. Pick up some groceries before Gavin gets here and a couple other things." He closes the door. "You want to ride with me?"

I nod eagerly, feeling like a little kid but not caring. "Give me ten minutes?"

"Take your time." He swings his key ring around his fingers before tucking it back into the pocket of his cargo shorts.

Fifteen minutes later, I'm sliding into the passenger seat.

Jude cranks the engine. "Hey, I have to run by the bank, and it's right by that little beach shop with the good saltwater taffy if you want to stop. They have postcards too."

"Ooo, yes! If you're sure we have time."

He puts his arm on the headrest behind me and turns to back out. "We'll make time."

"Would it help if I made a grocery list on the way?"

He slides the gearshift and passes me his phone. "Already done."

I tap the screen and laugh out loud when I read at the very top: *traditional undersized cereal.*

"You have any big traditions in mind for when my brother is here?" He keeps his eyes on the road, but this feels like a loaded question.

I scroll down the grocery list, adding *paper towels* and *coffee* at the bottom. He must have forgotten we were low. "Gavin wasn't part of the deal," I say matter-of-factly. "But after he leaves, we're going to have to double down if we're gonna stay on schedule. We have a lot to do before my family gets here."

"We need to pick up a net," he reminds me. I inspected the one under the house a few days ago and deemed it unacceptable for crab hunting.

"Right." I type in the addition and set his phone back in the cup holder between us. "How is it that running errands alone is a chore, but running errands with someone else instantly makes it a fun adventure?"

"I was just thinking the same thing." He puts on his blinker and turns onto the main road off the island. "Hey, I'm not sure what time Gavin will get in tonight, but if I'm not home yet, you guys order some food and I'll just join you when I get there."

I suck in a breath, horrified. "You really think he might get here before you're back?"

"It's going to be fine, Alex. It's just Gavin."

I don't know how to tell him that there's no such thing as "just Gavin," so I turn on the radio instead.

He takes a deep breath and pulls onto the bridge.

<h1 style="text-align:center">Chapter 14</h1>

We spent the weeks leading up to the summer of my eleventh birthday making our first business plan. Sutton, Elle, and I were staying at my Grandmama's house for the weekend when the idea struck: one afternoon of babysitting during the beach trip that would put some cash in our pockets for the rest of the week. Rebekah came up with the name after our enthusiastic pitch over the phone: Kids2Kids Family Day Camp. We made a list of activities to do with our younger cousins, set a price of five dollars per child, and drew some flyers to pass out to our aunts and uncles.

The next week, I ran dozens of copies on the machine at the library.

When the July day finally came, we couldn't have been more prepared. Set up under the deck of one of the beach houses, we had craft supplies, a basket full of sports gear, and an assortment of juice boxes and snacks we'd promised to reimburse my mom for once we'd been paid. Sure, there were a LOT of campers, but these were our cousins, little kids who knew and loved us. What could go wrong?

An hour in, little Katie Grace had cut Maria's hair with scissors, two of the beach balls had popped, all the snacks were gone, and Alan had tripped and skinned both knees so badly that Sutton had to carry him upstairs to my aunt.

"Maybe we should end early," a tearful Elle suggested. "This is a disaster."

"But we still have an hour and a half before the parents are supposed to be back." Rebekah sighed as she took another pair of scissors from our cousin Russell. Where were all these scissors still coming from?

I looked out across the backyard and to the right where Gavin and Jude had just walked out onto their deck. We'd told them our brilliant plan after dinner the night before. The two boys assessed the situation, eyes wide and mouths slightly ajar. I'm not sure if I mouthed the word "help" or just thought it, but they seemed to understand either way and came galloping down the stairs, our suntanned knights in shining armor.

Gavin rummaged through the sports equipment and extracted a red rubber ball. "Okay, everybody line up in the backyard!" The little kids took one look at the cool teenager with the shark's tooth necklace and willingly obeyed.

Jude set up orange cones for bases while Gavin divided the two teams as evenly as he could. What followed was a game of kickball so epic and hilarious that when our adult family members returned, everyone wanted to join in. Even Alan, both knees heavily bandaged, begged for one turn after another to kick the ball and be carried around the bases.

Once everyone had left to get ready for dinner and we'd cleaned up the remnants of our first—and last—day camp, we counted our earnings and divided out a share for the Alfords. They refused to take it.

"Nah, this was fun," Gavin deflected. "We were looking for something to do anyway."

They did, however, take my aunt up on her offer to join us for her famous chicken and rice casserole. Which, to be honest, was worth far more than all our money put together.

I've been a ball of nerves all evening. Who am I kidding? All *day*.

After Jude left for work this afternoon, I spent an absurd amount of time doing my hair and choosing an outfit that I hoped looked both casual and cute. For the past hour or so, I've sat in the living room with a book I have no intention of reading, listening for cars pulling onto the street and tensing every time one does.

Finally, the slam of a car door in the driveway drives me from my couch cushion and to the window. It's only Jude. I check the time; how is it already this late, and how close is Gavin now?

Jude jogs up the steps, and I sit back down before he has a chance to see me acting like a bona fide stalker.

"Hey," he greets me as if this were just any other night. "What are you reading?"

I hold up the book. "I borrowed it from your shelves. I hope that's okay."

"Of course. That's a really good one." He sits to unlace his shoes. "What part are you at?"

"Um." I close the book. "I really just started. I haven't gotten into it yet."

He frees his phone from his pocket and taps the screen. "Gavin texted a little while ago. He's here, but he's going out to play pool with some friends. He says it will probably be late, and he has a key, so we shouldn't wait up."

"Oh." All of that nervous energy, for this? I hate the way I have to fight not to tear up, but I refuse to lose it in front of Jude again this week. Especially over Gavin.

"Have you eaten yet?" he asks.

"I'm not very hungry." It's the truth.

"Want to play a game or something while we wait?"

I move the book to the coffee table and pull my feet up under me. "What kind of game?"

Jude shrugs. "Card game? Board game? Video games?"

"Video games?" I'm intrigued. "What system do you have?"

Jude grins and moves to the TV cabinet. He opens one of the doors under the TV to reveal, not one, but three different gaming systems and a plastic box full of games. "Did I or did I not reassure you when you got here that I am still very much a nerd?"

I laugh and join him on the floor. "Got any racing games?"

"I do." He pulls a cartridge from the collection. "But are you sure you want to challenge me to a race right off the bat?"

"What do you mean?" I squint.

"Not to brag, but I'm pretty amazing at this game. And didn't you tell me you failed your driver's test?"

"Why *did* I tell you that?" I swat at his arm. "And how do you know it wasn't for going way too fast or for throwing turtle shells at the other drivers?"

"Okay." He puts the game in and turns on the TV. "Let's see what you got."

He wins the first two races easily, but by the third, I'm keeping up. Right when I'm about to pass his car, I look over to see that he's taken his finger off of the gas button. "Jude! Don't you dare let me win on purpose. I will be personally offended if you treat me any differently than any other legitimate gamer. If—" His car slams into mine, and I spin out.

"Jude!"

"Just doing what you requested. Are you playing to win or not?" he challenges.

I reach for the cord of his controller and unplug it, then steer my car back onto the track and over the finish line.

"That was dirty." He plugs his controller back in and tamps down a smile. "But I admire your commitment. And now I won't feel as bad when I obliterate you on the next turn."

Several games and a whole lot of trash talk later, I've almost forgotten about waiting for Gavin. Almost.

When I check the clock on my phone around the tenth time, Jude pulls up his messages and shows me the screen. "Still no word. Sorry, Alex."

I sigh.

He turns off the TV. "I should probably do a little bit of work. You gonna write tonight? I could make us some coffee or cheese toast or something."

I finish wrapping up my controller and return it to the cabinet. "I'm kind of tired. I think I'm going to go to bed."

"Sure." He looks almost as disappointed in Gavin's tardiness as I am. "Goodnight, Alex."

Chapter 15

"Truth or dare?"

The six of us bobbed up and down on the rolling waves, watching them break a few yards in front of us while Sutton considered.

"Truth."

"Hmm." Elle smiled. "What's the best kiss you've ever gotten?"

It bothered me that she had to take so long to think about it, that she cut her eyes briefly to Gavin before she apparently scrolled through a lengthy mental list, like she was trying to impress him or something.

"Devon Thomas," she finally decided. "At the ninth-grade winter formal."

"No other details?" Rebekah prodded.

"Nope." Sutton nonchalantly looked to Elle's right. "You're next, Gavin."

Gavin scanned our group, and I silently prayed he wouldn't say my name. If he did, I'd already resolved to take the dare. I'd turned fifteen two days prior and had no real kissing experience to boast of.

"Jude." He turned to his brother. "Truth or dare?"

He must have been experiencing a similar internal conflict because it took him less than a second to answer. "Dare."

Gavin swept his wet bangs from his eyes and nodded. "All right. I dare you to switch bathing suits with me underwater and then swim to shore to see if Kelsey notices." He nodded toward their sister sitting on a towel with her headphones on.

Jude looked down as if to verify that the ocean was still dark enough that no one could see and then moved to the other side of his brother, putting a little more distance between himself and us girls. "Okay."

He'd gotten off easy for picking a dare, and we all knew it.

"On the count of three," Gavin instructed. As he reached for his suit and started counting, I looked away, just in case.

"One . . . two . . . three."

There was a brief pause before Jude shrieked, "Gavin!" and I turned my head to see Gavin swimming furiously toward the sand, Jude's shorts in hand.

Jude started to chase him but could only wade so far before he realized he was trapped.

Rebekah, Elle, and I stared in disbelief, unsure whether to laugh at the brilliance of Gavin's prank or cry on Jude's behalf.

It wasn't until Gavin reached the sand that I saw Sutton had followed him. She chased him all the way to Kelsey who, upon understanding what was going on, tackled him to the ground and wrested Jude's suit from his grasp. She tossed it to Sutton.

Her return trip seemed to take hours as the rest of us floated in silence, unwilling to even attempt to make conversation or eye contact with the mortified naked boy beside us. It was a real "bless his heart" moment as my grandmother would call it.

"Here you go, Jude." Sutton tossed his shorts when she was sure she was close enough for him to catch them.

He mumbled a quick, "Thanks."

"At least now you can cross skinny dipping off your bucket list, right?"

A small chuckle escaped Jude's lips as he redressed beneath the water. The tension was broken, and the rest of us finally gave in to the giggles we'd worked so hard to hold back.

Gavin stood proudly on the shore, his sister still chewing him out, and saluted us.

"Fantastic." Tyler throws his head back and howls with laughter. "Why have I never heard this story before?"

Jude takes a sip of his root beer and sets it back on the coffee table. We're all sitting on the living room floor, despite the fact that there is plenty of seating for four people.

I look over at Gavin and forget why I was so freaked out about seeing him again. When he walked in the door from golfing this afternoon, he'd wrapped me up in a giant bear hug, and it was almost like any other summer reunion, picking up right where we left off.

Well, not *right* where we left off. But close enough.

"So, what else have you been up to since you got here, besides writing? You been to see Jude's pirate show yet?"

Jude sighs.

"I'm not allowed," I pout.

"What?" Gavin shakes his head at Jude. "How's she going to meet anyone else in this town if you keep her sequestered in this house all summer, man? Introduce her to your friends!"

"Well, she's already met the coolest person he knows," Tyler boasts. "But, seriously Jude, you should at least bring her to one of Lincoln Shark's gigs sometime."

"Lincoln Shark?" I question.

"It's a band," Jude explains. "Ty's their drummer. They play a lot of local joints and small parties and stuff."

"Wow, way to really sell us, Mr. Publicist." Tyler leans back against the couch and addresses me. "We're very good, and you'd meet a lot of great people there. Only downside is . . . no pirates."

Jude rolls his eyes.

"Ah, come on, Jude. You always have fun at our shows; she'd love it. Although, she wouldn't get to meet you-know-who."

The words have an obvious effect on Jude, and if it were just me, I would probably leave the topic alone, but Gavin can't let this slide.

"Who?" he says. "Jude, is there a special someone you haven't told me about?"

"No."

Tyler fake coughs. "Norah," he whispers under his breath.

Jude turns to me for help which, at this point, is a mistake.

"Norah, huh?" I ask. "What's she like?"

"There is nothing going on with this girl. Let's talk about something else."

Tyler leans in. "Nothing other than the fact that she's totally obsessed with you."

"Hold on." I set my own drink aside. "Tyler's been to the pirate show? How does he know these people?"

"I'm going to bed." Jude starts to stand, but I tug his arm back down.

"Stop," I laugh. "We aren't trying to gang up on you. We just care about you."

"And so does Norah," Gavin adds. Tyler snickers.

I let go of Jude's arm. "But seriously, if this girl does like you, she obviously has good taste."

"Don't patronize me, Alex."

"I'm not! Jude, you are a *catch*. You're kind and funny and smart. You can cook. And you have an extensive book collection. I'm just saying. My only concern is if this girl is good enough for you, and how can I judge that if you won't let me meet her?"

"She makes a good point." Tyler nods.

"Oooh! We should host a dinner party!" I catch myself and lower my voice. "I mean, *you* should host a dinner party; it's your house. But I could help."

"A dinner party? I may know how to cook, but I don't know if I can cook for a crowd."

"Have you forgotten who you're talking to, Jude? We're at the beach. I *only* know how to cook for a crowd here. Just make sure this Norah is in that crowd, okay?"

"For the last time, nothing is going to happen. She's like, four years younger than I am."

"That's not that big of a difference," Gavin interjects.

"It is at this age. I'm twenty-one, and she's still in high school. I refuse to be some creepy older guy who preys on high school girls."

His words hang in the air, and he looks from Gavin to me and then quickly away. I'm positive now that he knows everything. The silence lasts just long enough to make us all feel weird.

"Well." Ty pushes himself off the floor and picks up his drink. "I should probably head home. I have an early lesson in the morning."

"Yeah," Jude says, standing. "I'm washing linens at six. Goodnight, guys."

"Early tee time for me." Gavin reaches over and squeezes one of my socked feet. "Hey, if Jude is working late again, why don't you let me take you out to dinner, catch up a little bit?"

"Yeah." I hope my face isn't as pink as it feels. "That sounds good."

We all say our goodnights, and I follow Gavin upstairs and settle into the room beside his. I know I won't sleep a wink.

Chapter 16

Two days after I turned twelve, I fastened a green bandana around my head to match the rest of my team. The adults had opted out of the simple footrace event now that we were old enough to oversee it ourselves, and we'd been allowed to choose our own teams. It just so happened that Gavin and Jude were on the beach that afternoon, and we had two open spots in our relay lineup.

"Listen up, everybody!" Whose idea had it been to give Elias the megaphone? "Down to the cones and back. You *have* to tag the cone and you *have* to tag the next person's hand before they can go."

Gavin caught my eye and nodded in mock solemnity; next to him, however, Jude was dialed in. The look of fierce determination on his face was so out of character, it was humorous.

"Ready?" Elias's voice boomed again. "Set? GO!"

Sutton, first as always, took off. Elle made sure the rest of us were lined up and ready to race, placing Jude at the back since he insisted on anchoring. It surprised us how invested he was in winning, but we weren't complaining. We all wanted those plastic gold medals and the accompanying bragging rights.

Sutton tagged Rebekah who ran up and down the beach before tagging Elle. I was next. As soon as Elle slapped my hand—harder than necessary, I noted with a wince—I ran as fast as my legs could carry me. Though I was making good time—and we were already in the lead before I started—I refused to concede even an inch to the other teams.

As I returned to our group, I nearly ran into Gavin; he had to catch me to keep us from both toppling over in the sand. We laughed as he set off for the second to last leg of the race. Jude waited at the line, fists clenched by his sides and already breathing hard. "You've got this, Jude," I offered.

And did he ever.

Gavin tagged his hand, and he shot off like a rocket, touching the cone at the other end of the beach and easily beating the next closest team back to the finish line by almost half a minute. He beamed as Gavin lifted him into the air and the rest of us cheered wildly.

"Gather around, please," Elias announced when every team had come in. "Let's give a round of applause for our new relay champs: the blue team!"

"What?!" Elle stepped forward. "*We* won!"

"Disqualified." Elias continued passing out gold medals to our second-place cousins.

"What do you mean 'disqualified?'" Sutton's hands flew to her hips, and Elias flinched.

"I mean," he calmly explained, "that this is the Henry Family Olympics. And you had team members who aren't part of the Henry family." Jude's face fell.

"Don't be an idiot, Elias," Rebekah chided. "Just give us our medals."

"No can do."

"It's not a big deal," Gavin assured a smoldering Sutton. But Jude had yanked off his bandana, thrown it to the ground, and had already stomped halfway to the steps leading back to the road.

We didn't often see Grandmama get angry, so when it happened, we remembered. And that evening when she heard us recount the story, she'd been furious. Elias had quietly emerged from her room a few minutes later and asked us to walk him over to the blue house to apologize.

"Sorry about earlier," he mumbled sheepishly to the two boys at the door. "I was just being dumb. And you guys are welcome to join in the games whenever you want, okay?"

"Thanks," Gavin said. But they never did again.

It's lunchtime, and I've finally reached the point of desperation. Rebekah is working a long shift, and Elle is likely on some exciting Spanish adventure because she isn't answering her phone. Sutton is my last and only option. I pull up her number and send the call before I can change my mind. I need to talk to someone, or I'll drive myself crazy.

"Alex!" She squeals. "I was starting to think you'd lost your phone. How's the beach? What's new?"

Just hearing her say my name makes me feel lighter, melts away my nerves. I pick up the bottle of nail polish I've decided on and head for the front deck. "Great. I miss you. How are you? And Marcie and Chris?"

She pauses. "You sound different."

I sit down in a rocking chair. "What do you mean?"

"I mean you sound different. In a good way. OH MY GOSH, Alex, have you met someone?!"

"What?"

"Answer the question. Have you met someone?"

"No."

"Hmm." She doesn't sound convinced. "Okay, well why did you call?"

"I just wanted to say hi. I told you, I miss you."

"And?"

The butterflies return to my stomach. I close my eyes and confess, "And I'm having dinner with Gavin Alford tonight, and I need you to tell me it's going to be fine."

"WHAT!"

"I ran into him yesterday," I half lie. "He's in town for the weekend visiting some friends, and he wants to have dinner and catch up."

Her silence is deafening, and I wish I could see her face right now.

"Sutton?"

She sighs. "I just want you to be careful. Okay?"

"What's that supposed to mean?" Now I remember why she was my last choice. This is not what I need right now.

"Alex." Her voice is dripping with the kind of concern that makes me feel both stupid and nervous. "I just don't want you to set yourself up to get hurt. You haven't seen Gavin in what, six years? And he's in town for the weekend. It's not like he's looking for a relationship."

"It's just dinner, Sutton."

"Right."

"Ugh, why did I think this was a good idea?"

She reads my mind. "Going on a date with Gavin or calling me?"

"It's not a date."

"Well, just make sure you keep reminding yourself of that."

I know my voice is too loud, but I can't help it. "Why do you do this?"

"Do what?" Her volume increases too. "Care about you?"

"Ruin things for me. Why can't I just enjoy catching up with an old friend?"

"Because you think of him as more than that. And you shouldn't."

Her words are like a slap across the face. I sit, stunned, and listen to my own breathing.

"Alex." Her voice is softer, quieter now. "The summer before Gavin kissed you on the beach . . ."

I somehow know exactly what is coming, and I want to stop it, but I'm still speechless.

"He kissed me too."

Of course she kissed Gavin. Nothing could be more Sutton-like. But then, she does the most un-Sutton-like thing possible. She stops talking and gives me space to process, lets me decide what happens next.

"Why didn't you tell me?" I finally ask.

"Because I knew it didn't mean anything." It sounds like she's crying now and that makes me even angrier. "Because what teenage guy isn't going to seize the opportunity to kiss a girl on vacation who looks at him like he's a celebrity? Look, you know I love you. And Gavin. But, Alex, be honest with yourself. Is what you've held on to all these years really Gavin or some version of him you've imagined but may not even exist?"

My chest physically hurts. "I have to go."

"Alex." Her voice is resigned. She knows I won't be calling her back.

At least my fury keeps my other emotions at bay. Opening the nail polish, I coat my toenails before starting on my fingers.

I'm so focused that I don't notice the white car pull in. I jump when Jude climbs the stairs.

"What are you doing home already?"

"I'm not staying long. Just came to change and grab something to eat before I head back out. You okay?"

"Yep."

He reaches for the door, then reconsiders. "You sure? You look kind of flustered."

"I'm fine." I sigh. "I'm just trying to paint my fingernails, and I forgot how hard it is to paint your own right hand. And none of my cousins are here to help."

He reads me almost as well as Sutton did. "That's all?"

"Yes," I snap. "That's all."

He squints into the sun, adjusts his glasses, and walks toward me.

"Here." He takes the bottle of polish and kneels on the deck beside my rocking chair, gesturing for my hand.

I watch as he carefully applies the color to each nail. Surprisingly, he's doing a good job.

"Thanks, Jude."

"Sure. But if you tell Gavin about this on your date tonight, you're in trouble, okay?"

I grit my teeth. "It's *not* a date."

Chapter 17

The bathroom counter was littered with curling irons, brushes, and every kind of makeup imaginable.

"With that shirt, this eye shadow will be perfect." I felt Sutton swipe the brush across my closed lids and knew instinctively the face of concentration she was making. "Done."

I inspected her work in the mirror as Rebekah finished curling Elle's hair.

"Think you used enough hairspray?" Elle coughed.

"Oh my gosh, Sutton. Did you stuff your bra?" Rebekah laughed as Sutton readjusted her shirt. "You're ridiculous."

I applied a final coat of lip gloss and yanked the cords from the outlets. "Come on. My dad's waiting for us."

Sure enough, my dad was standing at the bottom of the stairs, keys in hand. "You ladies ready for some seafood?"

We followed him to his SUV and crammed in. The smell of four different body sprays mingled in the air. "Y'all are awfully dressed up just for dinner with me. This restaurant you talked me into taking you to wouldn't possibly have anything to do with one of those Allman brothers, would it?"

"Alford, Dad. And Gavin is bussing tables there this summer, but we aren't going just to see him."

"He told us that the shrimp was the best in town, so we want to try it," Sutton explained.

"I see." He turned on the music and began to sing along loudly with the CD Rebekah burned for us before the trip.

"You aren't going to dance like this during dinner, right?" Elle asked from the back seat.

"Why not?" My dad met her eyes in the rearview mirror. "You're not going there to see anyone. And the shrimp won't care; they're already dead."

"Great," Elle murmured. But by the time the Spice Girls had reached the bridge, we were all singing and dancing too. To an outsider that day, it might have looked like we were trying to be more grown than we were, but in truth, we were all desperate to hold on to any sliver of childhood we could.

"Hold your breath!" Rebekah called as we left the island.

I take one last look at my reflection, wishing I had a second opinion. I've opted for shorts and a dressy pink tank top. I want to look cute without looking like I overthought it, which I most definitely have.

I add one more swipe of color to my lips before I turn out the light. Gavin is waiting at the bottom of the stairs, wearing jeans and a blue button-up shirt that matches his eyes perfectly. "Ready to go?"

"Yep. Where are we going?"

"It's a surprise." When he holds the door open for me and I walk past, I savor the scent of his cologne.

He spends the drive over the bridge telling me about his job while I scroll through photos of his new puppy on his phone. He's insanely cute. The dog. And Gavin. For a handful of minutes, I feel sixteen again.

But then he pulls into the parking lot of a building with a giant dragon on the sign, and the spell is broken.

"Gavin, I don't think this is a good idea."

He brings the car to a stop and cuts the engine. "Nah. It'll be fun." He studies my face. "He'll be fine, Alex."

I follow him into a lobby draped in pirate flags with swords mounted on the walls. A hostess in a themed dress scans the tickets on Gavin's phone. "Welcome aboard. You'll be in Buccaneer Jude's section." She gestures with her arm. "Second door on the left and enjoy the show."

"I don't feel right about this." I tug on Gavin's sleeve. But he rests a hand on the small of my back and starts walking.

As we enter the dark main theater, I gasp. It's so much better than I'd imagined. Long tables and benches surround a pool of water with a huge ship in its center.

"Where's the dragon?" I wonder aloud.

Gavin points. "It's under the water there; it doesn't come out until the third scene." We find our seats, and I'm so caught up in absorbing every little detail, I forget for a moment that we really shouldn't be here.

"Ahoy, Landlubbers," Jude's voice echoes as our whole section turns our heads to watch him descend the steps. He's in full costume with a bandana on his head and a scabbard swinging from his hip. He's even sporting the earring Ty mentioned. "Welcome aboard our ship. I hope you've all brought your courage with you as we will be hunting for treasure this evening and will likely encounter a frightful sea creature or two and maybe even the fearsome dragon rumored to guard the treasure." He smiles at a group of excited children to our left. "I hope you've also brought your hearty appetites." He scans the crowd, and I see surprise briefly flicker across his face as he recognizes me and Gavin, but he doesn't break character. "We'll be enjoying some of the finest fare in all the seven seas. So, make yourselves comfortable, and I'll be around to take your drink orders soon."

The lights dim, and several performers swing from the rafters onto the ship and start singing about a map and a quest. There is plenty to take in, but I can't help watching out of the corner of my eye as Jude makes his way down the table, introducing himself and listing drink choices. I feel terrible for showing up here when he specifically asked me not to come.

He stops in front of Gavin. "What can I get for you, sir?"

"I'll have sweet tea, thanks." The corners of Gavin's mouth turn up, but Jude moves along.

"And for the lady?"

I fidget in my seat, searching for a way to convey my own surprise and regret to him, but he won't meet my gaze. "I'll have the same, please." And then he's on to the next guest.

He comes back to bring our drinks and then later to deliver a meal of soup, chicken, corn on the cob, and bread. I watch him as much, if not more, than the show, noting how comfortable he seems in this role despite his apparent embarrassment anytime he's spoken of this job before. He takes extra time interacting with the kids in the audience, and I hear him answer at least a dozen questions about swords. When the fire-breathing dragon finally emerges, an excited little boy drops his cup of coke. Instead of treating it as just another mess to be cleaned, Jude brings out a mop and teaches him how pirate crews "swab the deck." It makes me proud to know him. And even more guilty for being here.

But the truth is: I'm loving this experience. The atmosphere is incredibly fun, the performance is amazing, and the food is delicious, especially the bread. I've almost finished the last bite before I look at the plates to either side of me and realize that mine is the only piece with melted cheese on top. A subtle olive branch, I hope. I finally relax and enjoy the rest of the hunt for gold, thinking of a thousand pirate-related jokes that I want to share. But not with the blue-eyed man sitting beside me.

Gavin is oddly quiet, both during dinner and afterwards on the drive back. But he doesn't seem angry, just content.

"Thanks again for this," I say as we travel back over the bridge. "I had fun."

"Me too, Alex. It's been really good seeing you again." He smiles. "I'm glad you're well. We think and talk about you guys all the time, you know."

I reach for my necklace. "Same."

"Hey, one of my buddies is having some people over tonight. You feel like coming along?" He turns onto our street. "Or we could just go home if you're tired."

I'm suddenly exhausted, but in a way I don't quite know how to explain. I do know, however, that while teenage me would have jumped at this chance, I have no desire to go anywhere else with Gavin tonight. "I have some laundry to do," I offer lamely. "But you should go. Will I see you tomorrow before you head back?"

"I'll make sure of it." He puts his truck in park, and I reach for the door handle.

"Alex."

"Yeah?"

"My brother's a great guy." His expression makes me wonder if he's feeling slightly unsettled about our choice of dinner venue too.

I look away. "I know."

He waits for me to climb the stairs and wave before he backs out. I'm not sure what I feel as I watch his truck disappear. But this is nothing like the disappointment or heartache that Sutton was worried about. Or the giddy nervousness I expected. It feels almost like . . . relief? Freedom, maybe? Closure.

I've just spent a whole evening with Gavin. He's still Gavin. And I'm still me. And I still care for him very much. But the Alfords are just the boys next door on vacation, and that's all they'll ever be. And I'm at peace with that fact.

My phone buzzes in my purse. Sutton. I turn it off and go inside to find my notebook instead.

Chapter 18

"Rome wasn't built in a day," they say.
And I know what they mean
But a lot can happen in the span of a few hours
And hasn't my whole life been built
And transformed
And rebuilt
Like a sandcastle
In handfuls of days at a time?

"Isn't it interesting," Grandmama said, her hair blowing around her face in the ocean breeze, "how we can come to this same beach every summer, but even from day to day or hour to hour, it's never exactly the same beach?"

I picked up a shell and inspected it while we walked. "What do you mean?" With so many cousins, getting time alone with her was rare, and I wanted it to last as long as possible.

"Well, think about it. The ocean keeps turning over and over, bringing things in, taking them away. The makeup of this shore is constantly changing. This isn't the same sand we walked on last year. Or yesterday for that matter. These aren't the same shells we saw, are they?"

My nine-year-old brain soaked in the words, tried to make sense of them. "I guess I've never thought of it like that before."

"That's not even mentioning all the ways we ourselves change. How we grow. The things we learn and unlearn and don't even realize we bring along with us." She stopped and closed her eyes. "And don't you think that changes how we see it all too?"

I finally set my notebook aside and climb out of the woven hammock. It's gotten colder since the sun started setting, but I'm not ready to go back into the empty beach house. I open the laundry room door, careful not to let it close all the way behind me, and flip on the light. Sure enough, there's a small load still in the dryer. I rummage around until I find Jude's band hoodie and pull it over my head. It smells faintly of laundry detergent but also of salt air and sunscreen and safety.

I turn off the light and check the color of the sky; he should be home any minute now. Sliding the notebook into the sweatshirt's front pocket, I curl back up in the hammock and wait.

It isn't long before his car pulls in and he steps out, still clad in his black work pants, undershirt, and shoes. "Alex?" He stops shy of the stairs leading up to the house. "Where's Gavin? What are you doing out here?"

"He went out to see some friends." I stand. "I was waiting for you. You have a few minutes?"

"Oh." He looks confused. "Sure. What's up?"

"The beach," is the only answer I give. He slides his keys into his pocket and starts walking beside me.

When we get there, I kick off my flip-flops, and he sits to untie his shoes. "It's worrying me a little how quiet you're being, Al. What's going on?"

"Nothing." I offer him a hand up. "I just thought we'd better start getting some training in is all. We only have a few more weeks."

"What are you talking about?" But he's smiling now.

"I think this is the summer you avenge your stolen gold medal. It's time."

He shakes his head slowly from side to side, still grinning.

"To the pier and back?"

"Let's go."

I keep up with him most of the way, holding my notebook still with one arm while I run, but I guess I've forgotten how long it's been since I've sprinted like this. My side starts to cramp.

"Slow down," I pant.

"That's not how a race works," he calls over his shoulder. He's back to the starting line when I decide to give up and start walking. A few steps later, I stop altogether and let myself collapse in the sand.

Jude jogs back to me and sits. "I'm not sure about the rest of your family, but if I'm pitted against you, I'm feeling pretty good about my chances."

I don't have the energy to come up with a proper retort. "I think maybe you deserve a gold medal just for putting up with me this summer."

He leans back on his elbows. "Nah."

"I'm sorry, Jude." I tuck my hands into the hoodie and wrap them around my notebook. "I didn't know Gavin was planning on taking me there, and I wouldn't have agreed to it if I had."

"I know you didn't. And I know you wouldn't." I can tell from his tone he isn't upset with me at all. "And Gavin means well. I'm just sorry you didn't get to see anything exciting happen. No grand proposals or birthday parties tonight. The dragon's head even stayed on all the way until it was supposed to come off."

"It doesn't always?"

"Every now and then, it malfunctions and falls into the water a couple scenes before the big fight. It doesn't happen that regularly but often enough that they had to write an alternate script just in case. I wasn't there the first time it happened, but apparently it was quite the disaster."

I laugh out loud. "Well, now I have to go back every night until I'm lucky enough to see it."

We listen to the ocean for a while, and Jude lets his smile slip away. "Are you all right, Alex?" I know what he's asking, and it means the world that he cares.

"I am." I sigh. "Really. I've been doing a lot of thinking tonight."

"Yeah?" He sits up and angles toward me. "About what?"

"I think maybe it's time for me to enter my Jo March post-New York era."

I expect him to ask what I mean, but instead he asks, "Book or movie?"

"Hmm," I ponder. "Movie, I guess?"

He waits.

"I just mean that I've been doing all this writing and kind of obsessing over what it should be. And maybe I've lost sight of what I meant for it to be. And who I meant it to be *for*. Don't get me wrong, I'd still love to be published one day. But maybe this isn't the book I'm supposed to write for the world. Maybe this one is just for me and the people I love. Maybe that could be enough?"

"More than enough," he agrees.

"I want to stop worrying about the writing itself and just tell our stories. It doesn't have to be all poetry. It's my book. And I don't care if my poetry is perfect or cutting edge or even that good, you know? I just want to let my soul spill onto the page. Anyway, I'm rambling."

My friend provides just the encouragement I need, as usual. "This sounds like a perfect plan to me. And you're right; it's your book. Make it what you need it to be. It will be every bit as legitimate whether you publish or not. I'm just sorry I won't get to buy it. But I can wait for the next one."

"Actually." I pull the notebook from the pocket of his borrowed shirt. "I thought maybe I'd see if your offer to read for me was still good? I'd love to hear your thoughts along the way, especially since your family is part of so many of these stories too." I hesitate, then extend the book. "No pressure," I add.

He reaches for it, and I'm hit with a wave of self-doubt. "Just, be honest. But don't hate it, okay? These are actual pieces of my heart in here."

"In that case, I'm sure it will be beautiful, Alex."

It's too dark to read anything now, but he still takes a minute to gently turn a few pages. The way he handles it, so carefully as if it really were my heart, assures me that I'm making the absolute right decision.

Chapter 19

I spent my sixth birthday throwing up.

No one was sure which cousin brought the stomach bug to the beach, but none of us escaped it. At first, our parents, many of them sick themselves, tried to keep us quarantined. But soon enough, they realized it was pointless. If we had to be sick on family vacation, we might as well all be sick together.

Rebekah and I were spread out on opposite sides of the couch while Sutton was curled up in the love seat with the remote control. Elle sat on a beach towel on the floor, an empty bowl in her lap as a precaution.

"Can I get you girls any ginger ale? Or maybe some crackers?" my mom asked.

"Ugh." Elle groaned and leaned over her bowl.

"Or maybe we'll stick with water." She walked back toward the kitchen area. "I want to make sure everyone stays hydrated."

Rebekah adjusted the blanket we were sharing. "Go back, Sutton. I like that show."

"I don't think it's appropriate for Elle." Sutton kept flipping channels.

"It's a cartoon."

"Not all cartoons are okay for all ages." Obviously, Sutton was feeling a little more like herself.

"I'm not a baby." Elle's voice echoed in the bowl. I was too tired to give my opinion.

Luckily, Grandmama chose that moment to open the beach house door, and everyone's mood instantly brightened.

"Just came to check on my best girls," she whispered sweetly. "And to bring this by." She pulled a movie from her faded leather purse.

"I've never heard of that one." Rebekah sat up and reached for the case. None of us had.

But when Grandmama pressed play, we were all enraptured by the story of a young girl learning to sing in the mansion of a mysterious stranger.

By the next day, we'd watched it so many times we had the songs memorized; and the day after that, we knew the lines as well. In fact, this would become one of our favorite films of all time, the premise of a dozen plays, and the inspiration for a whole new set of inside jokes and quotes.

Being stuck inside with a virus was not the present I'd have ever asked for on my birthday, but as many things do, it turned out to be a gift nonetheless.

"Tell your cousins hi for me and that I'm sorry I missed them. And I'm serious about you guys taking a road trip to Virginia. Anytime, okay?" He releases me from the warmest hug, and I feel teary all over again.

"Thanks, Gavin. I'm really glad I got to see you."

"Right back at you." He turns to Jude. "And you. Take care of yourself, little brother." They clasp hands, and Gavin shakes his head and pulls Jude in for a giant hug too. "Be good."

We watch him walk down to his truck and wave as he drives away. My fingers find the silver sand dollar. I thought about finally taking it off last night in some kind of symbolic gesture. But I'm not quite ready; it's too much a part of me now.

"Well?" Jude asks gently as we walk back inside while I dab the corners of my eyes with the back of my hand. "What do you want to do now?"

"Honestly?" I wait for his full attention. "I want to kick your butt in some more Mario Kart."

His concern melts away. "Well, since that's not gonna happen, would you settle for me kicking your butt instead?"

"You wish." I plop down on the floor and watch him set up the game.

"Here." He unravels the controllers and hands one to me, but I set it down when he comes to sit next to me.

The words almost catch in my throat. "What happened, Jude?"

"Hmm?"

"Six years ago." His brown eyes find mine, and he doesn't look away, so I keep talking. "Why did you guys disappear?"

He sets his controller aside too. "It's kind of a long story."

"We don't have to talk about it if you don't want to."

"No, it's cool." He shrugs. "I guess I owe you an explanation."

"You don't owe me anything. I just . . . care."

He takes his glasses off, wipes them on the hem of his shirt, and slides them back over his nose. I admire the way he always seems to be able to stop and order his thoughts before sharing them aloud, whereas there are times I'm not even sure what I'm feeling until I hear myself work it out verbally.

"After you guys left that summer, Kelsey called my dad to tell him she was pregnant. And that she'd decided to get married and was staying in Wilmington. She asked him if he'd bring some of her stuff. I'd never seen my dad come so unglued. He rented a trailer, made me and Gavin go with him to help him convince her to come home." His lashes flutter shut for the briefest moment. "She didn't, obviously. We came home in August, and Gavin went back to college. I think I knew at the time he was leaving for good too. So it was just Dad and me for a few months. We'd never really been close, and somehow the two of us in bedrooms next to each other in this big house felt suffocating. He took a new job that involved a lot of moving around and gave me two choices: come with him and finish high school remotely or stay with a friend until graduation. I couldn't stand the thought of no one being here. Or the possibility that my dad might sell the house if no one was using it. And honestly, I knew my dad didn't want me to come."

I can't imagine anyone not wanting to be around Jude, and I almost say that, but instead I ask, "So, you stayed with a friend here for *years*?"

"Tyler, actually. His parents were so unbelievably kind to me. They made me feel like part of the family, even put my picture on their mantel. I spent a lot of time after school working or hanging here at the house but always had dinner and slept there at night. Until the second half of senior year. I moved back here then."

"Why?"

"It was their last semester with Ty before graduation. I didn't want to impose on all those 'lasts' and memories they were making, I guess. And to tell the truth . . ." His voice changes. "I didn't think I could handle all the reminders of what I didn't have."

"Jude." I notice that my own voice is thick with emotion too.

"Please don't feel sorry for me. It is what it is, and I've made peace with it. You just . . . asked . . . and that's what happened. Or the main gist of it anyway."

I make myself count to ten before I answer. "I want to hug you because that's what I would need right now. But, what do you need, Jude?"

The corner of his mouth twitches, and he picks up the controller beside his knee. "Right now, I think I need to remind you who the superior driver is."

"I'm not sure that losing to me again is going to make you feel better." I try to sound as convincingly lighthearted as possible. "But if this is what you really want . . ." I grab my controller too.

With both our eyes back on the TV screen, he says, "And maybe a little later, we can get back to our list? What's next?"

"Seashell painting." It's one of my favorites, but I'm not sure if it will be one of his. "We decorate the shells and add fun little messages with markers and then leave them on the beach for other people to find. We usually take them to the other side of the island, so someone outside our family stumbles upon them."

"Do you bury them?" He asks as we start the race.

"Not normally. But I guess we could?"

"Wouldn't that be more fun for a kid to find? Like coming across a little treasure while they're building a sandcastle or something?"

I shouldn't be surprised anymore by how thoughtful and perfect his ideas are. "Spoken like a true pirate."

"I wondered how long it was going to take you to start making pirate jokes again. Almost a whole day since you were sorry you came to the show, huh?"

"If it really bothers you, I'll stop," I offer.

"It doesn't." He nudges my shoulder with his. "But, hey, speaking of shells?"

"Yeah?"

Something hits the side of my virtual car, and it spins out.

I can't even pretend to be mad, because Jude looks happy again. And if all it takes is video games to make him forget his pain for a little while, I'll play for as long as he wants to.

Chapter 20

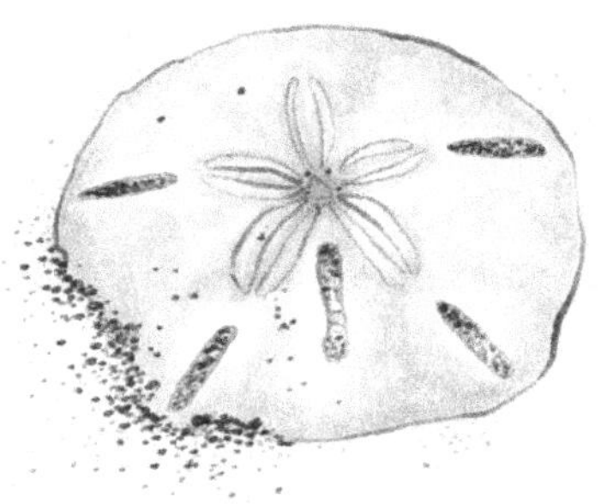

It's late morning, and Tyler and I have been watching the game for over an hour by the time Jude walks in.

"Hey! Where have you been?"

He perches on the arm of the couch beside me. "I didn't know you were a soccer fan."

"I'm not. But it's a World Cup year, so I have to be prepared."

He looks across me to Tyler and then back again. "For what?"

"For when my cousins come. One of the houses always has either live coverage or highlights on, and we play this game. It's called Lesser-Known Sibling." Jude doesn't look amused, so I keep explaining. "You pick out a player who looks like they could be related to a celebrity, and whoever comes up with the best one wins. Show him, Ty."

Tyler leans forward and points to the TV. "Okay, see this guy here? Number four? That's Chad Pitt, Brad's much less famous little brother. And the goalie on that side. Hold on." He waits until the camera pans over. "Marvin Short. You see it?"

I laugh. Jude does not.

"What's wrong, Jude?"

"Nothing. Why?" Something is definitely wrong.

"You just don't seem like yourself, is all."

He stands. "Tired, I guess."

"I thought you were coming down to the beach this morning," Ty chimes in. "The waves were insane."

"I had an appointment."

Ty winces. "Oh man. You told me that, and I completely forgot. My bad."

"It's fine." It doesn't sound fine. Nor do the pointedly silent moments that follow.

"I'm gonna head out." Ty hands me the remote.

"You can't leave now. We have to see if Chad scores another one."

Ty ignores me and stands up.

"You don't have to go," Jude grumbles. Why is he in such a sour mood?

The look Ty gives me is supposed to communicate something, I'm sure of it. But I have no idea what's going on right now.

"I'll see you guys later," he says as he slips out the door.

I scoot over to make room for Jude to sit. The game keeps playing, but neither of us is really watching.

I crack. "What's going on, Jude?"

"Hm?" He pretends to be engrossed in the action on the screen.

"Jude." I raise my voice the slightest bit. "You're acting weird."

His volume doesn't change. "Because I didn't show the proper amount of enthusiasm for your made-up game?"

"Because you're being mean," I shoot back. "And you aren't mean."

He turns his head and looks at me like I've just slapped him. "How am I being mean?"

"I don't know," I sputter. I'm so confused. "You just came in here in a funk and then kicked Ty out. And—"

"I didn't kick Ty out." He's on his feet now. "And why am I being attacked for coming into my own house and not being peppy enough?"

My cheeks warm, and I feel disoriented. "Why are you mad at me?"

"I'm *not* mad at you. Geez, Alex. What do you want from me?"

I forget for a moment that I'm not arguing with Sutton, that this is Jude, and I should probably proceed accordingly. "Nothing," I spit back. "I'll get out of your way." I retreat upstairs as quickly as my feet will carry me, the only sounds behind me the muffled voices of soccer commentators and a slamming bedroom door.

I don't risk resurfacing until a couple hours later when I hear the click of the front lock followed by tires backing out of the driveway.

Walking around the empty house, I feel more like an intruder than a guest. In a situation like this, I'd normally call one of my cousins, but that would require too much explaining at this point. And I can't write, because Jude still has my notebook somewhere; it wouldn't feel right to put my thoughts down anywhere else. I consider a trip to the ocean. Maybe I'll run into Tyler and he can give me some insight. But somehow that seems wrong too.

Eventually, I return to my room and pull out my plastic box of art supplies, moving aside the bottles of paint we used on the seashells to get to the stack of construction paper. I'd write an apology note if I knew what I was apologizing for. "I'm not sure what I did, but I can't stand the fact that something is not right between us, and how do I fix it?" doesn't exactly have greeting card vibes. Instead, I find a yellow sheet, cut a slow circle, and punch a hole at the top so I can string it on a piece of ribbon. On one side, I write "World's Most Patient Friend." Then I flip it over and add "Video Game Champion (for now)." It's not the traditional Henry Family Olympic medal, but hopefully, the sentiment will count for something.

This may not technically be the longest day of the year, but it's undeniably been the longest day of my year. I've had plenty of time to pick apart our interaction this morning. I've convinced myself at this point that, while I still don't understand why, something is very wrong and that I may need to pack my bags just in case.

My mom called a few hours ago, but I knew if I picked up, she would hear all my fear and ask questions I'm not ready to answer. Questions I'm not convinced I could answer even if I wanted to. While I texted her that I'd call later, a message came through from Jude:

Don't cook tonight. I'll pick something up after work.

I open the text again now. What does it even mean? He's bringing food home? Or he's going to eat while he's out? He wants to talk this through? Or he doesn't want to see me, so he's staying away?

I've almost made myself physically sick with worry by the time Jude walks in, carrying a pizza box. I stand from my spot at the kitchen counter and watch him walk across the living room, trying to read his face as he approaches.

"Jude, I'm so sorry," I blurt out as he sets the box down.

He looks up. "What are *you* sorry for?"

I open my mouth, close it again. I've rehearsed this for hours, yet my mind's gone completely blank.

"Alex, I owe you an apology. Earlier—" he starts, but I shake my head.

"I shouldn't have—"

He takes a step closer. "Hey, just listen for a minute, okay?" His words are so soft and kind that I almost cry with relief. I nod.

His hands move to his glasses, then to his pockets, then out again. "Sorry," he murmurs nervously as he leans against the counter.

"It's okay. Take your time." I resist the urge to reach out and squeeze his arm.

"A few years ago." He breathes. "I started seeing someone."

Definitely not what I expected. "Oh."

"Tyler's mom helped me make the appointment. She thought I might need some guidance working through everything. And she was right."

Oh. I switch mental tracks again and nod to show him I'm still following.

"I used to go every week, but now it's usually just once a month or so to check in. It's been helpful to process out loud with somebody." He sighs and runs a hand over his hair. "But it's not always easy. And I think the combination of seeing Gavin and talking to you about high school and then reading your poems was just . . . a lot. And I usually come home from these appointments and kind of crash for an hour or two; I'm not used to having someone else around."

"I'm sorry."

"Stop." He playfully widens his eyes. "It's not a bad thing. It's just something I'm still learning how to do. I *was* in a funk, and I wasn't ready to talk about it. And instead of telling you that, I was kind of rude to you. And I very much regret that. Will you forgive me?"

I put my arms behind my back and clasp my hands together to stop myself from trying to hug him. I can tell it's taking a great amount of courage for him to trust me with this, and I want to handle it with care.

"I was rude to you too. I think sometimes I forget that not everyone deals with things the way I do. And it threw me to see you act differently than I'm used to. But you are absolutely allowed to be in a bad mood. I shouldn't have pushed. I want you to feel free to tell me if you ever need to be alone or just want some space."

He shakes his head. "Alex, that's not what I want at all. Space is all I've had for years. I've navigated so many things alone, and I'm tired of it. But letting someone else see all the messy stuff is new. And scary."

"But you've seen me fall apart at least a dozen times. And you have my notebook. If that's not a figurative peeing of my pants at band camp, I don't know what is."

Jude's eyes snap up to mine. "What?"

"I just mean, you can trust me."

His eyes close. "Could I have been more of a nerd? I still can't believe I told you that." He looks at me again. "I'm sure you and your cousins got a good laugh out of that story at least."

"Of course not!" I put on my best offended face. "That conversation was just between me and you."

He reaches for one of the drawers on the side of the counter, the one where he keeps his office supplies. "Speaking of which." He pulls open the drawer and extracts my book. "I've read this twice already, but I'd like to read it again. And to see what you add." He passes it to me. "If you don't mind."

I turn the notebook over in my hands then pass it back. "Why don't we just keep it in the drawer when I'm not using it? That way, you can read my thoughts whenever you want to. And anytime *you* want to talk . . ."

"I appreciate that."

I unclasp my hands. "Can I hug you now?"

"Sure," he laughs.

"Seriously, Jude," I say as I wrap my arms around his middle, "you've given me a safe place to work through so much of my own emotional stuff this summer, in more ways than one. I'd like to do the same thing for you. That's kind of how friendship works, you know."

He doesn't let go. "Thanks, Alex."

"You can even wipe snot across my sleeve if you want to," I offer.

He chuckles. "I think I'm good. But our pizza's getting cold."

"Ooo." Pulling back, I watch him scoot the box over and lift the lid. "Pineapple and ham!" I squeal. "The best pizza there is."

"So I've heard." He smiles.

I lift a slice from the box and place it on one of the paper towels he just tore off. "Jude Alford, I'm about to change your life."

He slides onto the stool beside me. "I don't doubt it."

Chapter 21

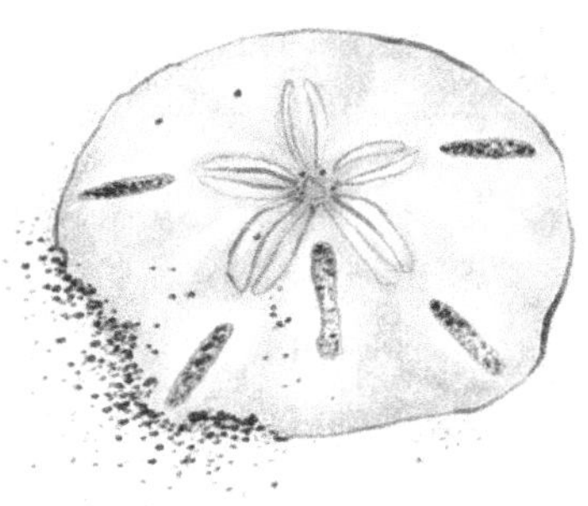

Peeling off a sunburn
Unwrapping birthday gifts
Shucking corn for dinner:
I've spent a lot of time
Pulling back the layers of things
Unveiling something new beneath
To only now be brave enough
To try it on my heart

"I understand, sweetheart, but you need to stay in and take it easy today." Mom inspected the stitches above my eyebrow with concern.

"But it's not fair," I sulked. "It's not like I busted my head open on purpose." I adjusted the strap of the suit I'd dressed in this morning before my parents ruined the rest of my vacation and I'd had to watch dejectedly out the window as my cousins carried sand buckets across the street. "What if I promise to be really careful? I won't even get in the ocean."

"Alexandria." Her tone assured me that this was the end of the discussion.

I stomped into the living room area and threw myself onto the couch, snatching up the remote.

I had just settled on some rerun I'd seen a million times already when Grandmama said a little too loudly from the kitchen, "I could really use an extra set of hands for this, but everyone seems to be busy today."

"Hmm," my mom answered. "Alex is here. I'm not sure if she's up for it, but you are welcome to ask her."

Intrigued, I rose from my throne of self-pity and walked to join them. "Ask me what?"

"Well." Grandmama grinned warmly. "You are just the person I need for this. And I was hoping to catch up with you today, hear firsthand the story of your bravery yesterday. Have you ever shucked corn before?"

"No. But I'm a quick learner," I assured her.

"Oh, I know you are." She opened the back door, and I followed her down the narrow steps and under the deck where several large cardboard boxes overflowed with green ears of corn.

When she settled on the ground and patted the concrete beside her, I sat and took the vegetable she passed me.

"Now." She held up the ear of corn in her hand. "We have to make sure we get all the leaves and silk off and clean them up good." I watched her demonstrate and marveled at how quick and effortless she made it seem, certain I wouldn't be as skilled at the process.

I was right. Getting the corn to the point where it was ready to cook was much harder than I'd have guessed. But as we sat and worked side by side, I was glad I'd stayed behind that morning.

As we finished up the first box and moved on to the second, a shadow blocked the sunlight, and I felt something wet drip on my bare leg. I squinted up at Sutton, Rebekah, and Elle.

"You guys are back already?"

"The waves were lame today," Sutton explained.

Rebekah tossed her towel to the ground beside me and sat. "It wasn't the same without you."

Elle turned to Grandmama. "Can we help?"

"Wow." Rebekah watched me strip the leaves off the corn in my hand. "You're really good at this, Al."

I waved her off. "Aw, shucks."

"Please." Sutton groaned. "That was the corniest joke I've ever heard."

Elle tried her hand at a pun next but failed.

Sutton scoffed, but Rebekah threw the green strings in her hand at her. "Leaf Elle alone."

"Kindness, girls," Grandmama reminded us.

"Yes," Elle agreed. "Kindness. Grandmama has spoken."

Grandmama nodded resolutely. "She who has ears, let her hear."

Even Sutton chuckled.

Corn, sausage, shrimp, and potatoes roll out of the giant upturned pot in Jude's arms and onto the table I covered with newspaper this afternoon.

"Yum," a tall girl with curly hair comments. "This looks incredible."

"Right?" the guy standing next to her chimes in. "I mean, it could be because it's after nine and I'm starving, but I can't remember the last time I've been this ready to tear into a meal."

Jude returns the empty pot to the counter where I'm filling glasses with ice. "Hey, thanks again for getting all this ready. I feel bad that I didn't do much to help."

"You were working. And, besides, I could make low country boil in my sleep if I needed to. I'm just excited I finally get to meet your mysterious work friends."

He turns back to face the room. "Everybody ready to eat?"

Close to a dozen people crowd around the table. I moved all the chairs to the living room this afternoon so there'd be room for everyone to stand and eat in the kitchen or fix a plate and relocate.

Jude opts for a plate, and I watch Miss Curly Hair, who I'm now guessing is the infamous Norah, trail him to the couch and sit a little closer than he appears comfortable with. He shoots me a pleading glance which I answer with a suggestive wink before returning to fill my glass with sweet tea.

My cell phone buzzes in my back pocket; it's a text from Jude: *Please help.*

Setting my phone aside and picking up my drink, I make my way through a small cluster of people and over to the couch where Jude is nonchalantly sliding his own cell back into his cargo shorts pocket.

"Hey there," I croon saccharinely. "Mind if I sit here?"

Norah looks at the empty cushion on her other side. I wait until she begrudgingly slides over and situate myself between her and Jude. "I'm Alex," I offer.

"Norah," she confirms.

"You work with Jude?" I lean into Jude's shoulder and watch her bristle. This is too much fun.

"I do." She fakes a smile. "And how exactly do you know Jude?"

"We're . . ." I purposefully hesitate for a beat. "Good friends. I live here." I can't look at Jude or my act will most certainly fall apart.

"Oh." She puts more distance between us, and her entire demeanor changes. "I had no idea. He's never mentioned you before." She blushes. "I mean, we don't talk much about life outside of work at work I guess."

"No worries; I get it. We don't usually talk about work much at home either." I imagine the horrified face Jude is making and almost crack.

Norah uncomfortably shifts her attention to her plate. "This is delicious."

"Thanks." I smile. "I made it."

"Mmm," she grunts around a mouthful of potato. "But messy. I forgot to grab a napkin." And with that, she stands and hurries away.

"Subtle," Jude comments under his breath as I scoot over into Norah's empty seat.

"You asked for help," I whisper back.

"I did," he concedes. "Thank you."

"Jude!" A burly redhead approaches from the kitchen and plops down beside me, forcing me back to the middle of the couch. "Your place is amazing. Why have I never been here before?" He turns to me. "And who is this?"

"Alex." I shake his hand as he tells me his name is Greg.

"I'm Jude's favorite coworker," he explains. "But don't tell the others." Jude's arm slides protectively across the back of the couch behind me.

"So tell me, Greg," I begin. "Have you ever seen the dragon lose his head before he's supposed to?"

"Heather!" Greg calls across the room. "This girl wants to hear about the alternate script."

And thus begins one of the most entertaining conversations I've ever been privy to.

It's funny in the way that things only are at one in the morning when you're simultaneously insanely tired and wide awake and have decided to do something spontaneous like leave a whole sink of dishes to soak while you go crab hunting in the middle of the night.

I swipe at the laughter-induced tears on my face as Jude turns off his phone screen and takes the net back from me. "That makes three people now who have asked when I'm hosting the next party and four who have texted just to say how much they like my girlfriend."

"Sorry about that." I shine the flashlight across the dark sand, watching for movement.

"For keeping Norah away from me or for majorly increasing my cool factor at work?"

"I don't know, that pirate earring is pretty cool. There!" A tiny crustacean freezes in the beam of artificial light, and Jude runs over to it, foregoing the net and pinching its shell between his fingers before hurrying back to drop it in the bucket I'm carrying.

"How many is that now?"

I angle the flashlight toward the bucket, watching the tiny transparent crabs climb on top of one another and trying to ignore how close they are to my hand. "A lot."

"You're not scared of crabs, are you?" he questions. "This *was* your idea. Don't you guys do this every year?"

"No, I'm not scared," I defend myself. "I just don't want to touch them."

Jude pulls his phone from his pocket again and chuckles. "'Thanks for dinner, Jude. Your fiancée is adorable.' Well, that escalated quickly."

"Nope. No way." I shake my head. "Your coworkers should know better than to think we'd be engaged."

"Yeah? Why's that?" He sounds insulted.

"Because the only marriage proposal I would have accepted would have happened at the show; they would have seen it."

"You're ridiculous." He takes the bucket from me. "Ready to set these guys free?"

"I guess so. We usually all stand in a big circle and my uncle dumps all the buckets in the middle at the same time. This feels sort of anticlimactic."

"I don't know. I feel like this might be just as much of an adrenaline rush." His words have hardly registered when he tips the bucket over and empties a pile of wriggling creatures at our feet.

I scream and drop the flashlight, watching in slow motion as the batteries pop out and everything goes dark. Then, I feel the tiny legs scurry across my bare toes. "Jude!" I almost tackle him in my attempt to escape. It's all over in a matter of seconds, but it's going to take hours for my heart rate to slow back down to normal.

"Ouch!" Jude yells.

"Did they pinch you?"

"No," he laughs. "But I can't feel my arm. Your nails are sharp."

I loosen my grip. "*Why would you do that*?"

"You told me you weren't scared. And they're harmless."

I realize I'm standing on his foot and move. "I also said I didn't want to touch them."

"I didn't know they were going to run straight for you. Or that you were going to scream loud enough to wake the whole island. We should probably get out of here before someone calls security on us." He turns on his phone flashlight and hands it to me while he locates the batteries and tries to repair the light I dropped. "I think this one's done for good," he says as he knocks it against his palm a few times. "Where's your phone?"

"Somewhere in your kitchen."

"Okay." He drops the broken flashlight into the bucket and slides his arm through it. "Grab the net, and I'll give you a ride back to the steps."

I loop my arms around his neck, and he hoists me onto his back while I struggle to hang onto the net and hold the phone steady enough to give him enough light to see where he's going.

"I'm going to have nightmares about crabs," I tell him.

"My fault." He keeps walking. "If you can't sleep, I'll watch *Little Women* with you."

If I didn't know he had to get up early to work, I'd suggest we watch it either way. "Sorry I broke your flashlight."

"It's fine. We'll put a new one on the wedding registry."

"The wedding is off. You're a great guy, but if dumping a bucket of sea creatures on someone's feet isn't reason to break off an engagement, I don't know what is."

"Fair enough. But do me a favor?" He sets me down on the steps. "Don't tell Norah."

Chapter 22

Part of me was buried with her
But parts of her lie buried in me

"She told me she was proud of me once," Jude says.

I pull the last cookie from the foil and set it on the plate in front of him. "Who?"

"Your grandma."

"What?" I try to be patient as I watch him pick up a cookie and take a bite. But the prospect of a story I've never heard before about Grandmama is too much. "When?"

"The summer before eighth grade. Auditions for the school play were always at the end of the summer, a fact that would have normally meant absolutely nothing to me. But I'd heard they were doing *Little Women* and was seriously considering auditioning for

Laurie." He passes me a cookie, but I'm only hungry for more of this memory. "Rather than just reading lines, they made everyone memorize a passage to perform for the audition. It was the scene where Laurie proposes to Jo." He shrugs. "You'd have thought I'd have an edge because I knew the character so well, but I couldn't decide if I should go more book-Laurie or movie-Laurie. And I couldn't get the lines down. I would sneak out super early in the morning to practice under the house; I knew Gavin would never let me live it down if he heard me. Anyway, that morning I had run through the thing a couple times before I finally felt good about it. And when I turned to go inside, I heard clapping from under the house next door. And there was your grandma, sitting on the porch swing with a Bible in her lap. She said I sounded great and that she hoped I got the part."

He pauses, and I lean forward, desperate for him to keep talking about her.

"I told her I wasn't sure if I was going to go through with the audition," he continues. "She asked if she could give me some advice."

"What was the advice?" How many times have I wished I could hear just one more piece of Grandmama's advice?

"If you want something badly enough, it's worth taking a risk." He notices my eyes filling and passes me a napkin. "I told her that was what I needed to hear, and that I was going to sign up for my audition as soon as I got inside. And that's when she said it. 'Well, young man, whatever happens, I'm proud of you.'" He studies the counter. "It wasn't something I heard often, so it meant a lot."

I swallow the lump in my throat. "She always made sure we saved some of her famous cookies for you guys, you know."

"She only saw us one week a year, but she always made us feel special. I think she probably knew we needed it, felt sorry for us."

"No. I think she just loved you guys like we did."

"Did?" he jokes.

"Do." I laugh and hand him another cookie. He turns it over in his hand.

"Hey, can I show you something?" He sets the cookie down, opens the laptop beside him, and starts typing. I walk around the counter to join him. I'm expecting to see a proposed change to Ty's website, but it's a job listing that fills the screen.

"Finally insisting I get a job and start pulling my weight around here?" I question as he pushes the computer over. I take in the island's city logo at the top of the webpage and scan the words "Community Outreach and Events Manager, Full Time."

"It's sort of everything I want to do," Jude explains, "without having to reinvent the wheel by starting my own business. And I could still help Ty if he wanted me to, maybe even steer some more tourists his way, create some kind of official promotional partnership with the city or something."

In typical Jude fashion, he's obviously spent a lot of time thinking this through, figuring out how it will affect not only himself but the people around him; it's one of my favorite things about him. I scroll through the list of job responsibilities. "Jude, you'd be perfect for this."

"Yeah, but it will still be a few months before I get my degree. And even then, it'll be in business, not hospitality." He frowns. "And they prefer experience."

"You have experience. You've been running Ty's surf company. And you're working in several tourism industries right now. Besides, I can't think of anyone better to represent this island than someone who's lived here his whole life. You have to apply." I sound like Sutton. "Sorry. What I meant to say was, whatever you decide about this, you have my support."

"No. The first thing was what I needed." He studies the screen as if he's not read the information multiple times, though I'm sure he has. "You really think I have a chance?"

"Absolutely. And like my grandmother would say—"

"If you want something badly enough, it's worth taking a risk?"

"No." I look him straight in the eyes and hope that he hears every ounce of sincerity in my voice. "Whatever happens, Jude, I'm proud of you."

"This one's kind of cool." He stops flipping through the binder of designs and points to the page that lies open on the store counter.

"No! You can't show me. It's got to be a surprise."

"Right." He resumes his page turning. "Any other rules?"

"It needs to be something meaningful. To you. Something that represents an aspect of this particular summer that you want to memorialize."

"Hmm. This feels like a lot of pressure."

"That's because it's your first tattoo. It's normal to be nervous."

The man behind the counter who'd earlier introduced himself as Big K clears his throat. "You do know this is just henna, right? It's not permanent."

"Don't ruin this for us, Big K. We want the full tattoo experience."

He holds up his hands in surrender. "Yes ma'am. Let's get you guys inked up. Who's first?"

"Me," Jude answers right away.

I survey the rows of T-shirts and beach towels and handmade jewelry. "I'll look around until you're done, and then we can switch." I rest a hand on his arm and say in mock solemnity, "You can do this. Be tough."

Big K snickers as I walk away.

Half an hour later, we step outside into the sunshine, and Jude says, "Okay, let's see what you got."

I balance on one foot as I turn my ankle to show him the still-raised shape of a tiny crab. "To remember my narrow escape the other night."

"It's perfect. I thought about getting a broken flashlight." Jude grins. "We would have matched."

"So what did you decide on? It has to be good if it beat out the flashlight."

He gingerly pulls up his sleeve, taking care not to bump the drying art, to reveal the outline of a tiny cereal box.

A sound of unfettered happiness bubbles out of me, and I open my phone to take a picture.

"So it's better than the flashlight? You like it?" Jude asks.

"Way better." I snap the photo. "And I don't like it; I love it."

It's late when I finally finish strategically skirting Sutton's questions via text and tell her my last lie of the day. *I should get some sleep. Goodnight.*

When I get down to the kitchen, Jude's laptop is open on the counter, but he's not behind it. I grab a drink from the fridge and pull open the drawer to retrieve my notebook. There's a loose piece of paper tucked into the spot where I left off. I unfold it and read the neat but distinctly masculine handwriting.

Someone once told me that
The human body is sixty percent water
And that my sixty percent is
Probably mostly ocean water
Because when you live next to the sea
It starts to live inside you
Maybe that's why
I spent sixty percent of my childhood
On the edge of this island
Dreaming of leaving it behind
But never could do it
And why the waves within me
Can only be calmed by the ones without
And why I fear if I ever lose the ocean
I might just lose most of myself

When I look up from the page, he's standing on the tiled floor, watching my face, waiting.

"You lied to me," I whisper.

His vulnerable countenance morphs into confusion. "What?"

"You said you weren't a writer."

His fingers flutter to the arm of his glasses. "I'm not. This is just . . ."

"Beautiful. And I feel really special that you let me see it." I smooth the page out. "Can I just make one tiny suggestion?"

He walks over to the counter and sits on the stool beside me. "Sure."

"Will you copy it into the book?"

He stares at the notebook I just placed in front of him. "Alex, this is *your* book."

"Maybe it's not just mine though." Why am I the nervous one here? "I've been thinking that there's no way I'm going to be able to fill all these pages by the end of the summer. Maybe I'm not supposed to?"

He picks up the pen, lets it hover above the paper, and finds my eyes. "Are you sure?"

"Positive."

I watch as he slowly tattoos the page, and—while I try not to scrutinize the thought too closely—I'm vaguely aware that something between us has just shifted permanently.

Chapter 23

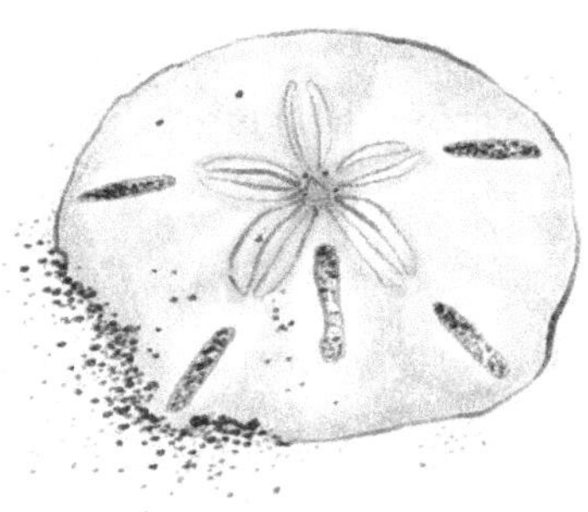

Tiny ghost thoughts
Scurry sideways
Through my mind
In the dark
The idea of catching them
Shining a light
Examining them up close
Thrills me
But I hesitate
Jumpy
Because I know
I can't hold them for long
I'll have to let them go again
And I'm not sure where

They will run next

I lower the sun visor on the passenger side and flip open the mirror. "It makes me sad that I missed out on six whole years of knowing you," I comment. "Elle tried to look you guys up on social media a few times, but Sutton said that made us seem like stalkers." I leave out the part about them finding Gavin and my refusal to look at his photos. Sutton may have been right about my need to preserve a version of him I wrote.

"Gavin found all your pages but wouldn't contact you guys for the same reason. Besides, I figured maybe you liked keeping your beach week life separate from everything else. I know how you were about keeping things special and all." I wonder if he knows how close to home his comment hits. "I don't really do social media anyway, aside from Ty's business pages. And, if I'm being honest, it's probably for the best that you missed the last six years of knowing me; I was kind of a mess for a while while I sorted through some stuff."

I close the mirror and shift in my seat. "Friends should be there for the hard parts too. I'm sorry these past years have been so tough. For what it's worth, I really like the version of you that's come out the other side."

"Thanks." He smirks. "Is it really that different from the version you grew up with?"

"Well." I gather my thoughts as he stops at a traffic light. "You're a lot taller now."

He laughs. "That's generally how it works."

"Hold on; I'm not finished." I make a face, and he steps on the gas when the light turns green. "You're more confident now. Less shy. Even more competitive."

"Competitive?"

"Jude. How many video games have I played with you this summer? And when I beat you . . ."

"Which doesn't happen often," he interjects.

"See?" I laugh. "Competitive. But also, you're like . . . still quiet and humble but certain of yourself in a way that I envy. You know who you are."

"You envy me?"

"Admire might be a better word." I try to lighten the mood. "But you don't spout off as many interesting facts about animals. Or go skinny dipping in the ocean anymore."

He cuts his eyes at me. "That *you* know of."

I rein in a giggle. "You're funnier than you used to be too. I can't remember the last time I laughed as much as I have these past few weeks." I pose the question before I can lose my nerve. "Do you think I've changed at all?"

He pulls into a crowded parking lot, and I know he's turning my inquiry over in his mind, holding his thoughts close until he's sure of them. "I think that, in most ways, you're very much who you've always been."

My heart sinks, my deepest fears confirmed. He slides the gear between us into park and keeps talking. "I wonder, though. Do you think it's possible that maybe I haven't changed as much as you think I have? That maybe I just knew you better than you knew me all those summers?"

My hand freezes halfway to my seatbelt, and I search Jude's expression.

He shrugs, a habit I've learned means that he's about to share something personal with me. "What I mean is that I've not always been the easiest person to get to know well. Intentionally. My counselor says I hold people at arm's length." He looks away. "But this summer's been different. And I like that you know me better now."

"Me too." I want to reach for his hand, to somehow try to convey the feelings I can't find words for, but I don't want him to think those feelings are romantic in any way. They aren't. At least, I don't think so.

He clears his throat and reaches for the keys in the ignition. "You ready for this?"

The bar is loud and packed with people.

"Whoa." I scan the room. "Lincoln Shark must be pretty popular."

Jude waves across the crowd to a group of guys and leads me to the merch table along the back wall. "There's somebody I want you to meet."

We've just come into view of a middle-aged couple when the woman squeals and drops the shirt she's folding onto the table. "Jude! Oh, it's so good to see you." She wraps Jude in a hug though she's only about half his size, then releases him and focuses her attention on me. "And you must be Alex. Tyler's told us so much about you."

I nod and look to Jude. "This is Ty's mom, Mrs. Becky," he explains, then gestures to the man who's just walked around to join us. "And his dad, Mr. Bruce."

"Nice to meet you." I smile. "I've heard a lot of wonderful things about your family."

Mr. Bruce shakes my hand. "Glad you could make it out to a show. You're in for a treat. I mean, I may be biased, but I've been at every single performance and have yet to resist the urge to rock out."

"Yes." Mrs. Becky rolls her eyes. "Which is why it may be a good thing that we're always manning the merchandise table."

The affection Jude feels for this couple is clear. "I don't know, Mr. Bruce," he says. "I think maybe you need to make your way into the mosh pit one of these days. It's a whole different experience." Mr. Bruce nudges his wife, and his hopeful expression makes my heart swell.

"Why not tonight?" I hear myself ask. "Jude and I can cover the table."

"I knew I liked this girl." Mr. Bruce winks at Jude.

"Are you sure?" Mrs. Becky asks. I defer to Jude, realizing I volunteered on his behalf without checking.

"Absolutely. Might be better to ease Alex into the craziness in stages anyway."

A microphone whines, and the chatter around us dies down as a man's voice rings out. "I'm supposed to introduce the band. But let's be real. These guys need no introduction. Ladies and gentlemen, here's your . . . Lincolnnnnn Shark!" The whole place erupts.

Four guys walk onto the stage and take their places, brandishing their instruments.

"You kids have fun." Jude nudges Mr. Bruce and Mrs. Becky forward into the crowd. I follow him behind the table, lean against the wall, and watch Tyler raise his drumsticks above his head, counting off the first song.

Whatever my expectations were coming in, the scene unfolding before me exceeds them all. The band plays a mix of cover songs and originals the audience seems to know just as well. The crowd—Ty's parents included—moves as one unit to the beat, not unlike the ocean itself.

After the fifth or sixth number, Jude leans over. "You having fun?"

"So much fun." I beam. "This might be my new favorite band."

"Don't tell Tyler that. It'll go to his head."

When the next song starts, I have to yell to be heard. "Do his parents really come to all their shows?"

"Every single one. They're really great."

"I can tell." I straighten the row of stickers in front of me. "They seem pretty fond of you too."

He tucks both hands into his pockets. "Mr. Bruce used to take me fishing with Tyler and his brothers all the time. And Mrs. Becky," he raises his voice above the music, "found out when I moved in with them that I'd never taken my own lunch to school. She told me school lunches were fine, but everybody should have someone pack them a lunch at least once. After that, she packed my lunch every day. Remembered all my favorites, put little notes in there and everything. Ty kept apologizing for how embarrassing it was. But I loved it."

As if summoned by this recollection, Mrs. Becky and Mr. Bruce step out of the mosh pit, cheeks flushed and out of breath.

"Well," Mr. Bruce pants, "that'll remind you of your age in a hurry."

Mrs. Becky steps around the table. "We'll take over. You two get in there." But before we make our way into the chaos, Jude pulls his wallet from his back pocket and hands Mrs. Becky a twenty.

"Which one do you want, Al?"

"What?"

"Everyone needs a T-shirt of their favorite band. Pick one."

I pick up the ocean-blue one I've been eyeing and sling it over my shoulder. "Thanks, Jude."

"I just hope you're prepared for this." I keep a hand on his arm as we're swallowed by the mob.

When we emerge an hour later, my ears are ringing and I'm sticky with sweat. But I'm smiling so hard my face hurts.

"Jude! Alex!" Tyler catches up to us at the merch table. "You made it! What did you think?"

"You guys are really good."

"Try not to sound so surprised," he jokes, then turns and slings an arm around his mom's shoulders. "You met my parents?"

"Yes. They're every bit as wonderful as Jude described."

Mrs. Becky beams. "Bring her over for dinner soon, Jude?"

"That sounds great."

"Hey, you want to meet the rest of the band?" Ty offers.

I'm so exhausted, I don't even open the drawer for my notebook. "Just wanted to say goodnight," I whisper.

Jude looks up from his laptop. "I'm glad we went tonight and that you had a good time."

I sit down, too tired to think straight but not ready to leave just yet, and watch him work for a few minutes. "Is Tyler your best friend?"

He stops typing. "One of them, yeah. Why?"

"Because I think you might be mine."

Something flickers in his eyes, and I hope my admission hasn't freaked him out. "Really?"

"Is that okay?" Maybe I should have just gone to bed.

"That actually makes me really happy."

I fold my arms on the cool countertop and rest my chin on top. "Sutton always said you can have a lot of close friends, but your best friend is the one you always want to share things with first, the one you'd think to call first if you ever got into trouble or needed help. And," I admit, "that's you now."

"In that case, I think you qualify as my best friend too." He scratches his head, considering. "But to be fair, Ty and your cousins are at a clear disadvantage. Because if either of us ever got into serious trouble, chances are calling them wouldn't be an option, since they'd be with us."

"You aren't wrong."

He closes his computer. "Hey, I know it's late, but are you up for some cheese toast?"

Suddenly, I'm not sleepy anymore. "Always."

Chapter 24

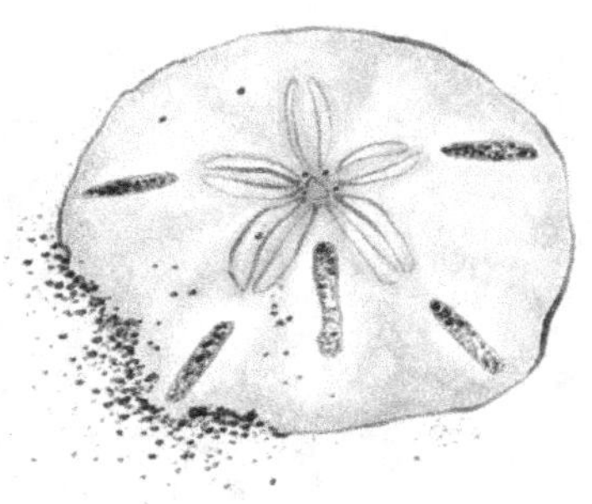

Is it strange that my favorite photograph of someone
Doesn't even show their face?
A mere silhouette
Just the outline, the shape of her
A shadow of the past
I wonder if it's because
All the details I'll never know
The face I have no memory of
The dark edges of mystery and loss
Are the things that have shaped me most

"This may sound weird, but I'd like to think she'd be proud that I'm doing this tomorrow. The thing my dad talked about more than anything was how much she loved this island."

I look across my plate of pancakes. "It doesn't sound weird at all." Jude hasn't touched his food. "Are you nervous?"

"A little."

"Understandable. But the fact that they called for an interview this soon is a good sign. They're clearly very interested."

He sets his fork down. "Thanks for helping me pick out a tie. Any interview advice?"

"Be yourself." He opens his mouth, but I cut him off. "I know that sounds cliché. But I'm serious; if they see the Jude I know, you'll be a shoo-in." I snap off a piece of bacon. "I wish I was brave enough to do something like this."

"You didn't interview for your job?"

"I did." He waits patiently for the rest of the story. "But it was a safe bet. I only applied because I knew I'd get it. And because I knew what to expect when I did."

"But you like it, right? Teaching?"

"Yeah. Most of the time. I just wonder if there are other possibilities I've overlooked because I'm—" I search for the right word.

"Scared?" Jude finds it. "You need to feel in control." He doesn't phrase the last part as a question. My vision blurs without warning, and his worried face swims across from me. "Alex, I'm sorry," he starts to apologize.

"No, you're right."

"Did something happen?"

I rein in my tears. "What do you mean?"

"You can tell me it's none of my business if you want. But I just can't help but wonder if there's a reason why you feel this way? What made you so afraid?"

I abandon my plate, no longer hungry. "That's the thing, Jude. Very few things that anyone would consider 'bad' have ever happened to me. When Grandmama died, it was the first time I'd ever experienced such deep grief. My childhood was a dream; I know no one's life is perfect, but I think I lucked out and got pretty close. And I feel like such a brat for even thinking this, especially after everything you've gone through, but I just worry that the rest of my life is never going to measure up. What if it's all downhill from here? What if it's just one loss after the next until all of it is gone?" The last word comes out as hardly a squeak, and I sit in silence under the weight of the words I just unloaded on him.

He pushes his own plate to the side and puts his hands on the table, taking a deep breath. "That makes sense to me."

A strangled half-laugh, half-cry escapes me. "Really?" I'm not even sure it makes sense to me.

"I spent a lot of years wondering if it would have been harder if I'd known my mom. If it would hurt more if I had all these memories of her like you do of your grandma."

"Jude." I'm bereft of any other words at the moment. At least three minutes tick by, the only sound the tapping of the rain against the window.

"Which ones would you trade?" Jude finally asks. "Which moments would you give back if it would lessen the pain of possibly losing them?" I let his eyes hold mine, the challenge in them laced with tenderness. I shake my head slowly. "We have to take it all together, Al. The good stuff and the hard stuff. And most of the best parts of life are both."

Though there are a hundred things I want to say right now, I can't. So I opt for, "Do you want to build a fort with me?"

"Huh?" Jude's brow wrinkles but his shy grin returns.

I gesture to the window. "We can't really go anywhere. Seems like a good day for a fort."

"Is this a Henry family beach tradition I've yet to learn?"

"Nope." I stand and pick up my plate. "Just something I used to do at home sometimes. You've never built a fort before?"

"Of course I have." He pushes his chair back. "It's been a while, but I'm pretty sure I could still whip up something epic. You get all the blankets from upstairs. I'll move the kitchen chairs to the living room. If we set it up in front of the TV, we can play video games from inside."

"I like the way you think, Alford."

When I return with my third and final armload of blankets and pillows from the second floor, he's already got the outside structure finished.

"This looks amazing." I duck inside. "Don't forget to tell the interviewers tomorrow that you accidentally left this skill off your résumé."

"I was just contemplating calling them to see if they wanted to meet here instead of their office." He joins me in the fort and helps me set up the pillows around the edges. "You know, for not being an official beach tradition, this might be one of my favorite traditions so far."

"I'm gonna let you in on a secret about traditions, Jude." I lower my voice to a whisper. "Anything can be a tradition. You just have to start it once, and then keep doing it."

"That settles it then." He stretches out and leans back. "Fort goes up on every rainy day from here on out." He pulls out his phone, types, and reads the screen. "And it looks like it's going to rain the rest of this week."

"Noo," I whine. "We still have stuff to do."

He passes his phone to me. "Good news is it looks like it'll be sunny by the time your family gets here." He lifts one of the blankets on the fort's wall and folds it back to let in more light. "You up for some video games?"

"I would be. But I'd hate to beat you so badly that it shakes your confidence going into the meeting tomorrow."

He tosses a pillow at me. "I'm not worried."

Another idea hits me. "Hey, do you have any Legos?"

"Do *I* have any *Legos*?" He pulls a face that I know is reserved strictly for me when he thinks I'm being absurd. "I'll be right back."

He exits our hideout, and I'm struck by the fact that I'm about to turn twenty-two next week and I'm currently sitting in a blanket fort waiting for my friend to return with Legos. I think about how much I've grown these weeks on this island with Jude. And how I feel both older and younger than I have in years.

Chapter 25

"Sorry for the mess"
She said as she gestured to the room
An empty coffee cup
An unfolded blanket
A stack of papers and a pen
The flip-flops discarded on the floor
"It's no problem"
I answered
But what I really meant was
Please don't stop
Leaving these reminders
That someone is living here
It's been too long since anyone has

It's been too long since I have

"I think the whole island might sink if it rains any more." I drop the remaining pieces of the jigsaw puzzle back into the box and replace the lid. We've spent the last few days using the hours around Jude's work schedule to play every board game he owns, put together two puzzles, and build an elaborate town out of Legos.

"You're finally bored of me?" He reaches into the container of snacks we set up inside our fort and fishes out a bag of gummy bears.

"Never." I open my hand, and he shakes some candy into it. "I'm just bummed that it's our last night before I leave and we can't go check anything off our list."

He takes the puzzle from me and moves it aside next to the LED lantern we've been using for extra light. "But you're coming back, right? You'll only be gone for a week, and then we'll still have time?"

"If you're okay with that." I've wanted to have this conversation all week but been too afraid to broach the subject.

"I'm counting on it." He twists the bag of gummy bears closed. "We have more traditions to cover, and the notebook still has plenty of blank pages. Speaking of which, did you finish the poem you were working on?"

"I haven't figured out where it's going yet," I admit. "I want it to end on a hopeful note. Like sure, sunburns do fade too soon like temporary tattoos, but there are also things that last. Maybe I should get a real tattoo at some point, and then I'll be able to relate to the sentiment that sometimes the pain and the beauty are linked like you said."

"Hmm." He considers. "But you do have a permanent tattoo of sorts."

Before I can ask his meaning, he lifts his hand to my face and carefully traces the scar above my eye with his thumb. Instinctively, I jerk away.

"Sorry," he stammers. "I didn't mean to—"

"No, it's okay. I'm just kind of self-conscious about it."

I watch the lamplight dance across his face, which is only inches from mine, and try to make sense of what just happened, what's going on inside me. "You shouldn't be. You have to be looking for it to notice it, and only the luckiest of us know to look. That scar is legendary, Al. Do you know how many times Gavin and I told the kids at school about the girl we knew who split her head open on the waterslide and woke up before the ambulance got there and shed not ONE single tear, because she was so busy trying to comfort her cousin while her aunt held a beach towel to her head and yelled at her to be still?"

I laugh, the memory as fresh as wet ink. "Elle was beside herself. And Sutton and Bekah were stuck at the top. I think Sutton probably wasn't very nice to your sister up there." Then the full force of his words hit me. "Wait. You were there that day?"

"I was there pretty much every day that summer. Kelsey was lifeguarding, and my dad didn't trust Gavin and me enough to let us stay home alone, so we tagged along with her. I usually just sat in the office with a book. Most days, Gavin teased me about being antisocial and afraid of heights, but I was glad I had a clean, dry towel to offer that afternoon. Which you ruined, by the way," he jokes.

For some reason, this revelation seems like a bigger deal than it should be. "How did I never remember this? And you *hate* blood."

"Yeah. But it was you. I didn't even think about it at the time; I just needed to know you were going to be okay."

My face heats, and suddenly the fort seems too small, too quiet, and Jude is too close. I look away.

He clears his throat. "You know what? You're right. We shouldn't let the rain spoil your last night before vacation. I need to make a quick phone call. Will you run up to the closet and grab a couple beach towels and the ponchos on the top shelf?"

Curiosity chases away whatever else I'm feeling. "What are we doing?"

"Starting a new tradition." Before I can ask another question, he crawls out of the fort.

The rain is really coming down when Jude pulls off the main stretch into the parking lot of the mini golf course.

"Are you serious?"

"What?" He cuts the engine. "I figured you'd be up for something crazy like this."

"Oh, I definitely am." I lift the clear hood of my poncho over my ponytail. "I just don't think you understand how good I am at Putt-Putt. I'm going to decimate you." To be honest, I'm only provoking him because I've become addicted to the way he looks when his need to win conflicts with the many exceptions I've noticed he makes for me.

"I apologize in advance for shattering this delusion of yours." He talks a big game, but I'd bet every penny I have he's going to let me win.

We dash across the parking lot and under the cover of the cashier's stand. There's a guy who looks vaguely familiar behind the register, shaking his head.

"And here I was thinking I was going to get a nice quiet night off."

Jude passes him a wad of cash and hands me the wire bucket of golf balls from the counter so I can pick out a color. "This is my buddy BJ. He's doing us a favor."

"I remember you," he says. "You were at the Lincoln Shark show." He pulls two clubs down from the rack behind him. "I'd pick the highlighter yellow ball if I were you, so you can see it out here in all this rain. For the record, I think you're both insane. But as long as there's no lightning or thunder, you're welcome to stay as long as you'd like."

"Thanks, man. I owe you one."

We make our way to the first hole, and I set my golf ball on the soggy green carpet.

"Hold on," Jude demands. "What are we wagering on this?"

I'm already freezing cold, but I don't care. "If I win, you have to make me hot chocolate and cheese toast tonight."

"That's fair," he agrees. "But I'd have probably done that anyway." He adjusts the poncho as the wind blows it around him. "*When* I win." He smirks. "You have to make me another medal."

"Deal," I laugh. "Now, can we play before I can't feel my hands anymore?"

By hole eight, we are drenched despite the ponchos, and when I reach down into the hole after my last putt, the ball is floating in a few inches of water.

"What was that? Four?" Jude calls from the tee.

"Three," I correct. "And I'm keeping score in my head too, so don't you try to cheat."

"I don't need to cheat, Miss Henry. I'm winning if you've forgotten." He putts the ball, and it rolls right beside me, almost a hole-in-one. Maybe he isn't going to let me have this.

My socks squish inside my shoes. "We might as well be in the ocean right now." I shiver.

"It is pretty chilly." He steps up beside me. "I'd offer you my jacket if I had one, though I doubt it would still be dry. We can just play to nine this time if you want."

"I knew it." I let myself stand closer to him than I normally would, justifying it with my need to be heard over the rain. "You're scared, because you know I'm about to make my comeback."

He stares me down, and without even looking, taps the ball straight into the hole.

By hole fourteen, he's "accidentally" missed a few shots, and I'm winning by one stroke. "It's because I can't see," he protests. His glasses are splattered with raindrops and starting to fog up.

"Here." I pinch an arm of the frames in each hand and carefully pull them from his face. I shake the water off. "If I had any clothing that wasn't soaked, I'd dry them off for you."

He leans in and squints. His hair is plastered to his forehead, and it's annoyingly cute. "Now, I *really* can't see."

"Sorry." I giggle and slide his glasses back into place. He blinks, focusing his eyes, seemingly surprised at how near I am. He doesn't step back.

"I forfeit," he states quietly.

My mind is too muddled to ask for clarification; all this rain is making me dizzy.

"Let's go home, and I'll start that hot chocolate. We can put on dry clothes, pile every blanket from the fort onto the couch, and watch a movie. What do you say?"

I find my voice. "You had me at 'dry clothes.'"

We run back to the car, BJ still shaking his head as we drop clubs and balls on the counter in passing. Once inside, I slam the passenger door and reach in the back for the towels. It takes me a minute to peel the plastic poncho off and swaddle myself in a striped towel that hardly does anything due to the fact that everything else I'm wearing is wet.

Jude finishes wiping his glasses, cranks up the heat, and tucks his own towel around me. "I'll drive as fast as I safely can," he promises.

I watch the water trickle in streams down my window as he drives, trying to distract myself from the idea of snuggling under blankets next to Jude on his couch.

"You're awfully quiet," he comments when we're almost to the house. "What are you thinking about?"

"Hot chocolate," I lie, braving a glance in his direction.

I watch whatever lighthearted retort he was planning to say die on his lips as he turns onto our street and curses softly under his breath. My eyes snap forward to take in the source of his sudden change: a silver car parked in the driveway.

He whips our vehicle in beside it and hardly has time to snatch the keys out before swinging open his door and bolting up the stairs, leaving me alone and bewildered.

Chapter 26

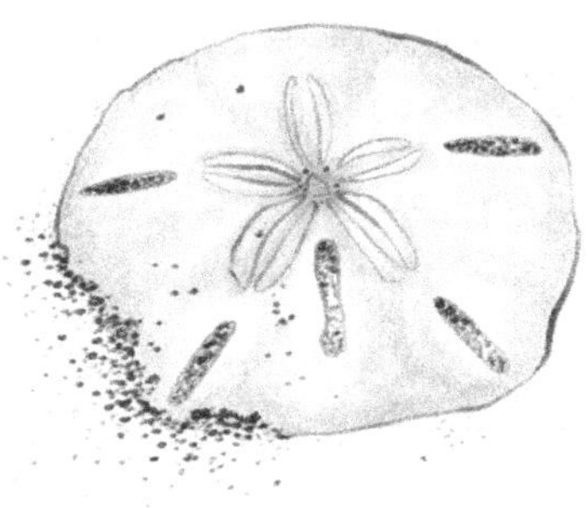

I'm only a handful of seconds behind him, but I hover by the screen door, listening, trying to piece this together like a jigsaw.

"... should have called first," she's saying. "But we just started driving."

"This is where you should have come. It's just as much your house as mine." He's standing there between us, rainwater dripping onto the carpet. "Where's Donovan?"

"I put him down in Dad's bed for tonight. Thankfully, he was asleep by the time we got here. It probably would have been hard to drag him out of a fort filled with Legos and junk food otherwise." She points to the structure beside her. "Should I even ask?"

Jude spins around and spots me just outside. "Shoot. Alex. I'm so sorry." He ushers me inside where the air conditioning only makes me shiver more violently. I can't tell if the tremor in his voice is from the cold or the understandable shock and disorientation he must be feeling right now. "You remember Kelsey, right?"

"Hi." I pull the towel more tightly around my shoulders and smile at her. "I'm sorry my stuff is in your room. I'm leaving tomorrow, but I can switch rooms tonight."

"We're fine down here. I didn't realize Jude had company." She looks at her brother apologetically again. "Let me check on Donovan; I'll be back in a few." She leaves us alone.

"Let's go change," he suggests. "And then I'll make hot chocolate and catch you up on what's going on."

"Actually," I counter, "why don't I start a pot of coffee before I head upstairs to clean up and turn in? Your sister needs you tonight."

He doesn't argue, just stands in front of me as I watch his mind spin behind his stunned eyes. It takes every bit of self-control I possess to walk past him into the kitchen and give him the time and space I know he needs right now.

I move the load of sheets and towels and my favorite borrowed hoodie to the dryer and push the button before quietly ascending the back stairs to the kitchen door.

I need to get down the words that rolled around in my head all night before I go.

What does it mean that
All my favorite pastimes

Are past times
And I pass time
By watching time pass
And crying, "Too fast!"
When I could sink my toes
Into the sand
Of this hourglass
And feel the sun on my back
And not look back
Or ask
How long it might last
But simply bask
In this moment
And unwrap
This gift, this Present
At last

When I close the notebook, he's there. "Morning."

"Sorry," I whisper back. "I was trying to be quiet."

"You didn't wake me up."

"I was hoping you might be able to sleep in this morning. You guys were up late last night."

He walks around the counter, and I can't stand how this tiny change in proximity affects me. "I'm cleaning houses this morning," he explains. "Trying to get an early start so maybe I can catch you before your family gets here for check-in."

"I've already packed my car." I pick up the notebook because I don't know what else to do with my hands. "I thought it might be better if I wasn't here when your nephew wakes up."

His gaze wanders to the living room where the blankets are neatly folded in a pile, Legos all packed back into their boxes. "But you *are* coming back? We had a deal."

"That was before you knew Kelsey would be here. We can still hang out after vacation, but I can figure something else out for those few weeks if that would be better."

"No." He says it so loudly that he winces and looks down the hallway. He lowers his volume again. "Please don't. They just need a safe place to stay for a little bit while Kels figures some stuff out. There's plenty of room here. After a week with a hundred people, three won't seem like that many, I promise. And you're going to love Donovan; he's amazing."

Why can't I look at him? "I'm sure I will." We sit, too close and not close enough, for a few minutes in the loudest silence I've ever heard.

He finally breaks it. "You excited to see your family?"

"Yeah."

"That didn't sound very convincing."

I sigh. "I am excited to see them. But it's like this every year: so much anticipation for this week, but the days leading up to it, all I feel is this . . . fear. What if it doesn't live up to my expectations? What if this is finally the year all the magic is gone? What if every-thing that came before gets tarnished somehow?" I bite the inside of my mouth, blink away tears. "I know, I have issues."

"We all have issues, Alex. And your fear stems from loving so much, which isn't a fault." I trace the outline of the notebook with one finger, positive that if I so much as glimpse his face, I'll lose my composure completely. "I'm not going to tell you not to be afraid," he goes on. "Because I know that's not how it works. Just don't let the beautiful moments be choked out by your need to hang onto them." How does he always know the perfect thing to say? Why do I want to stay here in this kitchen with him forever? Why do I want to run away?

"I'm going to get out of here and let you get ready for work. Thanks again for everything."

"I wish you wouldn't say it like that."

"Like what?" I stand and hug the book full of our words to my chest.

"Like you're leaving for good." He hooks his thumbs in his shorts pockets. "Look, maybe this is because I have issues of my own, but I just need to hear you say one more time that you're coming back next weekend."

I step to the side, making a decision for my own sake as much as his, and slide the familiar drawer open, deposit our book inside, and close it again. "I'll be back next weekend, Jude."

Then, I walk away as quickly as I can, before I say something stupid, before I even let myself think it.

Chapter 27

"She says they're about five minutes from the bridge."

I lean across the bed we're making and shout into the phone at Rebekah's ear. "Tell your dad to drive faster!"

"We're coming downstairs to wait for you outside. See you soon, Elly Bean." I'm halfway to the door before she even hangs up.

Rebekah was the first to arrive on the island this morning, and since the house wasn't open yet, we'd spent the time shopping, reminiscing, and eating our weight in shrimp at our favorite dockside restaurant. Once my aunt arrived with the keys from the realtor, we'd come over to help her stock cabinets and make beds before our wave of relatives rolled in.

"We couldn't have asked for more beautiful weather," Rebekah comments as we step out into the sunshine, all traces of last night's rain gone.

I walk down the deck steps and wonder how many times I've climbed them in my lifetime. "Hey, remember the year we sunbathed out here and listened to that old Mandy Moore CD on repeat?"

"And we thought those guys across the street with the binoculars were looking at us."

"How were we supposed to know there was an owl on the roof?"

"That was the year I had that pink suit too." She tosses her hair. "There's no way the owl was even close to that cute."

"Only you would be offended that some creepy guys *weren't* checking you out." I laugh. "I'm surprised your parents aren't here yet. Didn't you tell me they were leaving at lunchtime?"

"They're probably not far. Elias and Kade were going to meet them at the store to grab some stuff to set up for dinner." She shades her eyes and squints down the road. "There she is!" I watch her bounce on the balls of her feet as the SUV approaches, hardly able to keep still myself.

My uncle doesn't even have time to pull into the driveway before a back door opens and Elle jumps out, running toward us at full speed. I meet her halfway, colliding with her tiny frame and scooping her up in a massive hug. Rebekah, unwilling to wait her turn, envelops both of us.

We stand there like that for a long time, a pile of intertwined arms and souls, best friends reunited. Finally, Rebekah releases us, and I step back to survey the girl in front of us. She's wearing a flowy sundress and sporting a messy bun. Huge earrings dangle at the sides of her suntanned face. She's beaming. No, she's positively glowing.

"Elle!" Rebekah gasps, confirming that I'm not the only one who's noticed. "Look at you all grown up! You look amazing."

"We sent our little girl off to Europe and look at this stunning woman who's returned to us," I gush.

"Stop." Elle rolls her eyes. But it's true. How is it that she seems so incredibly different and yet somehow the truest version of herself I've ever laid eyes on?

"We'll help you carry in your bags." Rebekah walks to the now-parked van that my aunt and uncle and two of Elle's brothers are emerging from.

"That was quite the reunion." My aunt pulls Rebekah and me in for hugs in turn. "Your folks here yet?" We both shake our heads. "Well, it's good to see you girls together again."

"Is the infamous Dr. Dillon here?" Elle asks as we each grab a suitcase and carry them up to the house.

"He's coming sometime tomorrow afternoon," Rebekah answers. "He plays guitar for his church's band, so he'll leave after their service. But he'll be here until Wednesday."

"I can't wait to meet him." Elle enters the house and heads straight for the bedroom the four of us have always shared. "Any word from Sutton?"

"They'll probably be here later tonight," Rebekah reports. "Marcail threw up last night, and even though they think it's probably just her food allergy stuff, they want to wait a little bit to make sure. No one wants to be responsible for another Henry family vomit fest, right?"

"Food allergy stuff?" I drop Elle's backpack on the bed. "What are you talking about?"

"Oh, they've had a rough few weeks." Rebekah pulls open a drawer and starts unpacking Elle's clothes for her, neatly refolding the piles Elle clearly tossed in five minutes before they left the house this morning. "They're still waiting for some tests to come back, but it looks like it may be a long road ahead for our sweet Marcie."

The fact that I don't know any of this shouldn't hurt as much as it does. After all, I'm the one who has been avoiding Sutton's calls lately. But this is information I should not be getting secondhand.

Rebekah seems to read my mood and adds, "She's probably just talked to me more about it since I'm a nurse."

"Want to see what I brought you?" Elle drops onto the bed beside her backpack and wiggles her eyebrows.

Rebekah and I rush to join her on the starfish comforter. "I'm holding my breath for a matador costume," I joke.

"Next time," Elle says and pulls out three red soccer jerseys with yellow lettering. "In honor of it being a World Cup year." She tosses us each a shirt. "I've already come up with a long list of soccer star siblings, so I hope you guys are bringing your A game."

"My favorite this year is Tim Cruise," Rebekah tells her.

Elle grabs her hand. "Oh my gosh, I know exactly who you're talking about!"

"You guys want to go for a walk on the beach before dinner?" I suggest, setting my jersey on the nightstand while Rebekah meticulously folds hers in her lap.

"Yes!" Elle jumps up. "You don't think Sutton will mind if we go without her, do you?"

"We'll go again when she gets here," I promise.

The Atlantic swirls around our ankles, and I savor the familiar pull of the tide as I watch it take the sand from under my feet.

"It feels so good to be back at the ocean." Elle closes her eyes and breathes in the salt air.

"We're just thankful to have you on this side of it."

"If I'd known we were going to be out here for this long, I'd have put on sunscreen," Rebekah comments.

"You know you'll be burnt by Wednesday either way," Elle tells her. "But we should probably head back soon."

Rebekah pulls the phone from her back pocket and checks the time. "They'll be setting dinner up. And we don't want to miss fried chicken."

Arm in arm, we walk to the beach house that sits across the backyard from ours. Folding tables are set up in a row, loaded with buckets of chicken and tubs of mashed potatoes, slaw, mac and cheese, and green beans. At the end of the line sits a huge pile of buttery biscuits.

But an even more welcome sight than the feast is the faces of so many of my favorite people in the world. When we step under the house, we're hit with a wave of hugs and high fives and smiles and questions and updates. It's overwhelming in the best sense, and I feel my soul fill the way it only does this specific time of year.

After we've all exchanged greetings and my granddaddy has shouted a prayer over the yard, we line up and pile our plates high, then find spots to sit. I look out over the other tables, camping chairs, blankets, steps, porches, and concrete seating areas. These yards are more crowded than any popular restaurant.

I've just bitten into my biscuit when Rebekah gasps. "Sutton's here!" My stomach turns. I should be as ecstatic to see her as my cousins are, and I am, but I'm also keenly aware that things are not as they should be between Sutton and me. And keeping things at surface level is much easier over text than face-to-face. Still, I hop from the bench to join the welcoming party.

"Finally!" Rebekah takes Marcail from Sutton's arms, and Elle jumps into them.

"You have no idea how much we missed you, ElleBelle," Sutton whispers as Marcail starts screaming.

"I think she needs changing," Rebekah says.

"Story of my life today," Sutton grumbles.

"I'll take her upstairs; someone in this house will have diapers, I'm sure."

"I'll come with you." Elle kisses Marcie's red face. "Our nurse deserves a break from bodily fluids on vacation."

Three diaper changers seem like overkill, so I'm left standing in front of Sutton and Chris, searching for something normal to say.

"Glad you're here," I offer awkwardly. "Can I fix you a plate?"

"I'm pretty sure I can handle it." She smiles halfheartedly and walks away to load up on hugs and chicken.

Chris pulls me into a side hug. "Long day. She'll be fine."

But Sutton clearly is *not* fine all through dinner nor while we sit and catch up on the porch afterwards. And she's still not fine when she bids us goodnight and walks back early to the room she's sharing with Chris and the baby because "Marcie doesn't want anyone but mom right now."

Hours after she leaves, I slip under the covers of the bed I'm sharing with Elle. I don't even have to pretend to be tired as I tell her and Rebekah that I'm going to turn in but please not to stop whispering about charming doctors and Spanish cafes.

I lie awake until their voices die down, no longer drowning out the ones in my head. Out of habit, my hand finds the pendant at my throat, and I imagine I can see the kitchen light from the blue house next door. I wonder if Jude's typing away on his computer or writing something in the notebook. I wish I could walk downstairs and sit on the stool next to his, ask him about his day, talk to him about mine, and watch him work until he gives up and makes us both a snack.

Elle's steady breathing is the last thing I hear before succumbing to sleep, but the last thought I have is this: for the first time in all my summers of Henry family vacations, I feel homesick.

Chapter 28

Church at the beach is always at ten. But it never starts until at least ten-fifteen when the last group of teenagers shuffles into a row of metal folding chairs and a couple guitars start to strum. Most of the kids are having "Sunday School" led by my Aunt Clara in one of the houses down by the pier, but Marcail is sleeping on Sutton's shoulder. Judging by her and Chris's bleary eyes, they had a rocky night.

I'm situated between Rebekah and Elle, with my parents directly in front of us. I smile, remembering the way my daddy wrapped me in his arms last night and jokingly called me his "prodigal girl returned." I didn't remind him that I've been here the whole time and they came to me. "I thought something might be wrong because of how little we've heard from you," my mom said. "But you look happy. Seems like this summer is exactly what you needed." If she only knew how true that was.

We belt out two songs all together, and then Rebekah moves to the front and sings a solo, accompanied by Elias on guitar. She's always had the voice of an angel. As I watch Sutton stroke Marcie's back, I miss her more than I have in a long time.

Rebekah returns to her seat, and my Uncle James gets up to preach. Between beach trips and many childhood weeks spent at the summer camp he runs, I've learned from and been encouraged by dozens of his sermons.

When Elle opens her Bible, a faded photo of the four of us sitting in the hammock several summers ago falls out and flutters to the ground. I reach down to retrieve it, and that's when I hear it: the slam of a sliding door and a loud childlike voice that doesn't belong to anyone in our makeshift congregation.

Everyone's attention briefly pulls toward the porch of the house across the yard where a dark-haired little boy is climbing into his uncle's lap in one of the rocking chairs. Sutton audibly gasps, and Rebekah reaches over and squeezes my arm so hard I'm sure it'll leave a mark. Elle takes a second to let it sink in, but then her eyes go wide and a huge smile splits her face.

Here we go.

"I can't believe you didn't tell us!" Elle punches my bicep for the fifth time in an hour.

"I told you, I wanted it to be a surprise."

"So that white car was yours all along?" Rebekah asks Jude. "I knew it."

Jude nods and takes a bite of his sandwich, the one Elle made while she peppered me with questions I strategically dodged, the one that has mayonnaise on it because there is no reason I should know he doesn't like it.

"Sorry you guys missed Gavin," he says. "I know he would've loved to see you." I can feel Sutton glaring at me, but I don't look back.

"We're headed out to the ocean after lunch if you want to join us," Elle offers.

"Can we, Uncle Jude? Please?" Donovan implores around a mouthful of corn chips.

"I have to work in a little while, but we can see if your mom's awake and ask her if she's up for it."

"We can keep an eye on him if Kelsey is okay with that," I offer without thinking twice. Donovan nods his head enthusiastically. He looks so much like Jude the day we first met him on the beach.

Sutton yawns and stands. "I'm going to lie down with Marcie for a little while, but I'll join you guys later." She stacks her paper plate on top of her Styrofoam cup. "It's so good to see you again, Jude. I hope we can catch up more this week." And before I can dissect her tone or the hurt baked into the glance she throws me, she's gone.

Jude gathers everyone else's trash in a pile on the table in front of him and reaches over to tousle Donovan's hair. "Let's go talk to your mom, and then I'll see if I can find my old boogie board under the house."

The sun beats down on our faces.

Camped out on our towels, we watch Elias toss the little kids, Donovan included, into the waves in front of us.

Elle's laugh sounds like pure sunshine itself. Rebekah sighs contentedly. Chris sets Marcie down, the frills of her monogrammed bathing suit rippling in the wind. As far as I can see in either direction, the shore is dotted with people I adore. Marcie's chubby hand closes around a clump of sand, and she raises it to her face and giggles with delight. As Sutton watches her daughter fall in love with the beach, her whole countenance brightens. In this moment, everything is more than perfect.

"So." Rebekah leans over and lowers her sunglasses. "Other than reuniting with our long-lost friends and keeping it top secret, what else have you been up to these past couple weeks?"

I study the fading crab imprinted on the side of my foot. "Just waiting for you guys to get here."

Chapter 29

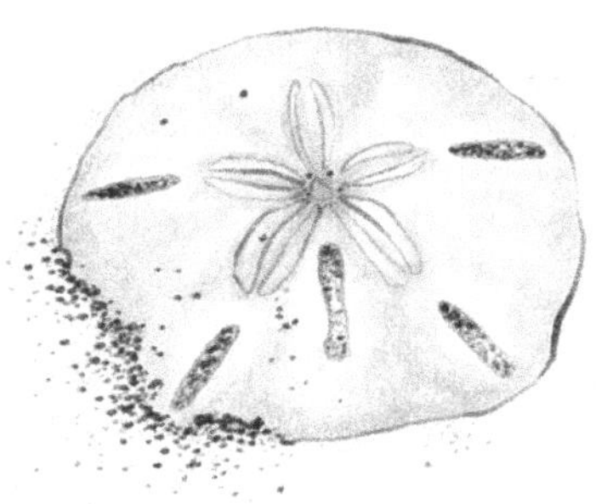

I set the sizzling pan back on the burner and start browning another pound of ground beef. The amount of prep work it takes to feed our massive family tacos for dinner is astounding. We started helping my aunt early this morning and have already packed one house's fridge full of meat.

Elle sits on the counter beside me, teaching me the Spanish words for everything in the kitchen. Sutton is taking a nap, and Rebekah is playing on the living room floor with Marcie while Dillon watches a soccer game with Chris.

"Oh, come on," Chris yells. "This ref didn't have any trouble finding his yellow cards earlier." Spain isn't playing today, but we're all wearing our jerseys anyway. The sounds of the game are accented with thuds coming from upstairs where my older cousins' little girls are practicing their gymnastics routine for the talent show. The front door opens constantly as people come and go, and an uncle keeps issuing loud reminders to "close that door behind you!" To some, it may seem overstimulating for a beach vacation, but to me, this is beautiful, peaceful chaos.

"Alex!" Uncle Zack walks into the kitchen and wraps an arm around me, squeezing my shoulder. "I heard you're finally working on that book! How's it coming along?"

I keep my reply to a bare minimum. "Okay."

"It's a very mysterious project," Elle chimes in. "She's hardly told us anything about it."

I stir the contents of the pan and watch the grease pop while I think. "Well, it's not exactly shaping up to be what I thought it would. It's sort of . . . evolved a bit."

"Good." My uncle opens the fridge and pulls out a can of coke, bends back the tab. "That means it's real."

"What do you mean?" I ask.

"I mean that that's how actual life works. We go looking for one story and find that another, better one has already been written for us. That's what you should document." I reach for the pan's lid, but he tugs on the oven mitts and takes it over to the sink for me, drains the grease into an empty can. "Didn't I always tell you you'd write a book one day? I can't wait to read it, Al."

But in my mind, I'm already in a different kitchen, thinking about the notebook in the drawer, wondering if parts of the story that I don't yet know about are being written right now.

"Want to referee for us this year?"

I look up from the table I'm wiping down after dinner to see Elias grinning, swinging a whistle from his pointer finger. Behind him, several teenagers are carrying buckets, sponges, and orange cones. A giant cluster of kids hovers around them. My Aunt Clara takes the dishcloth from my hand and nods, and I join the exodus to the sea.

This is my favorite time of day to be on the beach. The scorching heat has left for the evening, along with most of the other families, and the sky is just starting to change into her night clothes.

We're almost to the steps when we pass an exhausted mom with her chattering son in tow.

"Donovan. My dude." Elias stops to high-five him. "Catch any good waves today?"

"Yep!" He lights up, and I'm struck again by how much his face resembles a former version of his uncle's. And by how much time I've spent thinking about that uncle's face today.

"Question." Elias squats down to Donovan's eye level. "How fast can you run?"

"Real fast!"

"We're about to do some Olympic relays if you want to join us."

Donovan's head snaps up to Kelsey, his eyes begging for a yes.

"We'll make sure he gets back to you safely," Elias promises.

Kelsey takes the boogie board from her son's arms and whispers, "Have fun."

Once on the sand, we get to work setting up the course. The hopeful athletes stand in a circle around Elias as he reviews the rules. "Most importantly," he calls over the assembly, "let's have a good time together!"

The next forty-five minutes are a blur, flying faster than dozens of sprinting children, laughing and cheering and not yet fully realizing that they are having the literal time of their lives.

Joy leaks from the corners of my eyes as the last race ends with Elias placing a cheap gold medal around Donovan's neck and lifting him into the air. The green team whoops wildly. We spend the trek back to the houses singing silly songs we grew up on at my uncle's camp. My favorite is the one about how much we have to be thankful for because even though my little cousins insert the most random things into the verses, every single one of them truly is an undeserved gift.

Darkness settles in around the porch lights, but I spot Jude right away when we enter the busy yard. It's almost as if he's become a magnet since I moved next door. He's standing with Rebekah, Sutton, Elle, and Kelsey, still dressed in his black work clothes, a cup of lemonade in hand.

"Mom!" Donovan scrambles off Elias's back and runs to Kelsey. "Look!" He holds up the medal, turning it so it catches the fluorescent light.

Jude finds my eyes, and it's all I can do not to tell him on the spot how special his nephew is, how much every second with him makes me want to go back in time and relive every moment I've spent in Jude's presence, this time appreciating them as I should.

"You guys should all come crabbing with us tomorrow night," Elle suggests. "We won't be leaving until about this time, so you should be home from work, right, Jude?"

"Your job is really cramping our style," Sutton teases. "Didn't you tell them the Henrys were coming? They should have given you the week off."

Jude chuckles. "Well, you'll be happy to know that I'm working out my two weeks' notice at the restaurant. So next year, I'll be ready."

I almost choke on the sip of tea I've just stolen from Rebekah's red plastic cup. I watch the corner of Jude's lips fight to stay put; he knows this information will drive me crazy with questions.

"Hey." Chris jogs over with a basketball tucked under his arm and kisses Sutton's cheek. Someone across the yard has taken the baby for a while, and Sutton looks rested for the first time in days. "We need an extra guy, Jude. Up for a quick game?"

I half expect him to say no, to find some reason to head back to his place. But he sets his drink on the picnic table behind us and cuffs the legs of his pants. When the guys jog back over to the concrete driveway court, we girls stay at the table. A few aunts and cousins join us, passing stories and babies around and occasionally swatting a mosquito.

I trace the lines of condensation on Jude's half-full lemonade cup and try to keep my sight from wandering over to the game too many times. Something about watching him and Chris and Dillon enjoy one another's company is confusingly wonderful.

When they rejoin our group, Dillon slides onto the bench beside Rebekah, and I pass a sweaty Jude his drink. Chris takes Marcail from my cousin's lap and throws her into the air. She belly laughs, and Jude smiles as he lets his arm brush against mine for the briefest second.

I take in all the people around me, some I've known forever, some newer to the best week of the year, and I know in my spirit like I never have before—Grandmama was right. Some things can only be multiplied.

Chapter 30

"Please come with us, Sutton." Elle sticks out her bottom lip in her infamous pout. "Bekah's already ditching us for Jamaican food with Dr. Dillon."

"I know." Sutton sighs, offering a pacifier to her fussy daughter. "But the crab hunt is Chris's favorite. I know he'd miss it in a heartbeat for me, but I want him to have this."

"Okay," Elle relents. "I guess when you put it all gushy and sweet like that . . ."

I grab the glow sticks and Elle's arm. "Come on. They're getting ready to leave."

The anticipation is palpable in the crowd gathered on the street in front of the houses. I hand off the bundle of glow sticks to one of the teenagers who starts passing them out. Chris and another cousin help the littlest kids twist them into bracelets and necklaces.

Before I have a chance to locate him in the frenzy, Jude finds me. "Hey." He says it quietly while Elle is preoccupied helping someone reattach the handle to their sand bucket, and I like that this single spoken word, and the unspoken ones that seem to hide behind it, are just for me.

Donovan appears at his side, net propped on his shoulder and grinning from ear to ear. Elle turns around. "Donovan, that headlamp is *awesome*. What a great idea."

"Uncle Jude bought it for me." He flashes it on, temporarily blinding us.

Jude reaches over and clicks it back off. "I didn't want to risk him dropping my flashlight and breaking it if he got spooked. You know how kids are sometimes." He keeps a perfectly straight face, but I can tell he's reveling in the fact that I can't use any of the sarcastic replies that come to mind.

"All right!" One of my uncles shouts over our heads. "Stay with somebody you know!" When he starts leading the group to the beach, Elle and I look at each other and laugh at the same minimal instructions we've received every year since we could walk.

A high-pitched voice rings out from somewhere above the yellow glowing necklace dancing at our elbows. "Elle, can you teach us that Spanish song from the other day?"

"Si, chica." Elle lets her tiny student lead her further up into the throng.

At the very back, Donovan holds on to Jude's left hand; his right hangs at his side, close enough to mine that I can tell myself it's an accident every time they touch.

When it's our turn to descend the wooden steps and shed our flip-flops, there's already practically a mountain of shoes. Appropriate, I think; this is holy ground, after all.

The air is balmy, and it would be an exceptionally dark night if not for the myriad of glow sticks and flashlight beams crisscrossing up and down the shore.

Donovan switches his headlamp on and takes in the scene. "Is it okay if I stay close to you for now?" he asks Jude.

"I'm with you, buddy." Jude reassures him. "We can stick together as long as you want."

Donovan hesitates for a moment, then admits, "I'm not really sure how to do this."

"Well, first of all," Jude explains, "you have to shine your light all around until you find a crab." He places one hand on each side of Donovan's head and turns it toward the ocean before swinging it playfully back to the sand by the houses, then to the ocean again. Donovan cackles.

A triumphant scream is issued nearby. "Got one! We need a net!"

"Who's got a net?" I recognize Elias's voice. Donovan looks up at his uncle, and when Jude nods in assent, takes off. My heart swells as I watch him join my family. I have a ridiculous amount of love for this kid considering I only met him a few days ago.

Suddenly, I realize that Jude is standing much closer to me than he was a minute ago. I don't pull my eyes from the crab capture happening several yards away but tentatively allow the back of my hand to graze his. A second later, his fingers slide between mine.

The waves crash quietly behind us as peals of laughter sound in the glow stick-dotted distance. My brain tells me I should be experiencing the assault of all the conflicting emotions that have warred inside me these past days. But the only thing I feel is contentment. Peace. The distinct impression that whatever else might be wrong at the moment, this is very, very right.

"Uncle Jude! Look!" A small figure is tearing through the darkness toward us, a net balanced in front. "We got a big one!"

Jude squeezes my hand once before letting go. "Whoa." He kneels down and admires his nephew's bounty. "You're a natural, bud."

And that's when all the feelings come rushing in, flooding my heart and mind with questions and doubts, running rampant in my chest, clawing to get out.

The fan blades whir above us.

"We could go buy postcards," Elle suggests from her perch on Rebekah's bed. "We haven't written to anyone famous yet this year."

"Sure." Rebekah sighs, picking at a loose string on the comforter and looking like she just watched a puppy being put down. Dr. Dillon left early this morning to have time for a quick nap before a long shift at the hospital. In the past, I would have rolled my eyes at her lovesick moping, but it seems I have a newfound empathy.

I could swear one of my hands still feels warmer than the other, and every time I look at it, I physically ache. What is wrong with me?

"Come in!" Elle calls. I didn't even hear the knock.

Sutton's face appears around the cracked door.

"Did you seriously just knock?" Rebekah's brows pull together. "This is still your room too, you know." She scoots over to make space for our oldest cousin.

"Where's Marcie?" Elle asks.

"Chris took her for a drive." Sutton sets the box of candy and the laptop she carried in on the bed between us. "I thought our Bek might need some cheering up in the form of our favorite movie. Besides." She pulls her legs up under her. "Alex got too much sun yesterday. Did you put some aloe on?"

"Yes, Mom." I act annoyed, but I hope her bossing me around is a sign that things could be normal between us again. I yank the blanket from the other bed and arrange it around the four of us while Sutton starts the movie.

How many times have I watched this story play out on a screen? And yet, all I can think about is the most recent one, remembering how Jude laughed at all the right parts and tapped his socked foot along to the beat of my favorite songs.

I try not to dwell on the fact that my thoughts keep straying. Or the fact that I can't tell my best friends what my heart is doing right now, the way it's betraying me. Or the fact that I so very desperately want to.

Rebekah sighs again. "Falling for someone is wonderful. But sometimes it really sucks."

Sutton puts an arm around her. "Yes, it does."

"I wouldn't know." Elle shrugs. "But we're here for you, Bek."

I shove a handful of candy into my mouth.

Chapter 31

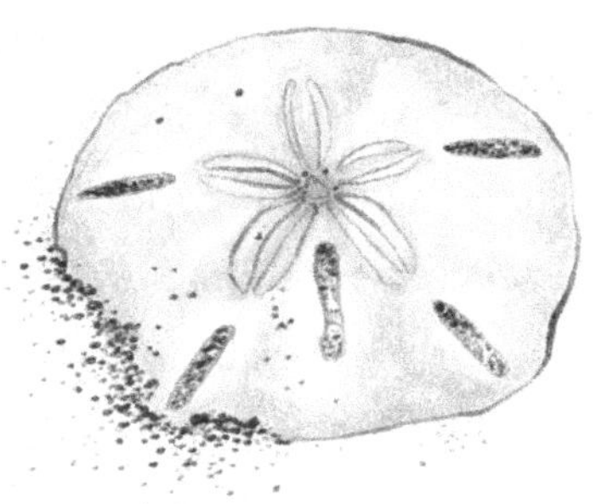

"Jude just got off work; he's on his way." Kelsey tucks her phone into her purse and sits back down at the table where an intense game of cards is underway. "Thanks again for letting us hang out for a while; I still can't believe I locked myself out. I swear there used to be a spare key under the back mat." The key that's attached to my key ring at the moment.

Elias draws two cards, discards one, and draws another. "It's no problem at all. The kids are excited to have an extra foosball player in the basement tonight. Plus, you get to see me and Elle wipe the floor with everyone else. Again." Rebekah flicks a gummy bear across the table, hitting him in the forehead. "Hey, now. Don't make me call Mom."

My granddaddy is on the couch, flipping back and forth between World Cup highlights from earlier today and a baseball game. Sutton's checking the batch of brownies in the oven with a toothpick to see if they're done.

A loud chorus of yells drifts up from the basement, and Kelsey starts to stand, but Elias waves her off. "He's fine, I promise. Someone will come up and tattle if things get too wild."

"It's a wonder Marcail's sleeping through all this," I comment.

"Oh, the magical powers of a day in the sun and a good sound machine. I'm sure she'll make up for it in a few hours, but for now, we'll take it." Sutton smiles across the room at Chris.

"Alex," Rebekah hisses as she kicks me under the table.

Elias beats me to it. "Cut!" Rebekah throws her cards down as Elle and Elias slap hands.

"Sorry," I mumble and try not to let my sight wander to the front door again.

Three hands later, it finally opens after a faint knock. "Jude!" Chris ushers him in. "Come watch some sports with us. We've got a little bit of everything going on." He points over to the kitchen area. "Or there's a cutthroat game of cards happening if you're looking for something a little less civil."

Jude crosses the room and drops his keys into Kelsey's hand before moving to stand behind my chair. If I thought it was hard to concentrate before, it's nearly impossible now.

Donovan thunders up the stairs with my cousin Lucas. "Oh, good." Kelsey shakes the keys. "Ready to head home, Donovan?"

"Not yet." He takes one of the Oatmeal Crème Pies Lucas has just pulled from a cabinet. "Just getting a snack." Before Kelsey can protest, the boys disappear to the basement again.

Elias chuckles. "I don't think you're going to be able to drag him out of here anytime soon. Your turn, Alex."

I reach for the five in my hand, but Jude leans over my shoulder and taps the three instead. I look at the cards on the table. It's a much better move, but Jude shouldn't know that.

"No cheating!" Elias scolds, then pauses. "You know this game?" He cocks an eyebrow.

"Ah, no." Jude clears his throat. "Just trying to figure it out by watching."

"Was he right?" Elias turns his attention to me.

I mentally apologize to Rebekah for blowing this hand and pluck out the five I had my fingers on first. "Nope. But I can see why he thought that. It's a complicated game, Jude."

"Sounds like it." He lets his hands rest on the back of my chair. "You'll have to explain it to me sometime." I feel my cheeks warm, thankful for the sunburn from yesterday.

Sutton walks around the counter. "Are you guys almost done? The brownies are ready, and I'd like to get in a decent porch talk before Marcie wakes up."

"Those smell amazing," Kelsey comments.

"They're even better when you eat them straight from the pan," Elle says. Then, "Hey, you should join us, Kelsey."

"Yeah," Sutton says as she starts to load the dishwasher. "Up for a little chocolate and girl talk?"

Kelsey stands. "Oh, I don't want to intrude on your family time. I probably need to get Donovan to bed soon anyway."

"You're not intruding," I say. "We invited you. And Donovan can stay a little while longer; maybe he'll even sleep in tomorrow."

"I'll bring him home in a little while," Jude offers. "I'd like to watch some highlights with Chris anyway, see how many goals Chad scored today."

My blood runs cold even as the room seems to heat up. Sutton fumbles the silverware in her hand, and Rebekah and Elle look at each other across the table.

Kelsey, oblivious, says, "I'm gonna go grab a sweatshirt. I'll leave the house unlocked for you if that's okay."

"Sure." Jude tucks his hands into his pockets and steps away from my chair. I don't dare make eye contact with him as I stand.

"I'll walk with you, Kelsey," I volunteer.

After a brief stop in Jude's living room, during which I very nearly check the notebook drawer just to verify that all of this is real, Kelsey and I head back over to the porch next door to join my cousins. I'm hopeful that her presence will deter them from asking me how Jude knows about our little game.

When we join them, they've already arranged the rocking chairs in a circle and are digging into the brownies. Sutton looks up, and I can tell right away that I'm not off the hook.

"So, Al," she starts.

I take the pan Elle extends to me and pass it to Kelsey before settling into my rocking chair. I squint into the porch light. "So?"

"You want to tell us what's going on between you and Jude now?" I don't know why I expected anything else; Sutton never beats around the bush.

My eyes shift to Kelsey, and all my cousins follow suit. "Don't look at me." She raises her palms. "I didn't even know she was living with him until I got here last weekend."

Elle spits out the sip of water she's just taken. "WHAT?!" Rebekah gasps. Sutton's practically shooting lasers across the deck at me.

"Oops," Kelsey mumbles.

I take a deep breath. "Okay, everybody calm down a minute. It's not that big of a deal." I fight to keep my expression neutral. "I needed a place to stay, and I ran into Jude. He had an extra room. He's mostly been working all summer, but he's helping me a little with my writing. And . . ." I'm not sure what else to say, how to end this conversation and get them to move on to another topic.

"And now the two of you can't be in the same room without having to stand as close as humanly possible without touching. And when Jude flirts with you, you can't keep from smiling and turning pink." Rebekah winks.

"Now you're just being ridiculous." I try my best to sound nonchalant, but there's no way I'm going to fool them when I can't even lie to myself.

"It's okay, Al." Elle leans forward. "This is a good thing. We love Jude. He's a great guy."

"He's not just a great guy," Kelsey chimes in; I'd all but forgotten she was here for a moment. "He's amazing, Alex, and he'd do anything for the people he cares about. No one I know would have more of an excuse to be bitter and messed up because of the crappy hand life has dealt them, and the people who haven't shown up for them like they should have. But somehow, my brother has held on to all the kindness and gentleness and goodness he's always possessed. He's pretty much the only reason our family can still be considered a family at all." She's staring at her fingernails, and none of us move as she takes the time to gather her thoughts before continuing. This is the most I've ever heard Kelsey say. "Jude put himself through school and even loaned our brother money to start up his real estate business. Up until a year and a half ago, he came up to see me and Donovan every Christmas; fixed stuff around the house, made sure we had what we needed, even stood up to Donovan's sorry excuse for a dad. And when my husband told him to get out and never come back, I let him." She shakes her head in disgust. "I hadn't talked to him since or returned any of his texts, but when I showed up the other night, he did what he always has." She smiles up at me sadly. "He loved us, no questions asked. My brother is a gem, and anyone who gets to spend time in his company is lucky."

Whatever defense I'd been building for myself crumbles. "I know," I whisper. "I'm the last person who needs to be convinced of how incredible Jude is, I promise. I just . . ." I run a hand over my face. "This is a new feeling for me, and I don't quite know what it is."

"Oh, but I think you do." Rebekah grins.

I bury my head in my hands. "I just wish I knew what *he* was feeling."

"You're kidding, right?" Elle laughs, and I raise my head again. "Jude's been crazy about you for, like, forever."

My puzzled eyes bounce from face to face, each one as incredulous as the last.

"I thought you just pretended not to notice," Rebekah says. "Surely no one is that oblivious."

"Alex is," Sutton scoffs.

I feel like the whole planet has just turned upside down.

Even Kelsey is nodding. "I'll never forget the summer he called from the little beach shop and spent the better part of an hour on the phone with me trying to decide between the necklace with a conch shell charm on it and your sand dollar one there. It was obvious before that he had a crush, but that's when I knew he had it really bad."

"What?" My hand closes over my necklace. Sutton rolls her eyes at me, and everyone else disappears for a moment.

"You knew?" I ask her.

"Of course I did."

My head is still spinning. "Why didn't you tell me?"

"For one thing, Jude asked me not to." She shifts in her chair. "But, aside from that, Al, you were so enamored with Gavin. It's like you couldn't even see what was right in front of you. And that summer . . ." I feel sick. "Alex, you know we all love Gavin, but guys like him leave a string of broken hearts behind them. I knew you were probably going to be disappointed. You had us; you'd be okay. But if you hurt our Jude —" She shakes her head. "I wasn't sure his heart would ever recover."

I tighten my grip on the necklace, still trying to reorient myself. "You did always have a soft spot for Jude."

"And why do you think that was, Alex?" Is it just the lighting or are her eyes damp? "When you see a person look at someone you love the way Jude's always looked at you, you can't help but love them too."

Tyler. Mr. Bruce and Mrs. Becky. Donovan. Isn't that what's endeared them to me so quickly? The way they recognize all the wonderful things in him that even Jude himself doesn't see? Isn't this what won me over to Chris? Even Dr. Dillon?

"Sutton." My voice catches.

She looks down at her phone, bringing us both back to the present. "I'm gonna go check on Chris and Marcie."

"I should probably head back too," Kelsey says. "Before the boys get home." She looks over at me. "Don't worry; I won't breathe a word of this conversation to my brother. I just appreciate you guys letting me be part of your girl talk. I was always jealous that Gavin and Jude had an in with your family and I didn't."

"You wanted to hang out with us?" Rebekah asks. "We thought you were way too cool for us."

Elle nods. "Way too cool. We wanted to *be* you sometimes. Living with our best friends at the beach year-round? I mean, really."

"Funny." Kelsey rises and slides her arms into the front of her hoodie. "Because all we ever wanted was what you guys had."

"I wish we'd realized that," I say. I wish I'd realized a lot of things.

Chapter 32

I linger on the beach a few minutes more, savoring the quiet of the early morning and the open space I have all to myself except for the two figures surfing in the distance. It didn't occur to me until just now that one of them may be Tyler, though it seems crazy early for him to be giving a lesson.

I search the shore above the surfers' positions, hoping that Jude may be out taking pictures or helping in some other way today. But the sand is empty.

The breeze is perfect, and the only sounds are those of the waves and a few seagulls. It's like a poem that's written itself. I wish I had my notebook. I'm glad I don't.

I watch the surfers emerge from the ocean and drop their boards side by side. One of them waves; it *is* Ty. The other starts walking toward me, and my heart rate picks up when it registers that I know him too.

He has a towel slung around his shoulders and a dry shirt in his hand; and why have I never noticed before how incredibly attractive he is?

He stops a few feet away. "You're up early."

"I thought you didn't surf."

He scrubs the towel over his wet hair. "I said I don't surf *well*. Doesn't mean I don't enjoy falling off my board while Tyler catches some good waves before his first students show up."

"Looked like you were doing okay to me."

His eyes light up. "You were watching?"

"I didn't know it was you."

He removes his glasses, cleans them with the corner of his towel, and slides them back in place. "Come here often to check out strangers on surfboards then?"

"I came to see the sunrise."

"Yeah?" He pulls the towel from his neck and drapes it over one of my shoulders, then tugs the shirt over his head. I look away.

"Last night, I realized that in all our years coming here and all my time here this summer, I'd never watched the sun rise over the ocean. That felt wrong."

"And?" he asks as he takes the towel back, moving closer and making my pulse quicken again. "What's the verdict?"

"It was amazing."

He smiles. "I could have told you that."

"But you didn't." I tuck a strand of hair behind my ear and fidget with the charm at my throat. "Some people need things spelled out for them. Otherwise, it could take entirely too much time for them to realize the goodness that's been right there waiting for them if only they'd woken up and really seen it." I scrutinize his face as he absorbs what I've just said. "Anyway, I'm going to head back for breakfast." I spin on my heel and start walking, still in too much shock to process my own candid words.

I'm halfway up the stairs before he calls my name. When I turn around, he's almost caught up. "Do you—?" He pauses, more breathless than he should be after such a short jog. "Can I buy you a cup of coffee?"

"It's breezy this morning." He sets his coffee cup on top of his napkin on the shop's patio table as the wind threatens to blow it away. "Are you cold?"

"I'm fine." I wrap my fingers around the warm mug in my own hands. "You're the one wearing a wet bathing suit."

"I'm good. But I should have run by the house to change; then we could've sat inside at least. Sorry."

He's nervous.

I am too, but my desire to put him at ease outweighs my own self-consciousness. "I don't mind. It just reminds me of the night I beat you at Putt-Putt."

He clears his throat. "You didn't beat me; I forfeited. There's a difference." A thrill of satisfaction runs through me at the tiny twitch at the corner of his mouth. And the fact that I knew how to draw it out.

"How's vacation been?" he asks, then grimaces. "Sorry about last night with the card game and the soccer thing. I wasn't thinking. Hopefully I didn't make things weird with your cousins."

"It's okay," I tell him. "They know about us now."

He hitches an eyebrow. "Us?"

"About me staying at your house, I mean." My face burns, and I try to coach my brain to chill out, act normal. This is Jude, after all.

But once a wave starts to crash, there's no stopping it. At this point, I'm hopeless and I know it. This is *Jude*, after all.

He gestures to the pastry on the plate between us. "Are you hungry?"

I'm about to answer when his comment from a few days ago hits me. I gasp. "You quit your job! Does that mean the city offered you the position?"

"I was wondering how long it would take you to bring that up. I half expected you to text me later that night."

"I wanted to," I admit, though I don't tell him how many times I actually pulled out my phone and talked myself down.

"I wish you had. I've wanted to text you so many times, but I didn't want to interrupt your family time."

I pick a piece of pastry from the plate. "Well, you have your sister and nephew there now. I didn't want to bother you either."

He breaks off a bite for himself. "I always want you to bother me, Alex. You're my favorite person to be bothered by."

I smile. "So? The job."

"The job," he repeats. "I haven't heard anything from the city yet; they said it could take a week or two to make their final decision. I put in my notice at the show a few days before you left; I sort of had a moment of clarity that night we built the fort."

"History is replete with epiphanies in blanket forts."

He smirks at my joke, and I pop another bite of pastry into my mouth before pushing the plate toward him. "Sorry, I'm listening."

He ignores the food and straightens his glasses. "Well, I guess it mostly had to do with the *reason* I took that job in the first place, the reason I've been working such insane hours at multiple jobs." He sighs and squints at me. "How deep of a conversation are you prepared for this early in the day?"

I set my coffee down, noting it's the exact shade of his eyes right now. "Whatever you want to share with me, Jude, I'll hold it carefully." He nods once, as if our hearts are shaking on a deal.

"A couple years ago, like I told you before, I was in a really bad place. There were days I wasn't sure I was going to make it through. There were days—" He swallows and stares down at his cup. "There were days I wasn't sure I *wanted* to make it through."

I reach my hand across the table, and he takes it, squeezing it once before continuing. "Mrs. Becky finally got worried enough that she ignored all my excuses and made me an appointment to get some help. I remember feeling so embarrassed walking in that first day. But a few weeks later, I didn't know why I hadn't gone sooner." His shoulders relax like he's relieved to have set this information in front of me, like it's been heavy to carry alone for so long.

"Anyway," he goes on, "the next years were a lot of hard work and just showing up and making changes to make sure I was taking care of my own health the way I would for anyone else I cared about. Two things my counselor recommended were to always have something to look forward to and to surround myself with other people as often as I could. When I was alone, I'd get in my own head and fixate on all the worst things from my childhood, all the reasons I thought they were my fault. Staying busy with work gave me somewhere to be other than an empty house. And people to hang out with besides just Ty's family. Plus, what's more fun than getting paid to pretend to be a pirate?" He winks at me, and I tighten my grip on his hand.

"Eventually, I got to the point where I could talk some of my deepest stuff out and work through it in a healthy way. I learned how to filter out what's true and to ask for help when I need it. I got more comfortable with being alone, not so scared to sit with my thoughts. This past year, I've been in a better place than ever. And then you showed up on my porch." He runs his thumb along my knuckles. "And suddenly, I wasn't only okay with being at home more; I wanted to be there. The idea of you coming back from your vacation and wasting any of the few days I had left with you doing anything but spending as much time with you as you'd let me was absurd. Especially when I could get another part-time job like this in a heartbeat. I want the job with the city; I really, really want it." His voice breaks. "But more than that, I want a life outside of work. I want to be able to take my nephew to the beach and spend time rebuilding my relationship with my sister. I want—" He lets go of my hand and straightens up. "I want to ask you something, but I need you to be completely honest with me." I nod. "Really, Alex. The last thing I want is for you to feel sorry for me or like you have to say or do something to make me feel better after I've told you all this; that's not your job. We're best friends, right?"

"We are."

"So one hundred percent honesty, okay?"

"Okay," I promise.

He's nervous again, and I wonder what's coming. "Remember our conversation about being willing to take risks when something is important to you? My last two shifts are next Wednesday night. On Thursday, I'd like to take you out somewhere. On a date. Would that be okay?"

This may be the easiest question I've ever been asked. I recapture his hand. "I'd love to go on a date with you, Jude."

"Really?" he breathes.

"I just have a couple questions."

His smile slips just a little. "Okay."

"Will the restaurant make you give the pirate earring back?"

He scowls at me, but it loses its effect with the laugh he can't hold in. "You are ridiculous."

"Have you . . . have you told Norah yet?"

He rolls his eyes.

"Are you regretting asking me on a date now?" I tease.

The look he sends across the table chases any further silliness from my mind, and something flutters behind my ribs. "Not even a little bit."

<h1 style="text-align:center">Chapter 33</h1>

I try my best to tone down the idiotic grin I can feel plastered across my face, but it's impossible. Rather than going upstairs when I get back to our beach house, I walk across the backyard to the tables where two of my aunts are still busy pouring pancake batter onto a couple large griddles.

I'm surprised to see Elle sitting beside my parents, Sutton and Chris on the other side of their table.

"Good morning." I snag a cup of orange juice from the breakfast buffet and sit by Elle. "Weird seeing you at breakfast; we used to always be the last ones awake."

"I'm still on Spanish time." She taps her juice cup to mine, an apparent toast to early mornings. "What's your excuse?"

"I went for a walk on the beach."

"Alone?" she whispers, and I elbow her in the side.

My dad cuts into his pancakes, oblivious. "All it took was one summer at the beach to turn you into a morning person? Maybe you should stay until Christmas."

"Glad you've missed me, Daddy."

"He's kidding," my mom chimes in. "But we do like seeing you so happy. I'm glad you've had this time for your writing."

I preemptively elbow Elle again, because I know her well enough to guess she has some suggestive comment at the ready.

"What are we supposed to wear for the family picture tonight?" Sutton rescues me.

Elle groans. Standing on the beach in dress clothes for an hour every year while my photographer aunt tries to get us organized and all the kids either melt down or run wild is everyone's least favorite part of vacation. But having a photo of our whole family to remember the year by is enough of an incentive to make it bearable.

"Navy and white," my mom tells her, then turns to me. "I brought that navy top from your closet just in case you didn't pack something already."

Marcail wiggles in Chris's lap and reaches across toward Elle's plate. "Hey, sweet girl." I break a tiny piece of pancake off the one Elle is cutting. But just as I stretch out my hand, Sutton slaps it away.

"She can't have that."

"Sorry." I wince. "I forgot."

"It's okay," Chris says. "A little bite wouldn't have hurt her."

"Then you and Alex can change her diapers today," she snaps. "We aren't supposed to be introducing anything new this week."

"I'm sorry, Sutton," I repeat. "I wasn't thinking."

She picks up her empty plate and swings her legs over the picnic bench. "I'm going to iron our clothes for the picture."

"Sutton," Chris implores. But she doesn't look back.

My mom frowns. "What was that about?"

I shrug.

But Chris turns his pleading eyes to me. "Talk to her, Alex. Please."

Elle loops an arm around mine. "I'll go with you."

I pace the room while we wait for Sutton to bring over the curling iron Rebekah requested. It seemed less confrontational to ask her to run up to our room than to all show up at her door.

"You should do the talking, Bekah. She listens to you."

"No ma'am." Rebekah pulls the elastic band from her ponytail and slides it onto her wrist. "We're just here for moral support. The two of you need to work through whatever this is, because we only have two days of vacation left, and we're not gonna spend them watching you give each other the cold shoulder."

"My shoulder is plenty warm," I grouse. "It's Sutton who has a problem."

"What?" Sutton pushes the door open, hair products in hand. "Did I hear my name?"

Rebekah takes the basket from her arms. "We were just saying we were glad you brought all this stuff. I can't believe I forgot mine."

"After I specifically reminded you in the packing list I sent to the group text." Sutton tsks playfully.

"She did," Elle verifies. "Though I barely remembered to pack a brush, so who am I to judge?"

I forget the speech I planned about how worried we've been about Sutton. "What group text?"

Sutton pretends not to hear. "I don't know why you're curling your hair now though, Bek. You're not going down to the ocean today?"

"No, I am. I just thought if you brought it on over, we could talk you into getting ready with us after dinner. Like old times."

"What group text?"

"I'll need to get Marcie dressed though. You can just run it back down to me after you do your hair."

"Chris can dress Marcie," Elle says. "It's not that hard."

"What. Group. Text."

Everyone freezes. Sutton sighs and turns to face me. "I sent Elle and Bekah a packing list to help them out. You were already here, so I assumed you didn't need it."

For having just been ready to make up with Sutton, I'm unreasonably angry at the moment. "So that was the only purpose of this group text? Or is it the one you created to talk about Marcail's food allergies and whatever else you decided to leave me out of?"

Sutton's icy blue eyes turn to straight fire. "No, Alex. This is the group we created to discuss why you suddenly stopped communicating with us when you left for the summer."

"I didn't stop communicating with y'all." My voice shakes.

"Sorry," she amends in the most patronizing tone I've ever heard. "What I meant to say was why you suddenly stopped communicating *honestly* with us."

"I didn't lie to you," I spit back, doing it even now. "I just didn't tell you everything."

Sutton reaches for the doorknob. "I'm leaving."

"Of course you are." I cross my arms.

Rebekah slides between Sutton and the door. "I don't think you should go until we've had a chance to talk this out," she suggests diplomatically.

"Fine." Sutton huffs. "Why then, Alex?"

"Why what?"

"Why didn't you tell us about Jude?"

Because I was trying not to overthink it?

Because I wanted to keep it to myself for a while?

I don't know why.

But how can I say any of these answers out loud?

"Because I was afraid you'd do what you always do, Sutton. You'd offer me unsolicited advice and tell me what I should be doing, what I should be feeling. Then, you'd hang up and leave me to torture myself with everything you said while you went back to your busy life and forgot all about me again."

Her face morphs, and she blinks once. Twice. Her voice is barely a whisper. "What are you talking about, Alex?"

"Sutton, you've always had an opinion about everything," I start.

"I know that; I didn't mean that part. What you said about me forgetting about you." She sits on the bed closest to her. "I'll acknowledge that I'm a little bossy sometimes. But it's only because I love you guys more than anything and I want you to be happy. How on earth could you think I'm ever too busy to think about you?"

I lower myself onto the other bed, and the tears start. "Because you guys all have these . . . real lives. Between Spain and the ICU and your husband and kid." I wave my arm around the room. "And I'm the odd one out now. And I don't know how to fix it, because this is just who I am: boring, safe, same-as-always Alex."

Sutton fixes me with a look of authority I've seen hundreds of times, but somehow this time it's exactly what I didn't know I needed. "That's the most absurd, least true thing you have ever said, Alexandria Henry. There is nothing about you that is boring. You are extraordinary." She pauses to keep her emotions in check, and Rebekah sits down beside her. "I keep waiting for you to wake up and realize that you could literally do anything you decided you wanted to. Why else do you think I keep trying to set you up with Chris's coworkers and nagging you to write your book? It's because I'm torn between wanting you to find all the insane happiness you deserve and being terrified that you're going to find it without me. And if anyone has become the odd one out—" She shudders with a sob, and it registers that she's crying now. "It's me."

Rebekah hardly has time to scoot over and slide her arm around Sutton's back before Elle and I are there too, undone at the sight of our ever-composed cousin falling apart.

"I love Chris and Marcie," she chokes out. "I really do. I feel like the luckiest woman in the world for having them. But after watching our moms and aunts do this seamlessly for so long, I just assumed—" She draws a shaky breath. "I didn't realize it would be this hard. Or that I'd worry so much. It's made me neurotic and snappy, and I hate who I've become." We're all crying with her now, even Elle as she rubs circles on Sutton's back. "I know it sounds selfish, but I'm sad I can't stay with you guys in here anymore or do all the things we used to. And then I'm even sadder thinking about how sometimes that's probably a relief for you."

"No." I wrap myself around her arm. "We miss you, Sutton. I miss you. I had no idea you were feeling this way."

Rebekah strokes her hair. "I feel like this all the time too. I'll reach for my phone at the end of a shift and think, 'No one wants to hear about the catheter I changed today or the patient who coded or the dad who broke down on my shoulder.' It's all so heavy, but the last thing I want is to put that burden on you guys. It's just weird not telling you everything. And I worry that you're all having fun without me."

"I *want* you to call me!" Elle exclaims. "I'm all the way over in Europe, missing everything. But I can't even complain about it, because I chose it. I can't explain it, but it feels so right to be there. And so wrong to not be with you guys. But I never want to reach out when things are hard, because you all still think of me as the baby, and I don't need someone to fix everything; I just need you guys to *know* everything. And tell me everything. All of it. I don't need you to protect me. Does that make sense?"

Sutton turns and pulls Elle into her lap. "Oh, Elle Belle. You have grown into a strong, beautiful woman who we all have so much respect for. You might be the bravest of us all." She kisses the top of her head. "But you'll always be our baby."

Elle laughs through her tears. "And you've always been neurotic, Sutton."

Suddenly, we're all laughing and crying and holding onto each other for dear life, and I can hardly breathe, and I can breathe freely for the first time in months. "You'd better add me to that group text as soon as we stop hugging."

"Let's never stop hugging," Rebekah says.

Sutton clasps my hand. "I just can't believe you fell in love and I missed it."

"You haven't missed it; it's still happening."

Rebekah and Elle both squeal. "Start talking," Sutton demands. "We want every last detail."

Chapter 34

Rebekah taps my phone to zoom in on the little cousin who's picking his nose in the front row of the picture on the screen. Classic. Definitely the best shot of the evening. My aunt emailed it out to everyone shortly after we walked back in our dress clothes.

Now, we're wearing our pajamas, crammed into one bed while the other sits empty across the room.

"I'm glad Chris let you stay with us tonight." Elle snuggles closer to Sutton.

"He didn't let me," Sutton responds. "He kicked me out, insisted that I needed this." She leans her head on my shoulder. "He was right."

"Two minutes." Rebekah taps the corner of the screen where the blocky numbers read 11:58.

"Jude's sister is really nice," Elle says. "She was a good sport tonight." Thinking about Kelsey juggling my aunt's giant camera as well as a couple cell phones and clicking the button every time my aunt shouted, "One, two, THREE!" while Donovan danced and made funny faces behind her makes me smile. I hope I can get to know her better these next couple weeks.

"Any second now," Rebekah sings. Elle and Sutton lean in. "Happy birthday!" They shout it in unison at the same time my phone buzzes. I drop the phone onto the blankets, and Sutton recovers my fumble.

"Ooo, guess who it is?" She shimmies under the covers. "Let's see what Jude has to say, shall we?" I blush but don't try to stop her.

"Happy birthday," she reads. "I know you're probably celebrating with your cousins right now, but I wanted you to know I was thinking of you."

"Aww," Elle croons. "Text him back and tell him Alex will meet him in the yard in five minutes for a birthday kiss."

I lunge for the phone, but Sutton pulls it out of reach. "Don't you dare," I bark.

She turns her back to me and starts typing. "Sutton!"

"Chill, Al. That's not what I'm saying." She finishes and turns back, tilts the screen so I can see her message before she hits send: *This is Sutton. Come have cupcakes with us tomorrow night. We'll wait for you to get off work.*

I wrench the phone from her hands and wait for Jude's reply. "You could have at least phrased it as a request." I watch the screen. "And now I think you've scared him off. He knows y'all are reading this."

"What do you think he'd say if he knew we *weren't* reading this?" Elle teases. "And Sutton doesn't make requests; she gives orders."

We all jump when the phone vibrates. Sutton yanks it back. "Hi, Sutton. Tell Alex I'll be there. And that she looks really pretty in the picture Kelsey showed me of the four of you."

"That is NOT what he said."

She passes me the phone smugly. It's exactly what he said.

"Whoa, Jude," Rebekah says. "Flirting boldly, my man. I like it." So do I.

"Okay." Sutton sends a heart and puts my phone on the night-stand. "No more boys allowed; this is cousin time."

The yard is bustling when we return from a late dinner out and an unnecessarily long trip to the beach shop. Rebekah was convinced we needed to buy friendship bracelets this year in addition to getting tattoos, and we couldn't agree on whether to get four of the same bracelets or just one bracelet that we would mail back and forth throughout the year. Sutton finally convinced us that it would end up lost somewhere in Spain ("no offense, Elle"), so now we're each sporting matching braided strings around our wrists.

Chris meets us halfway between the houses, and two squishy arms reach for Sutton. "My baby," she coos. "I missed you so much."

"Aw." Chris pecks her cheek. "And what about Marcail? Did you miss her too?" Sutton returns his look with one that may have made me cringe before. But now, I get it.

I search the folding chairs on the concrete until I locate Jude, sitting right next to my daddy, deep in conversation. Jude says something I can't decipher from this far away that makes my dad laugh.

"Look out!" A basketball whizzes past my head.

"Sorry about that." Elias jogs over with Donovan on his shoulders. "We're working on three-pointers."

Kelsey, who I didn't realize was right beside us, says, "Careful, Donovan. I don't think Alex wants a concussion for her birthday."

"He's doing great," Elias tells her before taking the ball from Elle and carrying Donovan back to the basketball hoop. My eyes follow them only as far as the row of chairs because Jude is now staring straight at me.

I cross the yard and take the empty seat next to him. "Hi."

"Hey, Birthday Girl." My dad leans around Jude to smile at me. "How was your ladies' night out?"

"We missed you singing Spice Girls."

"I could do that now for you," he offers. Jude indulges him with a laugh; if my dad didn't like him before, he will definitely get points for this. Who am I kidding? It would be impossible for anyone not to like Jude.

"Wow," Jude says. "That's a lot of cupcakes."

I look over at the tables under the house where Rebekah is helping my mom set out dozens of treats. "We thought you might like to share with everyone this year," she calls over to me.

I absolutely do. Sharing these sacred moments with others is a joy I wish I'd learned to fully appreciate while my grandmama was still here to see it, but I know she'd be happy for me right now no matter how long it took for me to come around.

"Come on, Alex," Rebekah calls as she pushes several candles into one of the cupcakes. "Time for you to make a wish."

I walk over and around the table where I have a perfect view of the yard. Of the family I was blessed to be born into and the members we've found along the years. The ones who have found us. I look at my parents. My aunts and uncles and cousins. The friends from next door. My closest confidants at my side. The boy with the brown eyes and glasses staring back at me with a look of adoration I don't deserve.

I hold my hair and the silver necklace against my chest as I lean over the flames and blow out the candles. But I don't close my eyes. What more could I wish for tonight?

Rebekah and Elle have already been asleep for over an hour when I give up trying and crawl out of bed. I pull out the envelope Jude handed me when we said goodnight and tiptoe to the door where I can read his words again by the light of the hallway.

It seems strange to say I've missed the familiar swirl of his hand-writing, the shape of his thoughts scrawled across a page. But I have.

I unfold the paper and feel myself smile as I re-read the title, a nod to our favorite story.

Sandcastles In the Air (for Jo)
I used to close my eyes at night and pray
I'd wake to something better than today.

Then, I'd name just one gift of Life's giving
That would make tomorrow's day worth living.
And every morning when I'd see the sun,
I'd search to try to find another one.
After some time, I found within my reach—
Like seashells gathered slowly from a beach—
A mound of treasured things I'd held in hand,
A "castle in the air" I'd made of sand.
It housed my heart and with each day that passed
Was reconstructed stronger than the last.
I didn't mind the waves that washed away
The lesser happinesses of a day.
For greater things than I had ever planned
Had built me solid places I could stand.
And gravity that pulled me to the sea
Brought breakers to reshape and bolster me.
And now that I have stood here way up high,
I listen to your fears and can see why
You worry that the life you've loved might sink
And panic overwhelms you when you think
The only way to go from here's downhill.
But what if what's to come is better still?
For I live somewhere sweeter now, it seems
Than any castle I've built in my dreams;
Which proves sometimes the future has in store
Everything you've dared to hope and more.
So enter this new year with open mind;
Who knows the joy ahead that you may find?

Below the poem, he's written just six words:

Happy birthday, Alex. See you tomorrow.

Chapter 35

I hadn't expected the onslaught of emotion when my family exited the seafood place this afternoon, hugged me goodbye, then drove away in dozens of cars. I stood there on the sidewalk between one part of my world and another before driving back across the bridge.

My dad had been especially stoic, telling me how much he loved me as he pulled me into his embrace. My mom was teary but beaming. And my cousins . . . I'm not sure any of us wouldn't have given just about anything for another day together.

"Sleepover at Sutton's before I fly out," Elle said. "You'll be there?"

"Of course."

Rebekah had held on to me the longest until Elias honked the horn of her car and waved her over. "Why did I agree to let him drive back?" she complained, then kissed my cheek once more before jogging off.

Chris pulled up next to the curb, and Sutton's window rolled down. "Listen." I walked over and she narrowed her eyes. "I'm going to give you space to enjoy this time with Jude, okay? But I need you to do two things for me."

"Yes, ma'am." I laughed and waited for her to go on. I was expecting a lecture about not breaking his heart or figuring out where the relationship was going.

Instead, she said, "Don't get in your own head, Alex. There's no script for falling in love. I know how you overthink. Just take it a day at a time and let this be what it is, okay? Let yourself be happy."

I nodded. "And the second thing?"

"If you need anything, or just someone to listen, call me."

"Promise."

I'd spent the rest of the day with Kelsey and Donovan. I was relieved when Jude came home from work and everything felt normal. The four of us ate a late dinner of pizza and watched a movie before Jude read Donovan a bedtime story while Kelsey and I cleaned the kitchen. Then she and Jude and I talked for hours in the living room like we were every bit as much family as the people I just vacationed with.

Now, I'm back in Kelsey's old room, sitting on the bed scrolling through beach week photos and trying to decide if I should sleep or tiptoe down to my regular spot at the kitchen counter. I've tried to tell myself that I'm just being respectful of Jude's space and the fact that dynamics have changed since last week; there are twice as many people living here now. But the truth is, I'm scared. Nervous that something has shifted and that things won't be the same between us now. What if we've lost something we can never get back?

Sighing, I reach for the band sweatshirt that was folded neatly on the corner of the dresser when I moved back in this afternoon.

I know he's at the counter before I even make it halfway down the stairs, and his hopeful eyes are fixed on me as I step into the living room and cross it to the kitchen. Just being in the same room, seeing him somewhere other than my mind, puts me at ease.

The notebook and a pen are already lying in my spot next to an unopened bottle of water. It's a simple gesture, but it makes me feel special to know he hoped I'd come down.

He focuses back on his laptop, and we fall into our rhythm. His keyboard clicks. My pen scratches across paper. The green numbers on the microwave clock count forward. My heart rests, feels comfortable enough to start untangling the thoughts swirling around my mind.

When I finish scribbling, I slide the open book next to his computer.

Petrichor
It hasn't rained in over a week
But the memory lingers
Of that cold night
That's kept me warm
These long, sunny days
It smells like towels
Washed in familiar detergent
And heat blowing from car vents
A half-eaten bag of fruity gummy bears

Abandoned in a fort
And the hot cocoa I'm still owed

He doesn't answer my written words with spoken ones, but his lips curl upward and he stands to turn the stove on and pull two mugs from the cabinet.

"Want to come out to the garage and help me pack up the tackle box?"

Donovan is out of his chair before Mr. Bruce even finishes the question. He's been talking about going fishing with him ever since he woke up this morning.

"I'm so glad it worked out for all of you to join us for church and lunch." Mrs. Becky smiles across the mostly empty dishes of pot roast and potatoes.

Jude stands and reaches for my plate.

"No, honey; you don't need to do that," Mrs. Becky says. "Tyler will get those."

Tyler makes a face but kisses his mom's head as he rises to help Jude clear the table. "Housework *and* fishing lessons? Y'all are keeping me busy today."

"Alex, you're welcome to stay and hang out with me and Kelsey while the boys fish." Mrs. Becky is helping Jude's sister research job openings and apartment listings this afternoon. Kelsey told me last night that between spending time with a healthy, loving family last week and Jude showing Donovan how a good man treats people, she can't imagine moving back to Wilmington.

"I think I'll ride back with Jude, but if you end up going to look at anything tomorrow afternoon, Kels, I can watch Donovan for you."

Jude reenters the room and stands behind my chair, resting a hand on my shoulder. "I should probably head back soon to get changed. You ready to go?"

"Wait." Mrs. Becky jumps up. "Let me wrap up some of this pie for you to have later."

Jude and I walk to the door, stopping to call a quick goodbye into the garage. Mrs. Becky meets us there. She tucks a plastic container into Jude's hands and squeezes his arm. "It sure is good to see you so happy."

"It's hard not to be happy when someone's just handed you pie." He winks at me, and I marvel again at what an idiot I've been all these years.

In the driveway, he passes me the container and opens the passenger door for me. I watch him jog around to the other side, fasten his seatbelt, and rest an arm on the back of my seat as he backs out and puts the car in drive. I don't realize I'm staring until he smiles and asks, "What?"

"I wish you didn't have to go to work this afternoon." I place my arm on the console between us, a subtle invitation, I hope.

His hand finds mine. "You and me both."

"Will you teach me to fish this week?"

"I would love to take you fishing. But I think we should go in the fall."

I wrinkle my forehead. "Fall fish are better?"

"No." His eyes flicker to the side and then back to the road. "I just think it might be nice if we make a list of things to do later. I want to give you every possible reason to come back and visit me."

Out of nowhere, a wave of panic rolls through me. I can feel my whole body tense.

He tugs on my hand. "What's wrong?"

"Nothing." I exhale and take a moment to make sure I say only what I mean. "You know how I have trouble sometimes living too much in the past?"

"And I have trouble sometimes living too much in the future?" He pulls out onto the main road. "Sorry. It's just that for so long I always needed something to look forward to. I didn't mean to make it sound like right now isn't enough. Because, in all honesty, this is more than I could have ever asked for, Alex."

I wrap my free hand around his arm. "There's nothing wrong with looking forward to things. I just get freaked out sometimes if I start to think too far ahead, and then I spiral. It's my problem, not yours. I'm working on it. But, you know. Baby steps."

We ride in silence for a minute, and I wonder what's going on inside his head.

I don't have to wait long. "I don't think I'll ever get used to this," he says.

"To what?"

"To you liking me." He holds up our hands. "Like this."

I more than like him. But he has no idea. "You should probably get used to it," I tell him. "Because we're going on a date this week."

"Oh, that's *this* week?" he teases.

I feign offense and start to pull my hand away, but he tightens his grip. "You know I'm kidding. I've been counting down the minutes."

"Me too," I admit. "See? Something I'm looking forward to in the future."

He smiles. "I just hope it lives up to your expectations."

"If it involves you and me spending time together, it's already the best date I've ever been on."

"Good." He turns into the driveway. "Pie in the kitchen while we work tonight?"

I reluctantly let go of his hand. "I'll be there."

Chapter 36

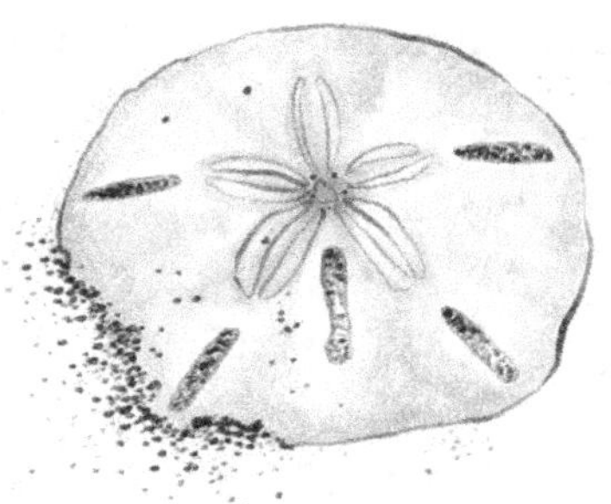

During the school year, I always dreaded Monday mornings. But it's a whole lot easier to wake up early when I know it increases the chance I'll get to spend a few extra minutes with Jude before he goes to work in the afternoon.

He and Donovan left before seven for Donovan's first surf lesson with Ty. It's almost nine, and there's still no sign of them, so I settle back into the couch and start another video on my laptop.

I'm halfway through a review of first aid procedures when the door opens and in walks Jude, hair a mess and towel in hand. Straight-From-The-Beach Jude might be my favorite version of him. He always looks so content, so *himself*, after he's spent time in the ocean.

"Good morning, Alex."

I pause my video. "Where's Donovan?"

"Kelsey took him out for breakfast. He did a really good job this morning, but he was frustrated he wasn't surfing like Tyler yet. He wasn't a fan of falling."

"I think he gets that from his uncle."

"Being terrible at surfing?"

I shake my head. "Being competitive."

He makes a face and steps closer to the couch. "What are you working on?"

"Professional development videos I have to watch before the new school year starts. I probably should have started before now, but I didn't want to think about it yet."

When he doesn't respond, I assume he's as dangerously close to overthinking what the end of this summer will mean as I am. "I can finish this later," I say. "Let's do something fun this morning."

"No, go ahead and keep watching. I need to shower anyway. I'll be back in a few."

I press play and try to distract myself until he returns. Like Sutton said, I can't afford to get in my own head right now.

I do my best to ignore him when he walks back through wearing a long-sleeved T-shirt and sweatpants and opens the microwave.

The sound of kernels popping finally gets me. "What are you doing?"

"Breakfast of champions," he calls back.

A minute later, he joins me on the couch with a big bowl of popcorn. "Okay. Catch me up."

"Well." I take a handful of popcorn. "We're on step three of the five-step weather emergency plan."

"Sounds riveting."

"You have no idea." I pause the video. "Seriously, Jude. I can watch these while you're at work. This is not how you want to spend your morning. It's not even how *I* want to spend *my* morning."

"You'll be with Donovan this afternoon though. Besides, I actually kind of love this."

"Boring safety videos?"

"The adventures and traditions are fun, Alex. But the regular stuff? Grocery shopping, sitting in the kitchen, this." He shrugs. "It's nice to do everyday life with someone you really like being around."

"Well, in that case." I move the bowl of popcorn to the coffee table, lift his arm around my shoulders, and snuggle in closer before clicking the button on my computer.

I don't absorb any of the last points of the presentation; I'll have to rewatch it later, but I don't care.

"You smell really good," I tell him as the screen goes dark. Part of me can't believe I said it out loud, that I'm flirting with Jude so unashamedly. But he doesn't seem to mind.

"Thank you." He chuckles, and when I turn my head, his face is mere inches away. The way his eyes scan my face makes me wonder for one beautifully panicked second if he's about to kiss me. But then, he clears his throat.

"What's up next?" He gestures to my laptop.

"Actually." I sit forward. "I was wondering if you might want to help me with a project. It's a normal everyday type task too, but it's more interesting than this."

"Sure."

I close the browser on my computer and open the photo files. "Every year, one of us girls compiles our vacation pictures into a photo book. It's my turn. But I was thinking about doing something a little different." I pull up a new window. "I thought I might take some of the stories I've been writing down and add them in with some older photos too."

"I think that's a great idea." He surveys the work I've pulled up on the screen. "I've reread those stories in the notebook more times than I feel comfortable telling you. They're really well written; I almost feel like I'm there when I read them."

"You *were* there for a lot of them, Jude. That's part of what made them so special." I enjoy his soft smile for a moment before I shift to the real reason I brought this up. "I want to make a separate book just for our poems, for us. So we can each have a copy. What do you think?"

His demeanor shifts. "Yeah. That'd be cool."

"That didn't sound very convincing."

He sighs. "It's a good idea. Just feels weird to think of our poems being anywhere other than the notebook in the kitchen drawer is all."

"I know. But there's only one notebook, and we can't both keep it."

"Exactly."

This is a conversation I cannot entertain right now, and I wonder how many times over the next few days we'll end up back here, fighting to stay in the present moment, pushing away the inevitable.

I need to change the subject, but I'm drawing a blank.

"You know what?" He steps between me and my painful thoughts. "I could show you how to use my camera, and we could take some pictures around the island to go with the poetry if you want."

I have to swallow the lump in my throat before I can answer. "I'd love that."

"Popcorn for breakfast yesterday and slushies on the beach today," I comment as I take the koozie and spoon he just bought from the cart. "I never thought I'd need anything more than tiny boxes of cereal, but now I can't wait for tomorrow morning."

"You're on your own tomorrow." Jude sits back down in his beach chair with his own slushie. "Wednesdays are my long days, remember? But." He takes a bite. "It's my last day."

"And then, our date," I remind him.

"I can make you breakfast Thursday morning after Donovan's lesson if you want, before we go. I was thinking of instituting a weekly pancake day anyway."

"You mean a . . . tradition?" I lift my sunglasses.

"I wish I'd put it together sooner that anything can be a tradition and that I didn't need anyone's permission to start one. I probably missed out on a lot of things that could have become fun memories like the ones you have."

"We're making up for it now." I push the crushed ice around my cup with my spoon. "In fact, I think we've covered most of the major traditions on my list. We should spend the next few days starting new ones, things Donovan can grow up treasuring."

"I've already been brainstorming." He holds out his slushie so I can try the blue, and I hand him my red one. "What do you think about a 'Christmas in July' day?"

I gasp. "I think that might be the best idea I've ever heard. Will there be a tree?"

"Obviously. And a movie marathon." He leans back in his chair. "I didn't get to see Kelsey and Donovan last year for Christmas, so gotta pull out all the stops."

I want to spend Christmas with Jude.

The thought pops into my head so suddenly and unexpectedly that it takes my breath away.

"Okay." Jude picks up his book. "Back to reading. I need to let you get into this story."

I stare at the thick volume in my own lap. "Mr. Tolkien is boring me with descriptions right now."

"Give it time. It'll grow on you."

I crack open the pages and shake my head. The things we do for the people we love. "We'll see."

Chapter 37

"Whoa!" I jump up off the couch and lift my hands up over my head. "Of all the things I guessed might be part of my Wednesday night, being held up at sword point was not one of them."

Donovan giggles and waves his new weapon back and forth. "Uncle Jude bought it for me."

"And how was the show?"

He lowers the sword and twirls it in his hands. "Awesome. I'm sad it was Uncle Jude's last night there, but he promised he'd take me back at Christmastime. And then, he can even sit with me. Right, Mom?"

Kelsey's eyes have the same sheen I've seen in Sutton's when she's watching Marcie have fun. "Right."

"Can we watch a pirate movie tonight?" Donovan asks me.

"No sir." Kelsey grabs his shoulders and turns him toward the hallway. "A dinner show and ice cream on the way home means now it's bedtime."

"But Uncle Jude should be home soon. I want him to read with me."

"Will you settle for me tonight?" Kelsey asks.

He pauses and raises his sword. "Will you do the voices?"

"Deal." When she exchanges a look with me, we both do our best to keep straight faces. "Now brush your teeth before I make you walk the plank."

"Can I hug Alex goodnight first?"

I melt. Kelsey nods, and Donovan wraps his arms around my legs. "Love you, Alex."

"Love you too, buddy."

Heart full, I sit back on the couch to wait for Jude. He walks in a few minutes later with a bag of takeout.

"Welcome home, pirate."

"Not anymore." He sets the food on the coffee table and sits beside me. "I've hung up my cutlass and vowed to live an honest life."

"Did you have a good last night?"

He nods. "It was a lot of fun having Donovan there. Did he already go to bed?"

"Kelsey's reading to him now."

"I hope she's doing the voices right."

"Jude, he might be the most precious kid in the world."

"I won't tell Sutton you said that," he jokes. "I know I'm biased, but I think he's pretty special."

"I'll admit though." I sigh. "I'm a little jealous that he got an invitation to the pirate show when I was expressly forbidden to come."

"You didn't let that stop you."

I open my mouth to argue, but he cuts me off. "I actually thought about taking you tomorrow. But I didn't want to show up there the first day after I quit." He lowers his voice. "And I'd feel weird taking you on a date to the same place my brother did."

I bristle. "First of all, that was *not* a date. And secondly, if you didn't notice, I spent that whole night watching *you*."

"Yeah?"

"Mmhm." I look into his warm brown eyes. "I think maybe that was when I started trying to convince myself I didn't think of you as more than a friend." I relish the way his eyes sparkle when I say this. "Honestly, there were a couple times I forgot Gavin was even there."

"But you can understand me feeling a little jealous. You definitely had a thing for him a few years ago." He shrugs. "I don't blame you. I'm still a nerd now, but I was super geeky back then."

"No. I was just super oblivious. Thanks for not giving up on me while I figured things out."

"Worth the wait." He jerks his chin toward the coffee table. "You hungry? I thought since Kelsey and Donovan ate at the show, we could eat in here tonight and maybe play some Mario Kart. Feels like the only appropriate way to celebrate."

"That sounds lovely. I'll grab some drinks." I stand, and he follows me.

"Don't you want to know what we're celebrating?" he asks.

I stop halfway to the kitchen. "I assumed you meant your retirement from piracy. Is there something else?"

He tucks his hands into his pockets and smiles shyly. "The city called this afternoon and offered me the job."

"JUDE!" I nearly knock him down with the force of my hug. "Why didn't you tell me this as soon as you walked in the door? Why didn't you text me the second you got off the phone with them?" I'm so overwhelmed with happiness for him I'm crying and shaking.

He wraps his arms around me. "And miss this reaction in person?"

"Congratulations." I step back and swipe at my cheeks. "I'm seriously thrilled for you. And for them. They could not have found a more perfect person for this job." I shake my head. "I don't even know what else to say. How are you so calm? I'm a mess."

"I can't explain how much better you being happy with me makes this." He's beaming, and his elation is contagious.

"I feel so lucky I get to be here to celebrate with you. We need balloons or streamers or something. Fireworks! Want me to run out and get some sparkling cider?"

He laughs. "We don't need balloons or fireworks or sparkling cider."

"But it's a special occasion! We should do something special."

"See, that's what I've been trying to tell you. Just being with you makes everything special. I just want to spend time with you."

The sincerity in his voice almost makes me start crying again. "Takeout and video games it is."

He walks to the refrigerator and pulls out two cans of ginger ale.

"Hey, Jude?"

"Yes?"

"Can I tell you something?"

He stops, sets the cans on the counter and waits.

"I just . . . I need you to know that I think you're amazing. I mean, in addition to being one of my favorite people on earth. You're a good man, Jude Alford, and the world is a better place because you're in it. I know you're going to be great at this job and make a difference in a lot of people's lives and bring a lot of families joy when they come here on vacation." I feel my face flush. "Anyway, I'll stop with all the mushy stuff; I just wanted to say that out loud. Let's eat." I reach for one of the drinks on the counter. "I can't stay up too late tonight, because I have a date with a really cute guy tomorrow."

He looks at me like I've just handed him a million dollars and steps close enough to send my heart into a tailspin again. "Well, now that you've said all these sweet things to me, I feel kind of bad that I'm about to beat you at video games."

I hand him the other can. "Not a chance."

Chapter 38

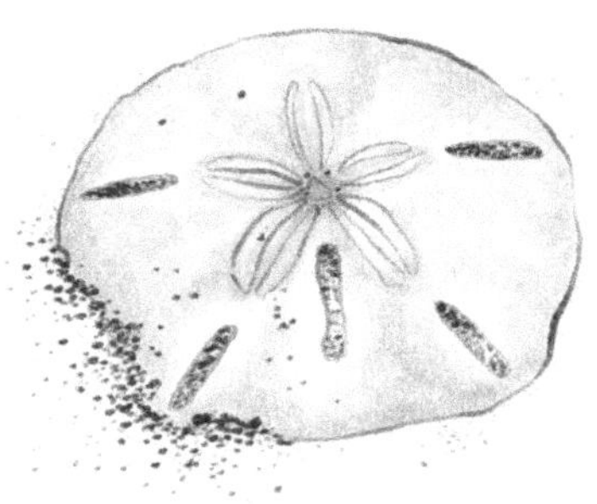

I smooth my hands over the skirt of my floral sundress and adjust the pin in the side of my hair one more time. I want Jude to know that I put time and effort into getting ready for this date, that he's the kind of guy who's worth dressing up for even though I know he'd be just as happy to be with me if I wore sweats and an old T-shirt.

"You look gorgeous," Kelsey says before we walk downstairs.

Donovan looks up from his game of Zelda. "I like your dress, Alex. It's pretty."

"Thanks. I hope your uncle thinks so too." I glance nervously at the hallway where his door is still closed.

Kelsey picks up my purse. "He will."

"Can I come?" Donovan asks, not for the first time today.

His mom laughs. "It's one afternoon, bud. We'll have fun here. And you have surf lessons in the morning, remember?"

"Will you come watch, Alex?"

"If you want me to. Maybe I can—" A knock at the door interrupts me.

Kelsey hands me my bag and turns me toward the door. "It's for you."

When I open it, Jude is standing on the other side, a bouquet of flowers in hand. He's wearing khaki shorts, a pink collared shirt, and the tentative smile that always draws mine out.

"Did you seriously just knock on the door to your own house?" I giggle and step back to let him in.

"I wanted you to get the full experience," he says, extending the bouquet. "These are for you."

I hold the blooms to my nose and breathe in their sweet scent. "Thank you. How did you know tulips are my favorite?"

"I have my sources."

"Would these sources happen to be slightly bossy and have just exchanged phone numbers with you last week?"

Jude chuckles. "Maybe."

"Can I come, Uncle Jude?" Donovan pipes up.

Kelsey reaches for the flowers. "I'll put these in a vase. You two get out of here before you end up with a third wheel."

Jude opens the front door again and holds out an arm, gesturing me through.

"Have fun!" Kelsey calls behind us.

The afternoon is warm, but a nice sea breeze tickles my skin. I feel like the younger version of me did every time she left the beach house to go on an adventure. We descend the steps, and Jude opens the passenger side of the white car for me before walking around and sliding into his own seat.

"You look beautiful, Alexandria. Have I said that already? Because I've thought it several times." He reaches for my hand, but instead of tucking it inside his own, he holds it up and studies my fingers. "Sorry I wasn't there to help paint your nails this time; I won't look at the other hand too closely."

I pull my hand away and fold down a rogue corner of his shirt collar. "Your sister helped me actually."

"Really?" He smiles and reaches for the gear shift.

"Yep. She did my hair and makeup too."

He backs the car out. "I like that you two are friends."

"Me too."

He puts the car into drive and takes my hand again, this time lacing his fingers through mine. "I can't believe we're on a date." He sighs. "Sorry, does that make me sound lame? I'm trying to play it cool here, but you have no idea how long I've waited for this."

"Not lame at all. I had trouble sleeping last night. It's been an exciting twenty-four hours. You finishing your job. Landing your new, dream job. Best pancakes I've ever eaten this morning. And now, this."

"I guess I understand it a little bit better now." He swallows.

"Understand what?"

"That feeling you described. Of everything feeling perfect. And being afraid of it all slipping away."

A cold wave of uncertainty slaps me in the face, and I grasp for a change of subject. "So when do you start?"

He turns the car and drives toward the bridge. "August thirteenth. It'll be a week of training, and then I'll start meeting with people from other beaches to gather ideas. They want me to plan some holiday events this year."

"That's fun!" I turn in my seat. "We can brainstorm during Christmas in July on Saturday."

"Yeah. It's hard to think about Christmas for real when it's ninety-something degrees," he comments.

"It'll be here before you know it though."

"Christmas in July or real Christmas?"

"Everything," I say.

His smile falters. "Exactly."

I don't want to spend our date—or any of the rest of our time together—dancing around this ticking clock-shaped elephant in the room. Thankfully, we pull onto the bridge and hold our breath, giving the topic time to dissipate, or at least giving me time to think of a different one.

When we exhale on the other side, Jude speaks first. "I'm sorry. I want to be here. Now. I promise."

I tighten my grip on him. "Good."

"Want to know where we're going?"

I nod eagerly, and his smile returns. "I thought I'd take you to the aquarium since you said you've never been. Then we could walk around the outlets a little if you'd like. And I made us a reservation at Ragazzo's for dinner." I've driven past the Italian restaurant multiple times but never dreamed of having an occasion to eat there.

"Ooh. Isn't that place super fancy though? I'd be just as happy with fast food."

"It is," he says. "And I know I won't be able to take you somewhere that nice every time we go out. But this is our first date, so I want it to be extra memorable." He jostles my hand. "That okay?"

The butterflies in my chest stir. "You make me feel special, Jude."

"You are special."

We ride in silence, both of us simply content to be in the other's company, until Jude steers the car into the big aquarium parking lot.

I unbuckle and reach for my door handle. "No. Sit tight," Jude says, ever the gentleman.

I wait for him to open my door and escort me inside, training all my attention on the man beside me rather than anything that lies behind or ahead.

Inside, just to the left of the ticket counter, a lady with a camera waves us over to a green screen. "Let me snap a quick picture of you guys before you get started. Here." She points. "Stand a little closer and hold your hands out together in front of you like this." She demonstrates. "Right. Okay, smile." The camera clicks a few times in rapid succession. "If you head over to that screen after you buy your tickets, you can see them."

"Looks like we came at a good time," I tell Jude. "It's not crowded in here at all."

He pulls out his wallet and approaches the counter. "Two, please. And can we also get tickets to the 3-D movie?"

"Yes, sir. Did you want to take a look at your photos and see if you'd like to add on a photo package?"

"They're already ready?" I pull Jude over to the computer screen. There we are, smiling back at ourselves. They've photoshopped a little turtle into my hands and a starfish into Jude's. We look good together. Like a couple.

"How much?" Jude asks.

The ticket agent smiles. "You can buy a package of two prints for forty dollars. Or you can purchase the digital file."

"Whoa," I whisper. "That's insane."

"We'll take the prints."

I pull on his arm. "That's way too much for pictures. We'll take our own."

He ignores me and swipes his card, takes the tickets as they slide across the counter along with the promise, "We'll have your pictures ready for you to pick up on your way out."

"Jude," I start as we walk away. I need him to know that all this isn't necessary, that I just want to be with him.

"I know what you're going to say." He tucks his wallet back into his pocket. "But I want you to have this picture." He shrugs. "I'm kind of hoping it might make it into that box of treasures you wrote about."

I loop my arm through his. "Oh, it's definitely going in the box. As soon as we get back to the house."

He guides me to the first wall of floor-to-ceiling tanks. "You ready for this?"

I am.

It's dark when we drive back onto the island, a box of leftovers on my lap and my stomach and my heart both full.

"You had a good time?" Jude asks again.

"The best," I assure him. "Thank you for everything. Today was perfect." It truly was. My only complaint is that it went by too quickly.

"Thank you for spending time with me." He parks in the gravel between my car and Kelsey's. "Can I see you again sometime?" he jokes.

I stifle a giggle. "I was just about to ask you if we could move in together."

"Slow down, Alex." He reaches for his door handle. "Let's not rush into anything."

I follow him up to the deck, wondering if Donovan's still awake and what show we might watch with Kelsey tonight. It's nice to have gained a whole new family I'm looking forward to seeing.

He pauses in front of the door and adjusts his glasses.

"Hey, Alex?"

"Yes?"

"Before we go inside, may I kiss you goodnight?"

My heart misses its cue to beat.

It's not like the question is unexpected. I've been ready for it, hoping for it even, for a while now. But I still feel unprepared for what it does to me. Everything goes fuzzy around the edges. I don't trust my voice, so I simply nod and take the tiniest step closer to him.

Before he leans in, he pauses and studies me, as if he's committing the moment to memory. I do the same, then close my eyes.

Everything else fades away, and there is no past, present, or future to worry about. Time stands perfectly still. His nose brushes against my cheek, and his lips find mine. And then, Jude Alford is kissing me.

There are no fireworks.

This is something stronger and much more beautiful, something far less fleeting. Like the warm glow of a fire in the hearth. Like the steady welcoming presence of a front porch light. Like coming home.

Too soon, he pulls away. I open my eyes.

His expression is uncertain and vulnerable, and it makes me want to kiss him again.

"Was that okay?" he whispers.

I let the words fall from my mouth before I think too hard about them, about what saying them aloud could set us both up for in the days to come. "I love you, Jude."

His face splits into a smile of relief. "I love you too, Alex. I have for a long time." He gently presses one more kiss to my forehead and reaches for the doorknob.

Chapter 39

Twisting my windblown hair up into a loose bun, I rub the sleep from my eyes and watch the guys get Donovan set for his early morning lesson.

Jude snaps one more shot of him practicing his stance on the board while he's still on the sand and then jogs over to me.

"Here." He fits the camera strap around my neck. "Just work on what I showed you yesterday with framing shots in thirds, okay? Have fun with it. We can edit them later."

I lift the camera and look through the lens. "This one's like my aunt's. You should have Kelsey out here; she has more experience."

He tugs on the end of one of my hoodie strings. "I like when you wear this sweatshirt."

"Brings back fond memories of band camp?" I ask.

He shakes his head. "Makes it feel like you and I are . . . a thing."
He lifts his eyebrows in question.

"Mmm." I slide my arms into the warmth of the hoodie's pock-et. "I'd say we're definitely . . . a thing."

"Good." He lifts the camera that's dangling from my neck, holds it above our heads, and leans in close. "Smile." He captures the moment, then passes it back to me, letting his hands make contact with mine a little longer than necessary.

"Hey, Romeo!" Ty yells from his spot at Donovan's side. "You gonna join us or not?"

"Yeah," he calls back. "Be right there." But his eyes don't leave my face.

"You'd better hurry," I say. "I think Donovan's still jealous I got you all to myself yesterday."

He gives me one more grin before slowly backing away and turning toward his friend and nephew. I frame a shot and wait for him to get halfway to the water. "Jude!"

When he turns around, I press down the shutter. I know right away it will be my favorite shot of the day.

"I'll make you a deal." Kelsey helps Donovan rinse his plate and load it into the dishwasher. "You go get jammies on and teeth brushed, and we'll watch a movie in the room tonight."

"What about Uncle Jude and Alex?"

Kelsey pulls the party hat from his head. "I think they'll be okay without us for a little while."

Donovan scrunches up his face but eventually relents. He comes back to the table to hug me and Jude and then prances off to his room.

"Thanks, Kels," Jude whispers.

She follows Donovan down the hallway. "You two behave."

Jude pushes his chair back and starts clearing the table. "Nope." He stops me when I try to grab the silverware. "You're not allowed to help clean up your own birthday dinner."

"My birthday was a week ago."

"Technically." He turns on the sink. "But I couldn't cook for you then. So we're making up for it tonight. Now, sit back and relax while I clean up, and then we can put on whatever movie you want. I might even let you win a round of Mario Kart."

I ignore his instructions and start to carry serving dishes back to the counter to put away the leftovers. He'd gone all out: Loaded macaroni and cheese, parmesan-topped breadsticks, salad ("Balance," he'd said), and for dessert, cheesecake. He even made a birthday banner with each triangular pennant transformed into a little wedge of Swiss.

"I just realized something." I reach around him to the drawer with the plastic wrap.

He pulls the roll away from me and takes over. "What's that?"

"I don't know when your birthday is." It still surprises me when I discover something new to learn about Jude; I feel like I know him as well as I do myself at times.

He keeps working. For a few seconds, I wonder if he heard me. "My birthday is October seventeenth," he finally says as he crosses over to the fridge. "But I celebrate it in April. We've always done half birthdays in my family."

"Ooh," I draw out the word. "A tradition? See, you had them too."

The fridge door closes, but he doesn't turn back around. Something isn't right. I walk to his side. "Jude?"

He inhales sharply and lets the air back out slowly. When he faces me, I'm sure it's the closest I've ever seen him get to crying. I clamp my jaws shut, determined to give him silence for his words to land on.

It takes him another full minute to speak. "October seventeenth was never a day my family could celebrate. My mom—" He closes his mouth along with his haunted eyes.

My knee-jerk reaction is to rush into his arms, but I hesitate, afraid it'll do more harm than good. I can't believe I didn't put the pieces together before now, and I'm furious with myself for causing him pain, even unintentionally.

He opens his eyes and reaches for me, pulling me to his chest. "I'm so sorry," I whisper against his heart. He kisses the top of my head and holds me close.

We stand there like that for a long time, my heart hurting with every beat of his, him granting me the unparalleled privilege of sharing in his grief. When he finally lets go, I look up at his still-dry eyes. "I didn't know."

"I know," he says. "I wanted you to. It's not my favorite thing to talk about, but it's part of who I am." He shrugs. "And I guess it probably sheds some light on my family dynamics for you, explains why my dad hates me."

"Jude." My tears make up for any he lacks. "I get that things are complicated with your dad, but I do know that he doesn't hate you."

"How do you know that?" He looks down.

I grab both his hands. "Because it would be impossible for anyone to hate you, no matter how hard they tried."

He attempts a smile. "Have you tried?"

"I haven't," I confess. "But I do have some experience with trying very hard not to fall in love with you."

His lips pull upward, genuinely this time. "How's that working out for you?"

"Not well at all."

He sighs, his shoulders relaxing again. "Can I give you some advice?"

I nod.

"You should probably just stop trying."

"I'll be right back," I tell him. "I want to show you something."

I hurry upstairs and reach into the top of Kelsey's closet where I stored most of the belongings I brought from home. Shoebox in hand, I take the steps two at a time and settle on the couch, waving Jude in from the kitchen.

He sits on the other cushion, eyeing the box in my lap. "So this is it, huh? It's smaller than I thought it would be."

"It's from a pair of jelly shoes I got for my sixth birthday." I run my hand over the label. "I loved those shoes so much. The box is kind of small, but this way, I can only keep what's truly special. Anyway." I transfer the box to his care.

He lifts the lid, sets it gently aside, and starts to unpack each keepsake. A couple of postcards. A handful of photos. A bottle cap. The real sand dollar that matches the silver one around my neck. A small piece of pink boogie board foam. A tiny wax candle. A waterpark wristband. A recipe card. A few faded receipts. I watch him carefully leave his fingerprints on the corners of my soul, waiting for him to reach the bottom of the box, where I've buried my latest treasures. The note with the little mouse drawn in the corner. The front of an empty box of cereal. A flashlight battery. A sticker with a band logo. A stolen Lego. A wrinkled minigolf scorecard. A birthday poem. A ticket to the aquarium and the picture of us on our first date.

After a while, he packs each item away and closes the box again, resting his hand on top. Somehow the moment feels even more intimate than our kiss. "Thank you, Alex. For showing me your heart. And for letting me be part of it."

"I was thinking." I take the box from him and set it on the coffee table. "What if we started something like this for you too?"

He shifts his weight and confesses, "I actually have a box. Not like this, exactly." He points to mine. "It mostly holds important papers—the deed to the house, my car title, stuff like that—but I have a few little things in there. Do you want to see?"

"Of course. If you want to show me."

He gets up and walks to his room, then reappears with a small metal lockbox, a very practical version of my tattered cardboard one. He sets it in front of me.

I unlatch the lock, leaning the top back on its hinges. The aquarium photo identical to mine rests on top. Underneath it are a few other pictures. One is a professional prom photo of Jude and a girl I'm immediately jealous of, but underneath that are several older ones of a beautiful lady who'd likely be envious of all the time I've gotten to spend with her son. My breath catches as I find all the similarities between her face and his. There's one of him and Gavin and Kelsey sitting on the bottom step and another of the two boys arm wrestling. The only other image of me in the collection is of Jude and me side by side at the ice cream place many summers ago. I can still practically taste that summer. Nestled between the photos and the stack of important papers he described is the gold medal I made him.

He takes it out of my hand. "I think I'm actually going to hang this one up so I can see it more often."

I almost make a joke about winning it back, but I get sidetracked by a playbill peeking out of the other papers. I pull the corner gently to free it. "*Little Women*," I read. "I thought you said you didn't get the part."

"I didn't get the part I auditioned for."

When he flips open the program, I scan the names, finding his on the right side and tracing the line to the left. "Professor Bhaer. Of course you were." I laugh.

"Laurie got all the attention." Jude takes the paper and tucks it back away with the others. "But Freddy got the girl."

"Yes." I watch him close up his box and think of all the room still left in it, the memories we could fill it with together. "Yes, he did."

There are moments
Like the clasp
Of a necklace
Making everything
Connect
Taking what once appeared

To be a line
A string of events in a row
And bringing them
Full circle
The past
And the present
Encircling a soul
Resting against a heart
One and the same
After all

Chapter 40

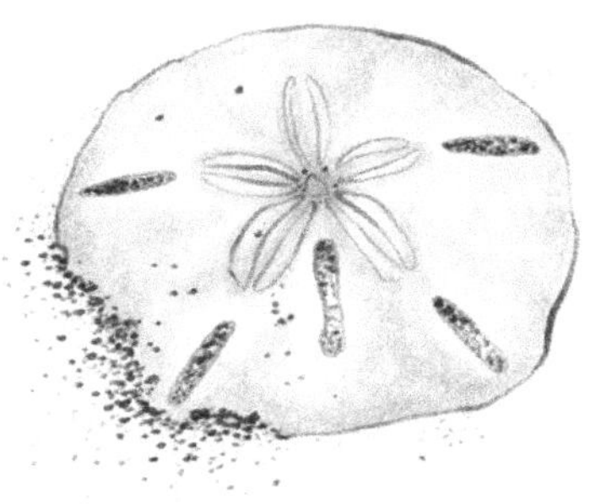

"Why are you standing so far back? Afraid the door's gonna latch on us?"

I watch Jude move the last few boxes from the dusty corner of the laundry room and drag out the large, upright one.

"I'm afraid another palmetto bug is going to run out."

He jostles the box back and forth as he scoots it across the cement floor. "It's entirely possible. I haven't pulled this out in years. I hope it's still in decent shape."

"If not, we'll just spruce it up Charlie Brown style." My phone buzzes on top of the washer, and I jump, still skittish from my encounter with the giant insect.

"That has to be the most active group text in existence. What are your cousins up to today?"

"Nothing as fun as putting up a Christmas tree." I pick up my phone. "But this is my daddy." I squint at the screen. "Checking in to see how my week went and if I had fun on our date the other night, which I did not tell him about yet. Sutton must have been over there."

He dusts his palms off on his pants and leans against the dryer beside me. "That was me, actually."

"Huh?"

"I told your dad."

"When?"

"On your birthday, before you and your cousins got back from dinner. I told him I'd asked you out and that I wanted him to know what my intentions were with his daughter and all."

"Are you for real?"

His hand shoots up to his glasses, and he tenses. "Is that okay? It felt like the right thing to do; it was important to me for him to know how I felt about you. How I feel about you."

"Which is?" I prompt.

"That I care about you very deeply and that I respect you a great deal. And that I will always treat you in accordance with those two truths."

That would explain the way my parents acted when they left last weekend. "Sometimes I think you're too good to be true, Jude."

He blushes. "Me? I'm still not convinced this whole summer hasn't been a dream."

"Well." I grab one side of the tree box. "Let's go celebrate Christmas before we wake up." I meant it as a joke, but the words taste sour in my mouth. Jude's face crumbles. "Jude, I—"

"I know," he says. "Let's just enjoy today. I don't want to waste a single second, okay? In fact, I've already lined someone up to cover my housekeeping shift next Saturday. This morning was torture."

He lifts the opposite end of the box and backs out of the tiny room, his eyes trained on mine, trusting me with where we're going.

But I bear the weight of something he doesn't know yet. Next Saturday, I won't be here.

Jude hefts Donovan's limp, sleeping form onto his shoulder as Kelsey turns off the third stop-motion Christmas classic of the night. Donovan's fingers are still wrapped around his new race car, and his cheeks are sticky with candy cane residue. Kelsey brushes her son's bangs aside and kisses his head before Uncle Jude, who has made this a day he'll never forget, carries him off to tuck him in.

As Kelsey watches them disappear down the hall, she says, "I'm mad at myself for keeping those two apart for so long."

"I love seeing them together," I tell her. "And I'm glad you're both here now."

She sets her empty hot chocolate mug on the coffee table. "I'm going back to look at that apartment Monday, and I think I'm going to go ahead and sign a lease. It's right by a fantastic elementary school and still close enough that we'll only be ten minutes from here."

"When do you start at Mr. Bruce's office?"

"They want me to start this week if possible. Mrs. Becky said she could keep Donovan."

I find a stray piece of wrapping paper and toss it in the bag with the others. "He could hang out with us."

She pulls her feet up under herself. "No. This is y'all's time. Have you talked to him yet about—"

His footsteps and a quick shake of my head silence the rest of her question. He looks from me to his sister and back. "Everything okay?"

"Yep," she says. "Today was so much fun. Thank you for making it magical for Donovan."

"I adore that kid."

"The feeling is very mutual." She stands. "I'm going to turn in. Y'all don't stay up too late."

"Night, Kelsey."

Jude settles beside me next to the tree, colorful lights dancing in his eyes. "Merry Christmas, Alex."

He reaches beneath the branches and hands me a small rectangular present, but I pull out the green gift bag and place it in front of him. "You first."

He moves the tissue paper aside, extracts the Lego surfboard set, and turns it over in his hands. "I love it. You'll help me build it?"

"Mmhm. Think it'll rain this week?"

"Not sure, but I don't think Donovan would mind if we built a fort anyway. Okay." He sets his gift aside. "Your turn."

I know it's a book as soon as I pick it up, but when I tear off the paper, I don't recognize the title.

"It's kind of obscure," he explains. "But it was one of my favorites in high school, and I really think you'll like it. I left you notes in every chapter." I instantly flip open to a random page, but he folds the book shut. "You have to wait and read them as you get to them."

More than the gift itself, it makes me happy to think about Jude sitting down to write notes just for me, about him thinking of me when we weren't in the same room and making sure I had a reason to do the same. I hug the book close. "I can't wait."

"But first you have to finish *The Fellowship of the Ring*."

I grimace. "Do I have to?"

"What if I read it to you? I think you're just imagining the voices all wrong." I like this idea very much, and I think he can tell. "We'll make a whole day of it. We'll wear no shoes, and after Second Breakfast, we'll cozy up at home and read all day. Next Saturday. Yeah?"

I swallow. I need to be honest with him, but I don't want to have this conversation right now. I focus on the gift in my lap, tracing the gold letters of the title with my index finger.

"What is it, Al? What's going on?" I should have known I couldn't keep something from him for long; he's always been able to read me.

"Elle." I inhale. "She's flying back to Spain next weekend."

Jude tenderly removes the book from my grasp and sets it aside. He gets to his feet and reaches a hand down, pulling me up into his embrace. "I'm sorry. I know it'll be hard for you having her so far away again."

I push back against his chest, feeling sicker by the second. I can't look at him. "Sutton invited us all to her house Thursday night for one more slumber party. And since there's only two weeks after that before teacher workdays start, it just makes sense for—" I make the mistake of glancing up. The sight of his face absorbing this information is even worse than I'd imagined.

"You're leaving on Thursday?" He blinks. I nod and try to say something else. But all that comes are tears that make me feel even more horrible because now he's holding me again, whispering comforting words when I know mine have just left him reeling. I hate that I always cry, that my emotions are so quick to spring to the surface, burying his even deeper.

"I'm sorry," I finally compose myself enough to say.

He catches my last tear with his thumb. "Let's talk about it tomorrow. It's still Christmas for a few more minutes." It's the kindest, costliest gift he could have given me.

I shake off my dread and try to pull myself back to this moment. "Today was wonderful, Jude. Donovan's face in those pictures . . . I can't wait to print them in the photo book."

"So you think I'll be okay at creating traditions for a living then?"

"Absolutely." I look around the room. "The only thing I was disappointed about all day was that you forgot to hang mistletoe."

His eyes, still slightly guarded, soften. "We could pretend."

I should be careful, more considerate of his heart, but right now all I want to do is pretend. Pretend that we don't both know what's coming. Pretend that we're not continuing to set ourselves up for heartache. Pretend that Thursday is more than five days away. That time doesn't exist, and that right now is all there is.

"I'd like that."

Jude frames my face with his hands and leans in. Where our first kiss had been tentative, this one is anything but. It's less of a question he's asking without words and more of a statement, a declaration, a case he's arguing for us. He kisses me until all other thoughts are chased from my mind.

Afterward, I stand there, breathless and bewildered.

"We should get some rest." Jude steps away and unplugs the Christmas lights.

I reach for the book on the coffee table. "Goodnight, Jude." I climb the stairs, sure of little other than the fact that I can't come back down to the kitchen tonight to write. I can't trust my heart to hold back the kinds of things I should probably stop saying to him now.

I pull the covers over my head, cradle my new book close, and cry myself to sleep.

Mementos are lovely things to collect.
But I want more than shells of things that once lived.
I want:
The warmth of a touch, a certain smile, blood rushing into cheeks
The feeling invoked by three words, eight letters lined up in
a row
Treasure buried under an island in my quiet kitchen
Standing next to you on the shore of a sea of possibility—
The same ocean I once tried to capture,
Back before I realized that the most beautiful things cannot be
contained in a box
or the palms of my hands,

no matter how badly I never want to let them go,
no matter how much it hurts to watch them elude my grasp and
slip away.
Even still, give me the moments that cannot be held,
And let them, like the ocean, hold me instead.

Chapter 41

Donovan giggles as he and Jude jump another set of waves. Though the sun is bright, the morning isn't too hot yet. I watch them from my beach chair at the edge of the water, sunhat shading my eyes.

Jude looks happy, settled in a way I can't describe. I feel it too. The waves crash, the seagulls call, and all is well on our little island.

"I'm thirsty," Donovan says.

"Race you to the juice boxes?"

Jude winks at me, and they both take off. Jude lets him win. "Shh." He laughs at the resulting celebration dance. "Don't wake your sister."

It's only then that it dawns on me that the boy isn't Donovan. He's too young, with hair a shade lighter. And there's something more than just peace settled on my chest; there's a baby girl, eyelashes fluttering.

Jude pokes a straw into a juice box and hands it to the boy before bending down to kiss her cheek, then mine.

I sit up suddenly in the dark room, book tumbling onto the comforter, and try to pull myself together. This was no nightmare, but my heart is racing and fear lurks close. Because for the first time in my life, I'm not dreaming of things I've pulled from my past but of a future my subconscious has dared to imagine, something lovely that could and may never be.

"I guess I'm just trying to understand why you didn't tell me sooner." His tone is kind, but I don't miss the edge of betrayal in his voice.

I pick at a loose thread on the skirt I wore to church this morning and watch the clouds as we drive to the ice cream shop. "Because I didn't want to think about it, much less talk about it."

"It would have been nice to at least have a heads up. Were you just planning to mention it on your way out the door?"

I knew when I saw him this morning that the reprieve he'd extended last night was over, that this conversation was coming the moment we found ourselves alone again. I keep my words as soft as possible; I owe him that. "You knew I was leaving soon."

"Not this soon. And I don't like thinking about it either, but at this point, I think we kind of *need* to talk about it."

My stomach tightens, and my head is still throbbing from crying last night. "What's there to talk about?"

"Everything, Alex. What the plan is. How we're going to make this work." He swallows. "Unless, you were never planning for this to last longer than this summer."

"I was never planning to fall in love at all this summer." I train my voice as best I can; the last thing this discussion needs is added emotion. "And of course I don't want it to end." I grapple for my next words.

"But?"

"Jude, long distance is hard." I sigh. I might as well tell him everything I'm thinking. "I'm just scared that we've made a huge mistake."

He pulls into a space next to the ice cream shop and turns to face me. "A huge mistake?" he echoes incredulously.

I close my eyes and take a deep breath. "I just mean that your friendship is one of the best things in my life, and I would never want to risk that for—"

He interrupts me, more worked up than I've ever seen him. "Why are you acting like we have to choose? Why can't we have all of it? And, long distance? It's not even a three-hour drive. Your cousin will be in SPAIN, and you haven't told her that maintaining your relationship long distance isn't worth it."

I will not cry. I will *not* cry. "I never said it wasn't worth it. I just said it would be hard. We're already fighting, and I haven't even left yet."

"That's not fair."

Should I reach for his hand or not? I'm handling this all wrong. "I don't want us to argue."

"Neither do I. But if the alternative is giving up, I'd rather fight every minute of the next four days." He turns up the air and angles his vent to blow in his face. "I just need to know that I'm not fighting alone. I need to know what you want right now."

"Honestly?" I ask him. "Right now, I want to get ice cream with my best friend."

He hangs his head, defeated.

"I don't want to be done talking about this," I promise. "It's important. But ice cream won't hurt, right?"

"I guess not," he relents. "I'm sorry I yelled at you." In a different context, it would be both humorous and adorable that he considered his slightly impassioned voice yelling.

When I rest my arm against his on the console, the contact seems to comfort us both a little. "What kind of ice cream are you going to get?"

"Strawberry."

"Since when do you like strawberry ice cream?"

"Since forever. But I never liked having to watch you pick either your beloved mint chocolate chip *or* cookies & cream. Now I can buy you a scoop of each."

I rifle through my mental files back to all the summers I agonized over the decision. Did he always get the other flavor so he could offer me a bite?

"See, Alex?" He opens his car door. "You don't always have to choose between two good things."

We're laughing again as we drive to the pier. The ice cream did help after all.

Jude's in the middle of a story about the time he and Ty caught a baby shark when his phone rings in the cup holder. I glance at the name on the screen and wait for him to pick it up.

He keeps his eyes on the road. "I can call them back."

"It's your dad."

"What?" He scrambles for the phone as the light turns green. "Can you answer? Put it on speaker."

I tap the screen with shaky hands and resituate it between us.

"Dad? What's wrong?"

The two seconds of silence feel like a full minute, likely longer for Jude. "Nothing's wrong, son. I just called to talk to you."

Jude isn't convinced. He keeps one hand on the wheel and searches for mine with the other. I hold on tight, hoping to provide him any small anchor I can.

"I talked to your sister late last night. She told me what's been going on with her and Donovan. How you took them in, helped her find a job and a place of their own."

Jude pulls off into the nearest lot and puts the car in park. Rather than picking up the phone, he takes my hand again. "I didn't take them in, Dad. It's just as much her house as mine. And Tyler's folks were the ones who really helped with the job and apartment and all."

Silence. And then, "She knew you were a safe place to go. And I'm thankful for that. It should have been me. I should have been that, for all of you." Jude's fingers clutch mine so tightly now that his knuckles turn white. He doesn't speak.

"She told me you seem happy," his dad goes on. "Said you've been seeing someone? One of those girls who used to come with that big family in the summer?"

"Yeah," Jude squeaks. "Alexandria."

His dad clears his throat, and it's only a noise, but I swear he sounds just like Jude. "This the girl you punched Gavin for kissing?" My mouth falls open.

"Yeah, Dad. Same girl."

"I'm happy for you, Jude." I can tell he means it. "And listen, I know I'm the last person who probably has the right to give you any kind of advice, but . . ." Emotion floods his voice and Jude's countenance. "When you find someone who makes you happy like that, hang on to her as long as you can. Don't take any of it for granted. Just, enjoy the time you have, okay?"

Considering the state he's in now, I'm shocked by the clarity of his answer. "I plan to."

A sniff echoes over the line. "I won't keep you. I just wanted to tell you how much I appreciate you being there for Kelsey. You've grown into a fine man, Jude."

The next words are hoarse, strained. "Thanks for calling, Dad."

"Love you, son." My fingers go numb.

"Love you too."

The call disconnects, and quiet fills the car like water rushing in. Jude lays his free arm across the steering wheel and buries his face in it. I watch helplessly as the person who has held me together all summer unravels.

His whole body heaves with every unbridled sob, but his hand remains in mine. So I trace my other fingertips lightly over his arm and wait out the storm by his side.

Eventually, his breathing slows and he sits up, releasing my hand and dragging both of his across his swollen face. "I'm tired."

I nod. "Let's go home."

Chapter 42

I wake to an empty house.

I knew Kelsey and Donovan were planning to leave early to swing by the apartment office before her first couple hours training with Mr. Bruce's staff. But I was surprised to see Jude's bedroom door sitting open when I crept down the stairs.

Yesterday, he'd gone to lie down for a few minutes when we got back, and I haven't seen him since. Maybe he went to the beach with Tyler?

I stumble into the kitchen, so preoccupied with thoughts of Jude that it takes me a minute to notice the tiny box of cereal on the counter with a note tucked underneath.

Ran out to take care of a few things. Be back this afternoon.

I consider pulling out our notebook to write out the things I can't say to him, but I think the best thing I can do for him right now is to keep my feelings locked away while he sorts through his. I've spent my life trying to shield my heart from loss, but his is the one I want to protect at all costs now. Is that what love is?

I trudge back upstairs and get dressed, brush my hair and braid it. In the mirror's reflection, I catch sight of the Tolkien book on my nightstand. I need to distract myself for a few long hours, and I want to feel close to Jude in some way; I guess this is as good an option as any.

I tuck the book under my arm and head to the hammock under the house where I can escape to a world of dragons and spiders and trolls, far less intimidating foes than the real fears threatening to consume me.

A hand on my shoulder shakes me gently back to consciousness.

"Tolkien isn't *that* boring," he whispers as I try to reorient myself and blink the fog out of my eyes.

I take the hand he extends, plant my feet on the ground, and roll out of the hammock. "Hey. Are you okay?"

"Yeah. But I could use a hug." He doesn't have to ask twice.

"I was worried about you."

"To be honest, I'm a little worried about you. Reading about hobbits without any prompting; are you feeling okay?"

I lean back and glower at him, relieved to hear him joking again. "For your information, I finished the book."

"And?"

"And then I took a nap."

He laughs, and I want to make him do it again. "I meant, what did you think of it?"

"It wasn't that bad. Not my usual kind of book but good enough to make me think about reading the next one."

He grabs both my hands and stares into my face. "Alexandria Henry, that is the most attractive thing I've ever heard you say."

I swat his arms away and roll my eyes.

"Are you up for a picnic?" he asks. "I want to take you somewhere."

I reach back to the hammock for my book and phone. I hadn't realized it was almost dinnertime. "What about Kelsey and Donovan?"

"They'll be okay. We'll make up some extra sandwiches and leave them in the fridge." He starts for the stairs.

"Jude?"

"Yeah?"

"Did you really hit Gavin for kissing me?"

He spins around and scrunches one eye shut. "I did."

I put a hand over my mouth.

"I told you, he means well. He did it for the same reason he asked you to dinner this summer, 'because if you don't make a move, Jude, someone else is going to do it first.'" His imitation of Gavin is spot on. I giggle.

"Appealing to that competitive nature, huh?"

He turns serious once more. "Except that it wasn't a competition. And you didn't deserve to be treated that way. I knew you had feelings for Gavin, and I didn't want him to hurt you."

And I don't want to hurt Jude. Before I can figure out a way to tell him that, he grabs the railing. "Let's go get that picnic ready."

Jude spreads the blanket over the concrete and sets our basket on top. When he said picnic, I was picturing a grassy park, not the middle of a paved-over swimming pool surrounded by a chain link fence.

"Sutton always told me they tore it down because of me, but I never believed her. Why would they have waited two years?"

"It wasn't you," Jude says. "You definitely weren't the only one to sustain an injury here." His gaze wanders across the area where the two blue slides once stood. "Kelsey just told me the other day that she's glad it's not still here; she would never have let Donovan near those rickety things."

"They weren't that bad." I pull out our sandwiches and a bag of chips.

He opens the bottle of lemonade and pours two cups. "You wouldn't believe some of the stories Kelsey has from her lifeguarding days."

"I'll bet." I wait for him to pick up his sandwich.

He taps the toe of my shoe with his foot. "Would it be okay if we talked about stuff for a minute? I don't want to pressure you, but I have something I'd like to tell you."

I set my drink down. "We can talk about anything you want to. I'm sorry about yesterday; I'm ready now."

"I've been waiting to bring you here all summer." He smiles when my forehead wrinkles in confusion. "I'll explain, but first I wanted to tell you that I went to see my counselor this morning and then spent some time sorting things out." He takes a deep breath. "As much as I never want this summer to end, as much as I never want this to end..." He gestures to the space between us and squares his shoulders. "Look, just because something is only for a season, doesn't mean it isn't just as beautiful and valuable as something that lasts forever. You've walked into and out of my life for a lot of summers, Al, and every one of them was special. But this summer." He scoots closer. "I think this summer we needed each other. And I think we're both better because of the time we spent together."

He pulls a napkin out of the basket and hands it to me. "Don't start crying yet. I have to make it through this."

"Sorry." I sniffle.

"It's taken me years to unpack what happened here that day when we were kids. But it left a lasting mark on me too."

"What do you mean?"

I study the way his jaw twitches, and I can almost see through his eyes and into a brain that's trying to untwist all this like a Rubik's Cube. "That year, my third-grade teacher said something several times. 'Hurt people hurt people.' I know now that she meant it as an explanation for some kids' behavior, but at the time, I took it as some kind of prophecy I was trying to outrun." He looks down. "It sounds absurd when I say it out loud now, but as a nine-year-old who was hurting all the time, I was so terrified I was going to cause someone else pain, that I was going to ruin someone else's life the way I ruined my family's just by coming into the world."

"Oh, Jude."

He holds up a hand, and I bite my lip. "But that day, I watched you hold Elle and calm her down while you were literally bleeding everywhere. And though I didn't fully understand it at the time, I think that's when the idea started taking root in my heart that I didn't have to be perfect or fixed before I could show up for other people. That everyone has their own wounds, and maybe we were made to hurt and heal side by side. To walk with each other through this life that's so, so hard but can be so good too. To witness one another's redemption stories." A tear slides down his nose.

"And I was way too young to be thinking about girls at nine years old, but I distinctly remember feeling that day that you were someone safe, someone I wanted to know, really know, not just run into on the beach. Someone I wanted to be known by." He takes off his glasses for a moment to run the back of his hand across his eyes. "This summer was life-altering for me in a lot of ways. And the fall is going to look completely different than any season has so far. And I guess what I'm trying to say is, thank you for being here beside me during this. I hope you'll look back and find that I was even a fraction as much of a part of your story this summer as you were of mine. You've been a big part of healing places in my heart that I didn't even know were there. And sure, I may end up with a couple new bruises here in a few days, but I wouldn't trade these past weeks for anything. I love you, Alex."

I will love this man until the day I die is the thought shouting in my head as Jude runs a thumb across my scar like he did that night in our fort; this time, I don't pull away. When he leans in and places a kiss where they stitched me up all those summers ago, my heart splits wide open. I'm not sure all the doctors in the world could stitch it back together again.

Chapter 43

"One more chapter?"

Jude marks our spot in the book on his lap with his left hand. His right arm is draped across my shoulders and bent at an angle so he can play with the ends of my hair. "You sound like Donovan."

I snuggle in closer to his side. "I could only dream of being as cute as Donovan."

"I don't know, I think you're pretty cute." He opens the book again. "Especially when you fangirl over Frodo."

I smile. "Frodo is definitely *not* the reason I'm enjoying this."

He kisses my temple, clears his throat, and resumes the story. We seem to be operating under some unspoken agreement not to acknowledge the fact that I'm leaving tomorrow morning. We've spent the past two days choosing these simple moments together over grand adventures and traditions.

Yesterday, I helped Kelsey clean her new apartment while Jude and Ty loaded Ty's truck with a bed and the extra couch as well as a few kitchen essentials to get her started. Other than that, we've filled the time with Legos, movies, walks, working on the book for my cousins, and reading. Neither of us has touched our poetry notebook.

He stops reading. "You hungry?"

There's an emptiness forming in the pit of my stomach, but it has nothing to do with food. I check the time, surprised and angry that the hour is later than I'd realized. "Not really. You?"

He shakes his head. "Let's go for a walk."

We walk until the sun is long gone and our feet ache like our hearts do. Maybe if we never stop moving, we can keep the dawn at bay.

"Hey." He pulls me close when the tears have overtaken me. I try to quiet myself, straining to commit the harmony of his heartbeat and the ocean to memory, like I'm cramming the night before a test. Rubbing my back, he murmurs into my hair. "I need you to know that this has been the best summer of my life."

It's crazy how I came here thinking my best years were behind me, how scared I was that nothing could come close to the kind of love I've known in my past. But my answer could not hold any more truth. "Mine too."

I step out of his embrace, reach for the hook on my necklace, unclasp it, and refasten it around his neck. "How did I ever go six years without seeing you? I'm not sure I'm going to make it through the first six hours tomorrow." I start to break down again.

"Shh." He pulls me close in the darkness, threads his fingers through my hair, and gently tips up my chin.

This time, his kiss is like the ocean, deep and beautiful and overwhelming. I love him. I love him with a love I didn't know existed back in May. I have never been happier. I have never been more devastated. Because here, on this beach that has drawn me back like the tide year after year, the love of my life isn't just kissing me. He's kissing me goodbye. And I'm drowning on dry land.

"I filled it up yesterday when I checked the oil, so you should be fine on gas. And traffic shouldn't be too bad."

We stand side by side in his driveway next to my car loaded with all my belongings except for the sweatshirt and our notebook in my arms. A tiny thread of silver glints where the necklace peeks out of Jude's shirt collar.

"Thank you. For everything." I don't know what else to say. Everything else, I've either already told him or can't say at all.

"Alex." I think he's about to reach for me, but he tucks both hands into his pockets. "I know this is probably not a fair question at this point, but I was wondering if I could ask you a favor." He eyes the notebook, and I pull it closer.

"Okay." I brace myself for the request.

"Don't leave."

My mouth goes dry. He steps closer, sincere eyes trained on mine. "Stay here with me," he pleads. "There are plenty of schools here still looking for teachers. Or you could focus on your writing. I'll take care of you. We can plan the city's events together. We can start our own traditions, our own family. Or, we could just be the coolest aunt and uncle ever. Whatever you want. I just want you."

"Jude."

"I can't give you the world, Al, but I can buy you tiny boxes of cereal and read to you and take you for ice cream and walks by the ocean. I'll build you a fort every day and let you win every game if you want. I think I could make you happy if you'll let me."

"Please don't do this." I close my eyes. "These last few days have been perfect. I don't want to leave like this."

"Then don't."

I'm not sure if the anger rising up in me is directed at him or myself. "My cousins are expecting me there tonight."

"So go be with them and then come back."

I step backwards until I'm leaning against the door of my car. "I have a job back home, Jude. A life."

He waits for me to look at him. "You have a life here too. We could have a life. Together. I just . . . this isn't just some vacation for me. And I refuse to pack up everything we have and shove it into a box." He juts his chin toward the shoebox in my backseat. "Love isn't a trinket. My heart isn't a souvenir."

"I . . . I can't." I stammer. I've been bracing for the impact of this moment for weeks, and suddenly the floor has opened up and I'm still falling. What happened to what he said about this summer being a season? I've already resigned myself to the fact that it's over, already started grieving him. Of course I want to make this work, but ending things now might be better for my heart—and his—in the long run. "I need time."

His face pinching, he nods. "Okay."

My throat feels tight, but I force the words out. "I don't want to hurt you. I don't want to be another person who leaves you, Jude."

"Look at me," he says, his tone kind but firm. "Guilt is the last emotion I want you to feel right now, okay? It is not your job to make sure I'm okay. I've lived through a broken heart before, and I'll do it again. I just want you to be happy."

These last words are making it even harder to think about getting into my car than his earlier plea.

He reaches for the notebook, and I'm too thrown to stop him. "I just need to borrow this last page."

"Wait. What?" I watch him tear the paper from the binding.

"I wrote it last night when I was hopeful this conversation might end differently. But it needs some editing now." He passes the book back. "Don't worry, I'll get it back to you, I promise. It just needs a little tweaking."

I'm positive this poem that I've never read is my favorite of them all. And now, I'll never read it.

Jude folds the page and slides it into his back pocket, then hugs me and says, "Drive carefully."

My body switches to autopilot as I open the door and get in, as I back out and drive away, as I watch Jude get smaller in the rearview mirror. I understand why he didn't want to let me go. He was right. I won't be able to do this again; I won't be back before next July.

By the time I reach the bridge, I have no breath left to hold. On the other side, I pull off the road and park my car, weeping so hard

I can barely see. I turn the air up, reach for my purse, and do the only thing I know to do: I call my cousin.

Chapter 44

"But I wanted to keep it!" I stood in the kitchen in my mermaid nightgown, my six-year-old eyes brimming with tears.

My mom stooped down to my level and cupped my gap-toothed face. "Sweetie, it's empty. You don't need it anymore."

"But it's special to me!"

Daddy sighed. "Everything is special to you, Alex."

"That's not a bad thing." Grandmama came to my defense. "Why don't I go look in the can outside? It picks up in the morning."

I ran for my new shoes. "I'll come with you!"

Minutes later, we were elbow deep in bags of paper plates and leftover food, coke cans, and torn red-and-white striped tablecloths. "It has to be in here somewhere," I wailed.

"We'll find it. We won't give up until we do." She lifted another bag. I leaned over her arm, holding my nose.

"There!" It sat at the very bottom of the green rolling trash can. Though its lid was slightly dented from the pressure of the bags we'd pulled off the top, it was largely unscathed, certainly salvageable.

Grandmama reached down and handed me the cardboard container. "There. Better than new."

I turned it over in my hands. "Better?"

"Mmhm. Because you loved it enough to come back for it. Sometimes we have to fight for the things that matter to us, work a little bit." She winked. "Like an old lady digging through the trash to bring back her granddaughter's smile."

Footsteps sounded on the wooden stairs next door, and two little boys emerged at the top. "Beat you," the younger one panted.

"You got a head start." The older one shoved him inside, and the door slammed shut behind them.

"Let's get you to bed," Grandmama said. "So you can dream of what you're going to do with your box."

"I already know," I told her.

"Oh?"

"I'm going to fill it with other special things."

She set the last bag back in its place and shut the lid. "That sounds like a wonderful idea."

I stand on the porch where my summer—my life—changed course and knock, even though the key still sits in the bag around my shoulder. I didn't handle last Thursday the way I should have, and I need to remedy that before I move forward.

When footsteps echo inside, I begin to sweat. It's only been a week, but it feels like an entire lifetime since I saw him last.

The door opens, and there he is, looking hesitant and a bit disheveled. He steps aside. "Come on in." I pretend not to see him stop by the couch after he closes the door behind me. I want to have this conversation in our usual spot in the kitchen; it feels like the only appropriate place to lay my heart bare. He follows me.

"Can I get you something to drink?"

I shake my head. All I want to do is run into his arms, but I'm here for a reason, and I can't lose sight of that.

"Are you okay?" I ask.

He sighs and shrugs his shoulders. "Not especially. But I will be."

"You're shaking." I can't talk myself out of taking his hand in both of mine, trying to press some kind of peace into it.

He swallows. "I didn't hear from you at all after you texted to say you made it back. And then, out of the blue, a message asking if we could talk? In person? I'm pretty sure I know what's coming."

"I'm really sorry." I am. "I didn't want to communicate with you until I had a grip on things; I don't want to hurt you any more than I already have." His hand moves, but I won't let go. "It's been an eventful week. Can I tell you a few things you don't know?"

His deep brown eyes flicker before he nods his assent.

"First of all, I stayed at your sister's place last night." I watch his face register my admission. "We've actually been in touch quite a bit this week." I give him a moment, then continue. "My principal called me into her office on Monday morning and let me go."

He gasps. "What? Why?"

"It seems a concerned citizen called her and told her I was heartbroken and wouldn't be much good in one of her classrooms this year. She offered to let me out of my contract and even to contact a friend of hers who works as an administrator in the district here." I smirk. "Did I ever mention that my principal is Sutton's mother-in-law?"

Jude smiles for the first time since I walked in.

"Anyway, I met with her friend this morning, and it's going to take a week or two for all the paperwork to clear HR, but—"

His hand flexes in mine, hope radiating from his face. "Alex, please tell me you're serious about this."

"As long as you're okay with it."

He's practically levitating. "Are you kidding me?!"

"Kelsey said I could stay with them for a while until I get settled and figure out what's next."

His reaction is every bit as satisfying as I dreamed it would be. When he's finished kissing me, he says, "If you're looking for input on that, I have a very strong recommendation." I follow his line of sight over to the drawer in the counter.

I let go of his hand long enough to walk over and slide it open. Where our notebook once lived, there's a single sheet of paper, still folded the same way I last saw it. And on top of that sits a small gray velvet box. Stunned, I stare at it as Jude starts speaking again.

"I wanted to give you time and space to figure out what you wanted, but I've known exactly what I want for a while, Alex." He touches his glasses, nerves overcoming him. "I don't want to freak you out or scare you off, so we don't have to talk about this right now if you don't want to."

I look up. "I do want to. I'm ready, Jude."

He moves next to me and picks up both the jewelry box and the paper.

"Did you change it already?" I ask.

He shakes his head. "I hadn't given up on the hope that maybe we could still edit the circumstances rather than the poem."

"Good." I lean against the counter. "Can I read it now then?"

"You can. But first." He inhales. "I need to ask you something."

I feel like I might explode with happiness.

"Alexandria." He pauses. "What time is it?"

Not the question I was expecting.

He leans around me to check the microwave display. "If we leave now, we can get there on time."

I'm lost. "What are you talking about?"

He sets the poem on the counter and tucks the ring box into his pocket. "How would you feel about making some Ye Olde Dragon history?"

"Shut. Up. Are you for real?!"

I can see my excitement painted all over his expression. He chuckles and leans in. "Unless you're ready to admit that a pirate-themed dinner show is the cheesiest place ever to get engaged."

I wrap my arms around his neck, stand on my tiptoes, and rest my forehead against his. "Jude Alford, I think you're forgetting a very important detail."

He moves his face until the tips of our noses are touching. "What's that?"

"I LOVE cheese."

His deep laugh rumbles through my chest, and it's hard to tell where his joy ends and mine begins.

"Let's go," he whispers and grabs my hand.

I'm not afraid as we walk to the door, just perfectly content holding tight to the boy whose past is interwoven with mine. He stops to kiss me once more and then ushers me out into the sunshine, into the rest of my life.

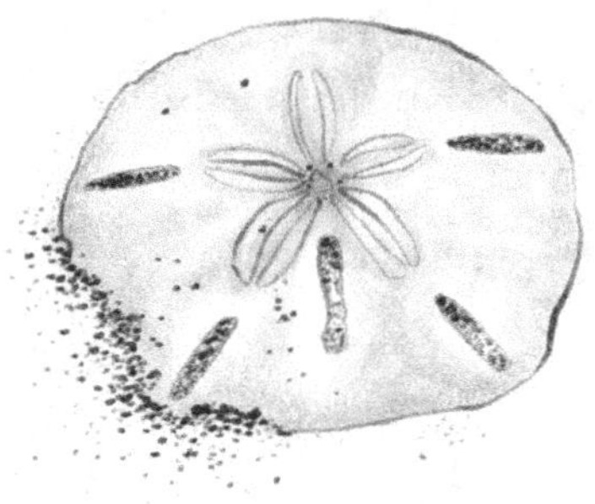

Epilogue

"There." Rebekah finishes knotting the braided blue bracelet around my ankle. It matches the ones my cousins transferred from their arms this morning. Though not intentional, I wonder now if the shade subconsciously factored into our decision when we picked out their bridesmaid gowns. Because they pair perfectly.

Sutton looks up from where she's pinning Elle's hair into an elegant side bun. "Though I'm not sure bracelets we bought eight months ago count as 'something new.' Or that you can use them for both that and your 'something blue.'"

"Sure they can." Elle's eyes sparkle at me in the mirror. She looks like she's grown up so much even since last summer, just as she should. "She's being efficient. Two birds with one stone and all that, Sutton. You of all people—"

Sutton cuts her off with a playful swat on the shoulder from the brush in her hand. "Okay, okay. I just hope Chris is being efficient. He assured me he could get Marcail up from her nap and have her dressed and ready in time for pictures. I promised I wouldn't check in."

Rebekah stifles a laugh, and I look down at the 'something old' and 'something borrowed' in my lap, running my fingers over the worn leather cover of the Bible my granddaddy pressed into my hands last night. I think about him walking down the aisle to be seated alone in a few hours, and tears gather in my eyes.

"Don't." Elle jumps from her chair and squeezes my shoulder. "You'll ruin your makeup."

Rebekah takes the tissue Sutton pulls from her bag and hands it to me, kneels down beside my chair, and rests a hand on my knee.

"I wish she was here," I whisper.

"She is." Sutton steps over next to Elle. "In your settled smile, Alex. And Bekah's caring touch. And Elle's feistiness."

"And your protectiveness," Rebekah adds.

I run the tissue carefully under my eyes and look into the three pairs around me to see myself more clearly. We've all changed in numerous ways. We're all still the same in more. I can't verbalize it without choking up, but it's us—*we're* my something old *and* something new. It's a wonder I didn't see it before, the way time and change only solidify what lasts forever.

When Sutton's phone chimes, she snatches it from the dresser. "Uncle Zack says they're ready for us." She frowns. "Why hasn't Chris texted yet? And why on earth did I promise not to check in?"

Elle laughs. "Bek and I will go assess the situation. We made no promises." She links arms with Rebekah, and they slip from the room, leaving me and Sutton alone.

It's quiet for a moment. I stare into the glass in front of us, watching our reflections stare back.

"You look beautiful. And happy." She smiles and reaches around to straighten the sand dollar pendant resting just above the neckline of my dress. I catch her hand. "Thank you, Sutton. For everything. But mostly for—"

She reads my mind. "Not interfering for once? I can assure you, it was the hardest thing I've ever done."

I giggle and sniffle at the same time.

"Let the record show," she continues, "I knew you and Jude were perfect for each other long before either of you did. And just as clearly, I knew that if I said a word about it, I'd ruin it."

I tighten my grip on her. "Thanks for knowing I needed to figure it out for myself. I just wish I'd done it sooner."

"I think the timing was just right," she says. "She would have told you the same thing." Her eyes fall to the book. "I think you were her favorite."

My voice comes out wobbly. "You do?"

"After me, of course." We both dissolve into giggles.

We need to head out onto the beach for pictures before my aunt sends a search party, but I want to read his words once more before getting swept up in the best day of my life; thus far, that is. I open the Bible and slide out the poem tucked between its pages. "I haven't shown this to anyone else yet, but I want you to see it."

Sutton nods, and I unfold the paper, knowing that just as holding it close all these months has made it special, sharing it will too.

Birthdays

When you asked me when my birthday was, my heart and mind
were torn.
I never marked another year on the day that I was born.
October's what the paper says, and April was the lie,
But I always felt the most alive the first week of July.
When we ate cake together and I finally got a taste
Of love, of family, of hope; and I didn't want to waste
A single wish I'd ever make, sent up from smoky candle.
The thought of this flame burning out is more than I can handle.
I want to make your dreams come true, offer you a life here,
To celebrate a love that grows year after hard-won year.
Every birthday I have left, you can have each one.
Trade the fragile candlelight for a home built in the sun.
I ask for just one present—a past and future too—
For the day my life truly began was the day that I met you.

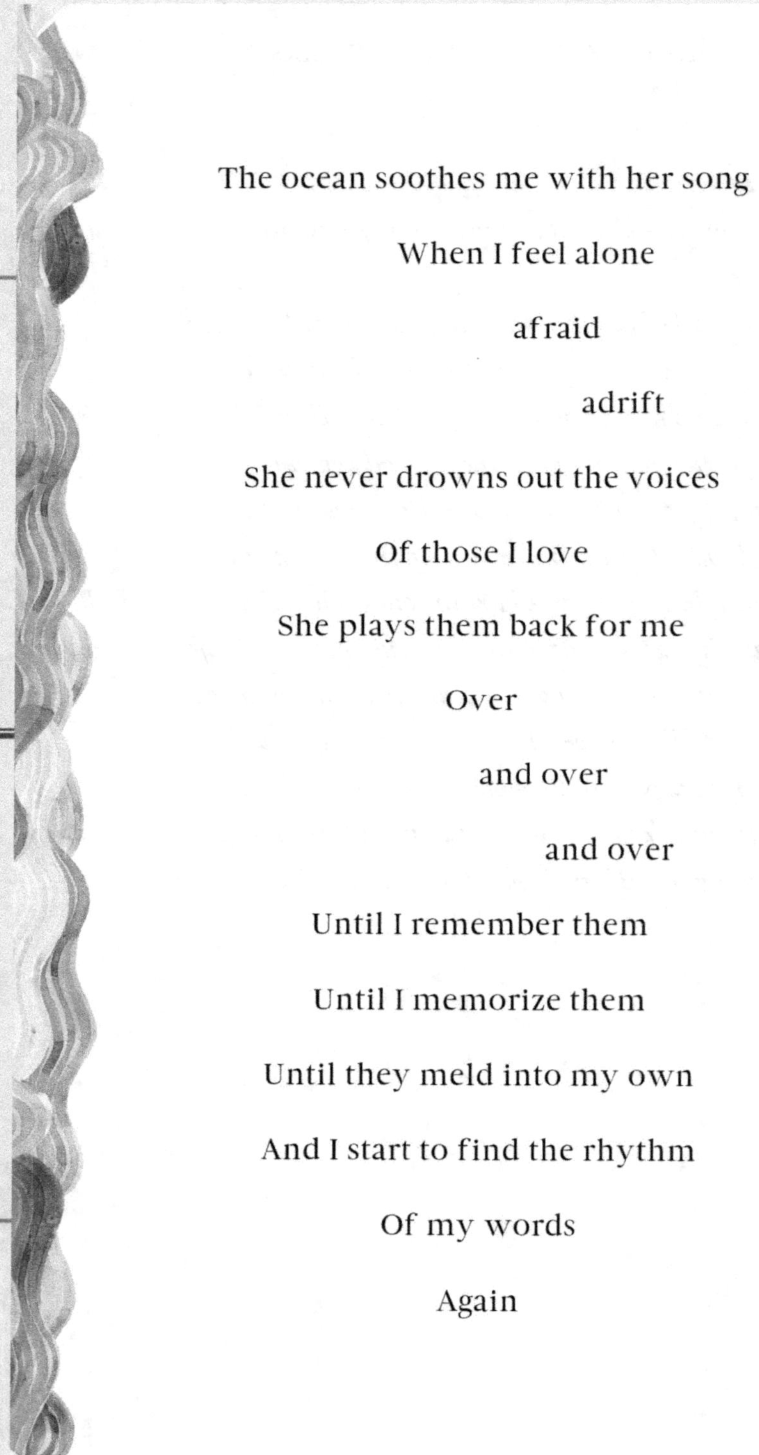

The ocean soothes me with her song

When I feel alone

afraid

adrift

She never drowns out the voices

Of those I love

She plays them back for me

Over

and over

and over

Until I remember them

Until I memorize them

Until they meld into my own

And I start to find the rhythm

Of my words

Again

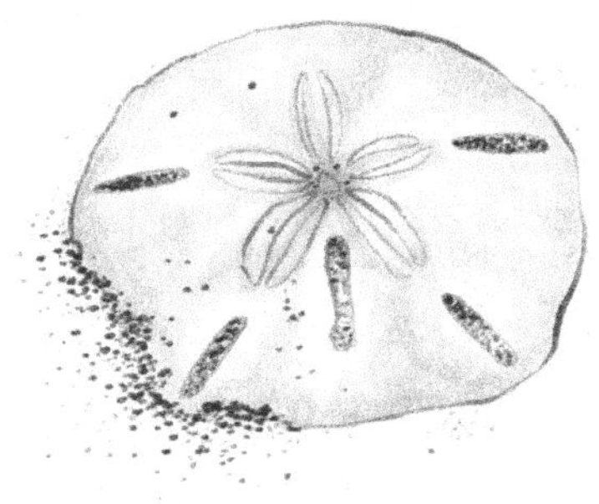

Author's Note

Some authors have the privilege of bringing a lovely tale to life, and some of us are fortunate enough to have been born into one.

As far back as I can remember, I've been surrounded by love, memories of the beach, and lots and lots of relatives.

In 1955, my dad's parents and grandparents took a trip to an oceanfront beach house for the first time. What began as ten people in two bedrooms has grown into an epic vacation of over 150 people in at least a dozen rented houses.

This week of summer is still one of the most anticipated events of the year and a touchpoint for me as I always get to celebrate my birthday there with my family and some of my very dearest friends, my cousins.

My dreams are often set on this island or have some random aunt or uncle show up as a character in them. And not only were many of the best stories from my childhood written on this beach, but I started to notice that the beach was bleeding into many of the new stories that began to flow from my fingers as I became a writer.

During an especially hard winter and a few months after saying goodbye to our beloved Ma-Ma, I decided it was time to memorialize this part of my life through a fictional novel based on my true recollections of sunshine and sand, crab hunts and talent shows, breakfasts and dinners for dozens, and obviously, tiny boxes of cereal.

Of course, the love story and plenty of the events in this book are purely fabricated (shoutout to the brothers in the beach house next door who were just friends), but underneath that, I want you to see the real beauty of a giant family with so much love for one another and a heart to share that love with others.

I hope you enjoyed *Seashells & Other Souvenirs*. As Alex says, there are "actual pieces of my heart in here."

-Rachel

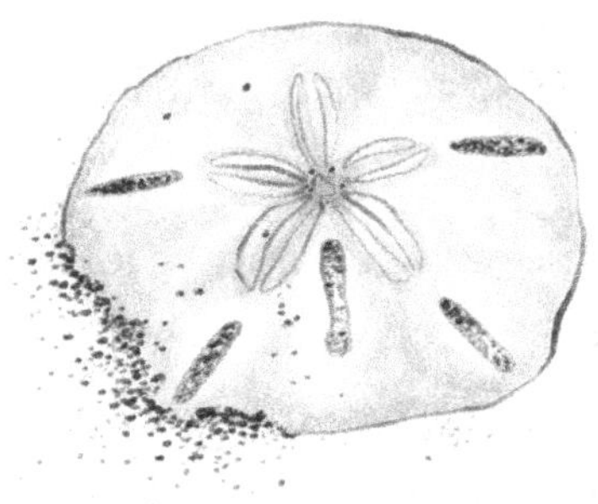

Acknowledgements

Sharing this story with the world is a literal dream come true. I still can't believe it. I couldn't possibly adequately express the depth of my gratitude or list every person I'm thankful for, but here is my meager attempt.

For my husband, who still builds forts and eats late-night snacks with me, who always cheers me up and cheers me on and points me to Truth. You are my best friend and the love of my life.

For my kids, who make every day an adventure. You are all my favorite.

For my Sola Sisters: Andrea, my first critique partner and dear friend. I wouldn't have had the courage to share this with anyone else without you (and Debra). Thank you for walking me through this and for the lovely sand dollar chapter art. I love you, and I'm obviously crying right now. Emily, my writing mentor. I want to be like you when I grow up; I hope you know I think the world of you. Kate, my practical family. Thank you for loving me and Jonathan and our kids so well and for doing dishes over Marco Polo with me. Amber, the Fen to my Marcel. Thank you for loving me even when you don't understand my weird emotions and for authoring my book soulmate.

For Katie, my kindred writing spirit. Thank you for sharing this journey with me, for always being up for swapping stories, and for pretending all our imaginary friends are real.

For my friend Shelby, who has walked through so much life with me and held me up when I nearly lost hope.

For the Cottage. I want to cry happy tears every time I think of our bizarre, creative little flim flam fam. You guys are a source of endless joy and inspiration...and memes and jokes and mummy screams. Adam and I adore you.

For AJ. Thank you for loving my story enough to invest in it, for holding my hand through this experience, and for becoming such a wonderful friend along the way.

For Maggie D. and Josh S., who both once said I should write a book—and kept saying it until I had the faith to believe it. Never forget the power of your genuine encouraging words.

For the delightful Quill & Flame team. You guys are talented writers and amazing people. I love you more than all the Oreos and pickles in the world. One day, I hope to write a musical about you.

For Jessica Gwyn, Denica McCall, and Stephany Araujo. Thank you for the work you put into making my story stronger and making it shine. You were a pleasure to work with.

For my street team and all the ways you've made me feel cared for and supported. Thank you!

For all the authors who came alongside me, offered me insight, beta read and gave me invaluable feedback, or gifted me such lovely endorsements. I am forever grateful.

For the family I was born into: Mom, Dad, Stephen, Tracie, all my nieces and nephews, my grandparents, aunts, uncles, cousins, and everyone in our giant circle (and my kind, supportive mother-in-law Mrs. Brenda). For my first best friends – Mantha, Becca, and Ally. I hope our kids and grandkids still vacation together. What a blessing.

And most of all, for the greatest Author and Storyteller, Love Himself, Who has always been faithful and tender in His care for me. May every story I write honor You and reflect Your love.

About the Author

Rachel Lawrence writes stories and poetry about the everyday joys and challenges of life, love, and choosing the perfect snack food for every occasion. She draws inspiration from her experience growing up in a huge family in the Carolinas and having her views expanded by new friends and family she's met along the way, both at home and across the ocean. Rachel is a wife, mom, and lover of inside jokes who plays Christmas music year round.